# SOMEONE *Is* KILLING
# THE *G*REAT *C*HEFS
# OF *A*MERICA

By Nan and Ivan Lyons

*Novels*

Someone Is Killing the Great Chefs of Europe

Champagne Blues

Sold!

The President Is Coming to Lunch

*Nonfiction*

Imperial Taste: A Century of Elegance at
Tokyo's Imperial Hotel

New York City

NAN and IVAN LYONS

# SOMEONE *IS* KILLING THE GREAT CHEFS OF *A*MERICA

*Mystery*
*Lyons*

LITTLE, BROWN AND COMPANY

Boston Toronto London

The authors wish to thank Jim Dodge, Dean Fearing, Larry Forgione, Bradley Ogden, Paul Prudhomme, Wolfgang Puck, and Jimmy Schmidt for graciously sharing their recipes — and themselves. The recipe on page 20 is published with the permission of Jim Dodge.

*First Edition*

This book is a work of fiction. Names, characters, places, and incidents are either the
product of the authors' imagination or, if real, are used fictitiously.

*Library of Congress Cataloging-in-Publication Data*

Lyons, Nan.
    Someone is killing the great chefs of America / Nan and Ivan
Lyons. — 1st ed.
        p.  cm.
    Sequel to: Someone is killing the great chefs of Europe.
    ISBN 0-316-54023-4
    I. Lyons, Ivan.   II. Title.
    PS3562.Y449S64   1993
    813'.54 — dc20                                        92-38576

10   9   8   7   6   5   4   3   2   1

MV-NY

Published simultaneously in Canada by Little, Brown & Company
(Canada) Limited

*Printed in the United States of America*

*This book is for Samantha,*
*our best sequel*

"Never eat more than
you can lift."

MISS PIGGY

# SOMEONE IS KILLING THE GREAT CHEFS OF AMERICA

ACHILLE VAN GOLK wore only gray velour sweatpants and a pair of hospital clogs. He sat bolt upright as Dr. Enstein taped the electronic sensors to his head and neck and then tightened the straps across his muscular chest and flat stomach. Neither man spoke. For five years they had done nothing but talk — two hours in the morning, one hour after lunch, one hour after dinner. There was nothing left to say.

Enstein placed the suction discs over Achille's heart, inserted the temperature probe under his arm, and wrapped the blood-pressure sleeve around his firm bicep. Achille stared straight ahead, careful to avoid eye contact with the only person who really knew him.

The doctor sat down at the computer console and turned it on. There was the hiss and buzz of electronic chips and semiconductor parts and then simultaneous flashes as three screens lit up to monitor the polygraph readings for blood pressure, heartbeat, breathing, and perspiration; the Zeiss-Freimeister test for brain waves; and the Bell evaluator for irregularities in the voice. Enstein picked up a glass and slowly sipped his Perrier, giving the printer stations a full minute in which to establish normal patterns against which Achille's reactions would be compared.

Enstein tapped his finger on the microphone and glanced over at the dials on the tape deck. Finally he ran a nervous hand through his unruly white hair and picked up the list of questions he had been preparing for years. He knew how much depended on the answers — a man's life.

Enstein spoke with a soft German accent. "What do you think of when I say *crème brûlée?*"

Achille paused. "Politics."

Enstein searched the monitors for the slightest sign of irregularity. "Please. Go on."

"It is not of French origin. Grilled cream originated in the seventeenth century at King's College, Cambridge. A rather simpleminded variation on vanilla custard, it first appeared in America on Thomas Jefferson's table. In my opinion, his cook Julien gave the dish a French name, *crème brûlée*, to make it more digestible for the anti-British ruffians."

The readings on Enstein's printout were steady. He looked down at his notes. "How do you feel about beef Wellington?"

"A notorious waste of foie gras. No one with an IQ above that of an anchovy would consider eating such a disaster. Its day, like the dinosaur's, is over."

Enstein sighed with relief. The horizontal centerings had not shifted. All parameters maintained their original zones. He cleared his throat. "Lobster bisque."

"Crayfish is superior."

Enstein held his breath. There was a sudden jump in the brainwave pattern. "Go on."

"It has to do with the difference in shells. You see — " Then Achille's memory caught up with the waves. "There's something else. A dream."

Enstein looked up quickly. "Please."

Achille hesitated, knowing that his response had already registered on the monitor. He had no choice but to go on. "I dreamed that I was floating in a ramekin filled with *crème anglaise*."

Enstein tensed. There were marked changes on all three screens. The graph pens arced dramatically. "And?"

"I opened my mouth to taste it, and I drowned."

Enstein's eyes filled with tears. "What a gift from your subconscious! When did you have this dream?"

"Some months back."

"So you see," Enstein announced triumphantly, "it has been there all the time!"

"What has?"

"The proof of the pudding!"

Enstein had begun gathering proof five years earlier. Achille, after killing three of the greatest chefs in Europe, had entered a plea of insanity in return for which the Crown had agreed to his being remanded to Enstein's clinic near Geneva. Indeed, the Crown would have sentenced him to the Bridal Suite at Claridge's to avoid a public trial. Anything to spare further embarrassment to the Royal Family. Achille had been a frequent dinner guest at Buckingham Palace.

Although Enstein's theory of a link between criminality and obesity had been ridiculed throughout Europe, Achille had continued to fund the research. Enstein was convinced that intensive analysis coupled with a traumatic change in physical appearance would liberate the healthy side of the psyche — the thin person screaming to get out. Indeed, the documentation was all there. As Achille spent year after year modifying his eating habits, he began to lose his psychotic tendencies. He had passed dozens of psychological evaluations with flying colors.

Enstein was about to declare that the former homicidal maniac, and ex-publisher of the world's leading food magazine, *Lucullus*, had been cured of the delusion that he could not survive without gorging himself. Trim and repentant, no longer a threat to society or to himself, Achille had been brought back from the obese. Enstein had given him a new life.

Enter Alec Gordon — his new life. Achille van Golk, according to a bogus death certificate signed by Enstein, had died three years earlier. "Enstein's monster," as Achille had referred to Alec, would soon be free to go among the gourmets in peace.

The doctor's voice was tense. "Please watch the overhead screen." There was still one final test.

Achille looked up, narrowing his eyes as that infamous headline from the London *Daily News* flashed on the screen — SOMEONE IS KILLING THE GREAT CHEFS OF EUROPE. Then a photo of Louis Kohner, smiling, followed by one of the London police removing his charred body from an oven.

Enstein scanned the printouts and monitors, hardly daring to breathe. The next image was the bloated body of Nutti Fenegretti being lifted from a fish tank by the police in Rome.

The parameters held. No erratic activity.

Then the monitors exploded with images of Jean-Claude Moulineaux, his head crushed in a duck press. No discernable reaction.

"Excellent," Enstein whispered. All the readings were normal. The doctor's red-rimmed eyes fixed on the graph pens and their plotter points. He held his breath and asked, "Did you kill the great chefs of Europe?"

"I did not."

"Who did?"

"Achille van Golk."

"Where is Achille van Golk?"

"He is dead."

"What is your name?"

Pausing to modify his voice, Achille spoke in the newly acquired American accent he would use from that moment on. "Alec Gordon."

"What does the name Achille mean to you?"

"Fat."

"What does the name Alec mean to you?"

"Thin."

"Alec, do you understand your dream now?"

"The *crème anglaise?*"

"It was no coincidence that you remembered the dream today. I have always told you to listen to your inner voice. It is the voice of truth. But you were not ready until now."

"Until the *crème anglaise?*"

"Exactly. You said you were floating in a pot — "

"I said a ramekin."

"You open your mouth . . ."

"Yes?"

"And you drown."

"Yes."

"You eat the pudding, you die."

"Yes," Achille said.

"Extraordinary."

"Extraordinary."

All the readings were perfect. Enstein pressed the button for the last slide — a picture of Achille that had been taken nearly six years earlier. He waited for a response as Achille stared at his former self.

The man strapped in the chair not only had lost 175 pounds, but also had undergone an arduous exercise program, countless liposuction treatments to remove the last traces of fat, months of extensive plastic surgery to tighten his skin, and even a hair transplant to achieve a full head of dark brown waves streaked with silver at the temples. Achille studied the photograph of someone he had not seen in years. Someone he viewed as a total stranger. "Odd."

"What?" Enstein asked. "What is odd?"

"How much I used to look like Robert Morley."

Enstein's eye began to twitch with excitement. The reversal was complete. There was nothing further to be done at the clinic. It was time for his patient to be exposed to a new environment, after which Enstein would gather the final results that were sure to make medical history. He walked over to Alec Gordon. Without a word, he removed the sensors, the pressure sleeve, and the straps. Enstein's eyes filled with tears. "I have delivered lectures to thousands of psychiatrists eager to unmask me as a fraud. But now my theory has become reality. At the moment of my greatest triumph, facing not my critics but my creation, I am suddenly at a loss for words."

Alec stood up and drank a glass of Perrier in a single gulp. He took a deep breath and, feeling the flush of victory, turned and smashed his glass in the fireplace.

Enstein embraced him. "My dear Alec, you are every bit as sane as I."


ALEC GORDON, the thin man who had struggled to get out, was out. He left the Enstein Clinic on foot. He carried with him no baggage, nothing but the clothes he wore, which had been hand-tailored to lie flat against the muscular geometry of his new physique. He had left behind everything connected to his former life. Soon even the memories would begin to fade.

It was a beautiful day. He walked along an Alpine path that led to town. He heard cowbells in the distance and stopped to listen, enjoying most of all the luxury of time. His own time.

The path led to a paved road, and the road turned off onto a winding cobblestone street. Intuitively, Alec raised his wrist to check his watch. He smiled. It would have taken a calendar to time the walk from the clinic.

Alec stopped at a flower stall to buy a red rose for his lapel. A little girl standing nearby watched him. He bowed slightly and offered her the rose, pausing to bask in the warmth of her smile. He continued down the street straining to catch shards of conversation that never once mentioned inner voices, compulsions, or the

7

subconscious. As he turned the corner, Alec found himself standing in front of the town bakery.

He went in.

"*Bonjour, monsieur,*" the baker's wife said. "How may I help you today? We have some beautiful *napoleons. Eclairs.* A *gâteau aux marrons? Tarte aux fraises?*"

"How much?"

"For the *tarte*, monsieur?"

"No."

"The *éclair?*"

"No! All of them."

"You wish to buy all my *éclairs?*"

Alec banged his fist on the counter, nearly toppling a tray of petits fours. "No, you cream-filled cretin! I wish to buy the *éclairs and* the *napoleons* and the *tarte. And* the *gâteau. All* the *gâteaux!* I don't suppose you have a *Schwartzwalder kirschtorte* tucked away somewhere?"

The baker's wife stood frozen. "You wish to buy everything in my bakery?"

"At last, the dough has risen."

She reached nervously for a stack of boxes. "It will take time to wrap them."

"Don't be a danish," Alec snapped, shoving her aside as he stepped behind the counter. "I'll eat them here!"

NATASHA O'BRIEN ran along the jetway as the ground crew held the cabin door for her. It was an old trick she had learned while working for Achille: a call to the head of public relations was sure to open a five-minute window.

"You were great!" one of the stewardesses called out. Natasha had just appeared on the eight-thirty segment of the *Today* show. "I couldn't believe what you said about Martha Stewart."

"Please thank Captain Foster," she said breathlessly as the door slammed shut behind her. "They're waiting for me to make dessert at the White House."

The stewardess's eyes opened wide. "Really?"

"I guess they're tired of Hillary's cookies." As Natasha was led into the first-class cabin, Barbara Walters looked up, caught her eye, and smiled.

Natasha wondered if the smile was because Barbara remembered her or if it was simply one of those "I'm worth it!" glances women give each other going into and out of ladies' rooms at expensive restaurants.

"Hello," Barbara said, reaching for Natasha's hand. "You're looking wonderful. And doing wonderful things, too, I hear."

Natasha tried not to look as stunned as she felt. It must have been five years since the interview. "You were so kind to me that day," she said, gently squeezing Barbara's hand.

Natasha was suddenly uneasy as she walked down the aisle to her seat. How many people must that woman have interviewed over the years? How could she have remembered? Not that Natasha could ever forget. There it was again, that ache in the pit of her stomach. It made no difference how hard she had worked to put her life back together: Barbara Walters hadn't forgotten.

Natasha sat down, careful not to crush the jacket of her favorite mauve Chanel suit. Slipping off her raspberry suede Ferragamos, she reached into her matching purse for a tissue. Natasha was eager to remove the rouge on her cheeks and the lip gloss. Although nearly forty, she looked more suited to the cover of *Vogue* than *Gourmet*. She rarely wore makeup. Certainly never lip gloss. Except on television.

After returning from Europe, Natasha had been eager to keep a low profile. But that was nearly impossible. The gruesome killings had made international headlines. Natasha had narrowly escaped being murdered herself. She was news. The call from *20/20* implied that, in the national interest, she had to allow Barbara Walters to interview her.

But at the last minute Natasha felt she couldn't go through with it. Entering the studio, she saw photos of the mutilated bodies of Louis, Nutti, and Jean-Claude on the monitors. Then the footage of Achille, his massive, bloated frame coming toward her just as he did in her nightmares.

Natasha grabbed hold of Barbara's hand. "I'm sorry," she said, tears streaming down her cheeks. "I can't do it."

Barbara embraced her and spoke softly. "Trust me. This will help put it behind you." She smiled. "By tomorrow, it will all be yesterday's news."

She had been right. There was something cathartic in reliving the horror in front of millions of people. The demons, no longer locked up inside her, became public domain. As did Natasha herself. The world was eager to give her a second chance. But it wasn't until she received the news of Achille's death that Natasha finally put the past behind her. Determined to create a new image, she turned her back on the classic cuisine of Europe and embraced American regional cooking. She began with a PBS series on American chefs, published two cookbooks, and then took on the most difficult challenge of all: creating the first magazine devoted solely to American food.

As Achille had always told her, there was no place to start but the top. It had taken nearly a year, and her last penny, to raise the financing for *American Cuisine*. The cover shot firmly in her mind

(Natasha surrounded by half a dozen of America's great chefs), she convinced the White House to break with tradition and serve an all-American state dinner.

Natasha couldn't help smiling. It was a coup worthy of Achille himself. If only he knew. He'd turn over in his grave.


NATASHA WALKED ALONG the ground-floor corridor toward the White House kitchen, flanked by two Secret Service agents who had numbered and photographed each of the knives in her case. She felt as relaxed as Clarice on her way to interview Hannibal Lecter.

The only sound she heard was that of her own footsteps. They passed the White House florist, and a bouquet of inquisitive eyes looked up. Natasha suddenly had a sense of impending doom, as though she were walking the last mile. But then the familiar scent of onions sweating in a sauté pan wafted over the five-and-a-half-foot wall to her left. She breathed a sigh of relief.

The White House kitchen was smaller than those of many restaurants and had a permanent staff you could count on one hand. But it had been transformed into a six-ring circus presided over by six superstars of American cooking.

Natasha stood in the doorway and allowed herself a moment of self-satisfaction. There they were: Wolfgang Puck, Paul Prudhomme, Bradley Ogden, Larry Forgione, Jimmy Schmidt, and Parker Lacy. It was like opening a box of Cracker Jacks and finding it filled with prizes.

While the state dining room was being set for a hundred of the world's most diplomatic people, Natasha knew that the kitchen was simmering with a bouillabaisse of egos. Her "impossible dream" could still blow up in her face at any moment. No matter how smoothly she had negotiated its passage through culinary canyons and across hostile ethnic borders, she still didn't have the recipes and photos that would make or break the inaugural issue of *American Cuisine*.

"Natasha!" Wolf shouted on seeing her. "My gorgeous artichoke!"

"My delicious ham hock," Brad chimed in, smiling.

Jimmy looked up. "My beautiful chanterelle!"

"My precious salmon!" Larry said, waving a filet hello.

11

"At last!" Paul held up a fistful of Louisiana oysters. "Venus on the half-shell!"

"You guys nuts?" Parker shouted from the grill. "Get a load of those thighs. Those breasts! The lady is pure pheasant!"

"Miss O'Brien." The greeting that sounded more like an accusation came from White House Executive Chef Alain Caranne, whose résumé read like a map of the restaurants in Lyons. He was less than delighted to share his kitchen with a band of culinary outlaws. It had taken Caranne over half an hour merely to copy the menu onto the blackboard. And then he stared at it, as though trying to decipher a gastronomic Rosetta stone:

ROASTED ONION SOUP
with Roasted Garlic and Ham Hock Crouton
(Bradley Ogden, The Lark Creek Inn)

CEDAR-PLANKED SALMON
with Old-Fashioned Egg Sauce
(Larry Forgione, An American Place)

PARADISE PASTA
(Paul Prudhomme, K-Paul's Louisiana Kitchen)

OVEN ROAST PHEASANT
and Pumpkin-Molasses Puree
on a Sauce of Apples, Tequila, and Ancho Chilies
with Crispy Tortilla Relish
(Parker Lacy, The House on Money Hill)

ROASTED TENDERLOIN OF BEEF
with Wild Mushroom Ragout
and Tri-Colored Polenta Terrine
(Jimmy Schmidt, The Rattlesnake Club)

CHINO CHOPPED VEGETABLE SALAD
(Wolfgang Puck, Spago)

VERY BERRY POT PIE
(Natasha O'Brien)

"My darling Chef Caranne!" Natasha sang out. Hoping to defuse him, she went to Caranne first, kissing him on both cheeks. "I feel just like Snow White and the Seven Chefs."

Paul, wearing his signature pea cap, smiled and rolled his eyes. "I can tell you which one is Monsieur Grumpy," he said, glancing at Caranne.

"Not as grumpy as I'm going to be," Brad said, studding a suckling pig with garlic slivers. "My soup will never be ready if I don't set up a spit over that grill."

"Hey, dude. Don't blame me if Frenchie forgot to preheat." Parker Lacy spoke with a Texas drawl preserved as fastidiously as his physique. Parker, the dean of Southwest cooking, was based in Dallas — despite numerous trips to New York during his yearlong affair with Natasha. "Sure wish I could get my hands on whoever talked me into this gig."

Ignoring Parker, Natasha went over to Brad and kissed him. "Where's that boyish grin we all know and love?"

"Thank God you're here," Larry called out. "He's been driving me crazy. Worry, worry, worry."

Brad began to laugh. "He's the one who's worried. I keep telling him, 'Don't worry, Larry, someday you'll cook as good as I do.' "

"Sure he will," Jimmy said from across the aisle. "That's not much to ask for."

"All right, children," Natasha said. "Mommy's here."

Wolf, wearing his Spago baseball cap, winked. "And not a moment too soon, *liebling*," he said, dicing celery.

Natasha put her arm on his shoulder and whispered into his ear. "You're beautiful when you chop."

"And you, Tasha, are even more delicious than my Chino Farm veggies."

"Even better than what they buy at Safeway?"

Wolf threw his head back and laughed. The Safeway market on Wisconsin Avenue was where the White House shopped. Chef Caranne sent two or three chefs in an unmarked van. On their return, everything was checked in by a security guard.

"Listen, it wasn't easy to get clearance on your carrots."

He shrugged. "Love me, love my carrots."

"Hey, break it up, you two!" Paul said. "I'm getting jealous."

Natasha whirled past the sixty-quart mixer and went to the worktable where Paul was sitting. "You want to talk jealous?" she asked. "Talk the chicken cacciatore recipe in your new book."

"You think I should make that instead of pasta?"

"And miss out on the fabulous oysters you brought?" She reached for one and sniffed its shell. "From Pointe à la Hache?"

"On the nose."

Natasha kissed his cheek. "What makes you so luscious?" He offered her his coffee cup. She took a sip of the dark roasted Louisiana coffee flavored with chicory. "You don't miss a trick."

He leaned over and whispered, "I've got a dozen oysters just for you. After we feed the hicks."

Natasha groaned. "Oh, you are bad! I can't wait."

"*You* can't wait? What about Mr. Pig?" Brad asked, stuffing the cavity with onions, garlic, and oranges.

Natasha spoke confidentially. "Listen, you incredibly handsome brute, I'm walking on *oeufs*. I can't be rude to Chef Caranne."

"But coach, all I want is my turn at bat!"

She leaned over to see what Brad was doing. "Such vibrant colors, such robust flavor — "

"Such baloney!" He flashed her one of his famous smiles. "I've got something I want to make for you after dinner."

"Your place or mine?"

She turned to Parker and motioned for him to hurry up.

"Don't blame me, darlin'. Ask Merci Bocuse."

Natasha was dancing as fast as she could to keep the peace between her dream team and the French foreign legion. She couldn't believe Caranne had simply forgotten to preheat the grill, especially after she had been so specific with her instructions for the prep work. Was it bad form to scream in the White House?

Larry held up his salmon. "Better go over there and do your stuff," he said, nodding toward Caranne. "I need the grill, too."

"I already did my stuff," Natasha said between gritted teeth. "I've been on the phone for months now, telling him exactly what we needed and when. You can't get blood from a foie gras." She changed the subject quickly and picked up one of the cedar planks Larry had brought with him. "How'd you ever think of cooking salmon on a wooden board?"

"Shh. The Indians in the Northwest did it first. Except they didn't have to wait on line for the grill."

More fast footwork. "You know what I'm going to do?" Natasha said, running her fingers across the embroidered American flag on

14

his chef's jacket. "I'm going to speak to the Secret Service again. I really don't see the harm in having a few smoldering planks in the dining room. It's a dynamite presentation."

Jimmy Schmidt was very dapper in his checked Armani cook's pants and white jacket. "I think for the best presentation, you should substitute a pastrami sandwich."

Larry started to laugh. Natasha leaned over and took a sip from the glass of Schramsberg champagne Jimmy was nursing. She ran her hand over his Appaloosa horsehide knife case. "You shoot this yourself?"

He nodded and glanced toward Caranne. "Just practicing."

"Jimmy, darling, you must do me a favor."

He stamped his foot. "No! I won't invite him to my birthday party."

"Promise you'll save me a slice of polenta."

"Sure. But I've also got a great veal chop with crab apples, cider, and sage that has Natasha written all over it." He leaned over and whispered, "Listen, I'm really getting worried. I'm last on the list for the grill."

Natasha spun around and without missing a beat shouted, "Enough already, Parker!" He was the only one at whom she could yell. "I thought you were grilling pheasants, not buffalo."

"Thirty pheasants, missy. You can afford to sashay around here being sexy. All you've got to do is fill ten pies."

Parker's words struck terror in Natasha's heart. She turned full face to Caranne, who had been following the conversation as though it were a tennis match. Everyone became quiet. All eyes were on her. She walked toward the dessert table as Cleopatra had walked toward the asp. More frightening than a deadly cobra was the sight of ten blind-baked thirteen-inch pie crusts. They were stacked in two pie racks. Five pies each. A total of ten.

Pausing to catch her breath, she shut her eyes and counted in a flat, emotionless voice. "*Un, deux, trois, quatre, cinq, six, sept, huit, neuf, dix.*" Then, just like the little girl in *The Exorcist,* her voice echoed through the room. "My instructions called for one hundred pies!"

Caranne stepped back. "One hundred pies for one hundred people?"

As though pointing to the Ark of the Covenant, she tapped the listing for Very Berry Pot Pie on the blackboard. "What does that say? That last item. My dessert?"

Caranne cleared his throat and spoke as distinctly as possible. "Veree Beree Poh Pie."

"Pot pie!" she corrected, exploding the *t*. "As in chicken po*t* pie! Very Berry Po*t* Pie is a culinary turn of phrase."

The White House chef shrugged and raised his hands in amazement. "*Je regrette*, but I, too, turn the phrase. I check the ingredients. Raspberry. Strawberry. Red currant. Blueberry. '*Ecoutez*,' I say to my sous with a big smile on my face, 'she is making the joke. She is making a *poh* pie.' " He waited and narrowed his eyes. "As in *pot*-pourri."

"As in chicken po*t* pie!" she snapped. "One hundred individual po*t* pies!"

His voice began to rise. "Chicken po*h* pie is not always *un petit* pie!"

"Right you are! But if you're having one hundred people for dinner and the recipe calls for one hundred pies, what is the logical conclusion?"

"I conclude that you make a mistake."

Natasha began circling Caranne. The room was silent. You could hear a sprig of parsley drop.

Parker came to her side. "Whatcha gonna do now, little lady? Reckon it's too late to round up a hundred head of pot pies."

"Reckon so, Tex." Natasha felt tears of frustration well up in her eyes. But she knew everyone was waiting to see the great Natasha O'Brien save the day.

It wasn't as if she'd never faced a crisis before. If you were a world-class chef, every day was filled with one crisis or another. But this was just a stupid mistake. She couldn't let it ruin a state dinner or destroy a new magazine that was fighting for its life.

She turned to Caranne, put her hands on his shoulders, and said, "Not to worry. A simple misunderstanding. It happens all the time. Oedipus Rex. The *Titanic*. Ollie North."

An audible sigh of relief swept through the kitchen. But then, very slowly, Natasha moved her hands closer to Caranne's neck. As his eyes widened, she tightened her fingers and screamed, "What the fuck am I going to make for dessert?"

*　　*　　*

CARANNE HAD OFFERED Natasha a small room near the kitchen. She hung up her jacket, took off the rest of her clothes, and slipped under the sheet on the single bed. She had to think. Natasha always thought best on her back.

What would Julia Child do? She had eight quarts of strawberries, eight quarts of blueberries, eight quarts of raspberries, and eight quarts of red currants. She had ten thirteen-inch pie crusts and no time to make the hundred that she needed — unless she made them out of meringue. No, they'd leak or get soggy. But not if she lined them with chocolate. Tricky. Perhaps white chocolate.

There was a rap at the door. "Knock knock."

"Who's there?" she asked.

"Tex."

"Tex who?"

Parker opened the door, stepped in, and locked it behind him. "Tex two to tango."

"Oh, Parker. Do you realize what a terrible position I'm in?"

"Don't look so terrible to me," he said, unbuttoning his white jacket and unzipping his trousers. He wore bikini shorts with an American flag pattern.

"Three cheers for the red, white, and blue," she said wistfully.

Parker slid in next to Natasha. "Ain't lust grand?" He leaned over and kissed her breasts.

"Tex, we can't do this in the White House."

"Why not? It's time somebody did."

"I'm so worried."

"I know," he said, reaching for his trousers. "But I didn't forget." He held up a package of condoms.

"Sex is the last thing I need now."

"What the hell kind of dessert chef are you? No one is ever too full for sex." Parker got up onto his knees and straddled Natasha. He moved up and sat gently on her stomach. She positioned the condom and slowly, very slowly, unrolled it millimeter by millimeter. He groaned with ecstasy.

"All I can think about is a thirteen-inch pie!"

"Hey, you want to give me a complex?"

"Parker, we've got to do this fast."

17

"Fast is good."

"I need inspiration."

He smiled. "That's what I'm here for." He kissed the top of her head and worked his way down to her toes. "Giddyap!"

"Tex, I've got to think about pies."

"I was thinking more about *cock au vin*. But all right. Let's think about pies before this thing chokes me to death."

Natasha put her arms around Parker and sighed deeply as he entered. "Pies, pies, pies."

Parker whispered, "Who was it stuck his thumb in a pie?" He began rocking back and forth.

Eyes closed, she held tightly to him. "Little Jack Horner."

"There you go, missy. What kind of pie?"

"I can't remember."

"Think harder," Parker gasped.

Natasha went through all the obvious choices. Berry tart with apricot glaze and vanilla ice cream. Berry cream pie. Red berries in blueberry sauce? Perhaps with a spun-sugar dome. Like the Capitol building.

Parker nibbled on her ear. Breathlessly, he whispered, "How you coming?" He buried his face in her breast, massaging her nipples with his lips.

Perhaps a thin lid of dark chocolate studded with white chocolate stars.

Parker began rocking faster. "Did you say 'stars'?"

"I said I was seeing stars." It was then that she remembered Parker's American flag shorts. She reached for them. "Hey, Tex," she whispered, putting them around his head, "I love your red, white, and blueberry undies."

"Depends on where you put the blueberries."

Natasha gasped. "Oh my God!"

"Thanks, baby. It's great for me, too."

"Tex, I've got it!"

"Wait for me, missy. I'm gettin' it!"

Natasha held tight to Parker. "I can see it!"

"Jeez, you're really hot today."

"Listen to this . . ."

"Talk to me."

"I know what to put in the pie crusts!"

He began to groan as he thrust deep into her. "I never thought about doing it in a pie crust!"

"A circle of red currants . . ."

"Oh, yeah!"

"Then a circle of white-chocolate mousse . . ."

"Destry rides again!"

"Then a circle of raspberries . . ."

"Then white, baby."

"Red, white, red, white . . ."

"Oooooooooh!"

"Then strawberries . . ."

"Aaaaaaaaah!"

"More white mousse."

Parker laughed. "I never saw a white moose."

"The red and white stripes of the flag."

"I love it!"

"And a big circle filled with blueberries. Blueberries covered with white-chocolate stars."

"Shootin' stars!" he shouted. "Holy jicama! I'm gonna shoot stars just for you!"

Natasha began to gasp. She dug her fingers into Parker's back and tightened her muscles around him. "Oh, say, can you see!"

Parker began to groan and rock faster. "Hold on, darlin'. The cavalry is coming!"

After a few moments, they lay motionless in one another's arms. Parker took the underwear off his head. "You are some wild filly. You on something?"

"Does my ass count?"

"I don't know." Parker sat up. He turned Natasha facedown and stared at her buttocks. "How much is two and two?"

She began to laugh. "Oh, Parker, promise you won't ever fall in love with me. I'd really miss the sex."

He took her chin in his hand. "What about the inspiration?"

Natasha shrugged. "You know me. I'll think of something." She threw her arms around Parker while she began to work out her battle plan for "Red, White, and Blueberry Pie."

# RED, WHITE, AND BLUEBERRY PIE

TART DOUGH
1 1/2 cup unbleached all-purpose flour
1 teaspoon sugar
1/4 teaspoon salt
1/2 cup unsalted butter, cold
1/3 cup whipping cream

Blend flour, sugar, and salt together in a large bowl. Cut
butter into 1/2-inch cubes and toss into flour. Press butter
between thumbs and fingers, blending it into flour mixture
until a coarse meal is formed--its texture will resemble that of
cornmeal.

Add cream and blend with a rubber spatula or spoon until it
is absorbed. Press together with hands until a dough forms.
Work the dough gently if needed. Shape into a ball, dust with
flour, and roll into a 13-inch circle. Roll around a rolling pin.
Unroll over a 10-inch tart pan. Lift the edges, allowing them to
fall to the inside edge of the pan. Press dough against the pan.
Fold the extra dough over and against the edge of the pan,
forming a double edge. Press the double thickness of dough
into the rim of the pan, forcing some of it above the top. Move
the extra dough out beyond the rim. Trim this with the bottom
pad of your hand, cutting it against the rim. Chill for 30
minutes. Preheat oven to 375° and put rack on lowest level.

Line the inside of the shell with heavy aluminum foil. Press
the prongs of a fork through the foil and dough repeatedly, an

inch apart each time, covering the bottom. Bake for 30 minutes or until golden brown. Remove from oven and set aside to cool.

## WHITE-CHOCOLATE MOUSSE
2 large eggs
1/2 cup sugar
1/4 cup lemon juice
4 ounces white chocolate, chopped
1 cup whipping cream

Beat eggs until blended. Stir in sugar, then lemon juice. Cook in the top of a double boiler, stirring occasionally until thickened enough to coat the back of a spoon. Remove from heat and stir in white chocolate until melted. Set aside to cool, stirring occasionally. Whip cream to firm peaks, cover and chill until needed. Fold cooled lemon mixture into whipped cream. Reserve 1/3 of the mixture and spread the rest evenly into the prebaked shell. Chill for 1 hour.

## FINISH
1 pint strawberries
1 pint blueberries
1/2 pint raspberries
1/2 pint red currants
1/2 cup sugar
1/4 cup water
1 tablespoon fruit pectin
4 ounces white chocolate
1 cup whipping cream

Wash the berries separately by submerging them in cold water. Drain and dry on separate towels. Alternate rings of raspberries and strawberries from the center of the tart out, leaving a ring of mousse visible between each ring of berries. The final outer ring of the tart should be about 2 inches wide. Fill with blueberries. Put the remaining 1/3 of the mousse mixture into a pastry bag and pipe over existing mousse rings to make them level with berry rings. Cover and chill until ready to serve.

Crush the currants in a blender or food processor. Combine in a stainless steel saucepan the currants, sugar, and water. Bring to a boil and reduce to a simmer. Cook until sauce coats the back of a spoon, about 15 minutes. Stir in pectin, remove from heat, and strain, discarding the skins. Set aside to cool.

Cut chocolate into small pieces and place in the top of a double boiler, covering top with plastic wrap. In the bottom of a double boiler, heat water to a simmer. Turn off heat and place pan with chocolate on top. Let stand until chocolate is almost melted. Remove plastic and stir with a metal spoon until completely melted. Spread evenly, 1/8 inch thick, over a piece of parchment or wax paper. Set aside to harden. Using a small star cutter, cut 24 stars. Place 12 evenly around the outer ring of blueberries on the tart.

Cut tart into 12 servings, each containing a star. Whip cream to firm peaks. Center servings on individual plates, pour currant sauce on the side, and pipe a whipped-cream rosette next to each serving. Finish with another white-chocolate star against rosette.

ALEC GORDON stood up and waved at Miss Beauchamp as she entered the domed salon at the Ritz in London. His former secretary, the woman he had married by proxy in order to protect the van Golk fortune, the only person other than Enstein who knew that his death had been staged, was meeting him for tea. Meeting Alec Gordon. A friend of van Golk's. If he could fool her, he could fool anyone.

Beauchamp (pronounced *Beechum*) was a riot of beige. Everything about her was colorless, from her tan fedora to her sensible shoes. She was one of those women who looked fifty the first day of kindergarten.

Alec stood up nervously and extended his hand. "Miss Beauchamp?"

Her grip was tight. She stared intently at him. "What news?"

Alec smiled. "Won't you sit down?"

Beauchamp nodded. She pulled her chair close and spoke in a hush. "Is he all right? I'm so worried. He won't take my calls. He doesn't answer my letters. The last time I heard from him was nearly a year ago." She burst into tears. "A three-word telex."

Alec nodded. " 'Send more caviar.' "

She gasped. "How is he?"

"Quite fit, actually."

"If only I could be certain. Can you help me? I must see him."

"Of course."

Beauchamp's mouth dropped open. " 'Of course'? When?"

"Right now."

She put a hand to her breast. "He's here? In London?"

"Yes."

23

Beauchamp whispered, "He escaped?"

"In a manner of speaking."

Her eyes opened wide. "Where is he?"

"Here."

Beauchamp moved her lips, barely making a sound. "Here? At the Ritz?"

Alec leaned forward and took her hand. "Here. At this table."

Beauchamp paused to process what she had heard, then pulled back and sat straight up in her seat. She narrowed her eyes. "Mr. Gordon, what is it you're up to?"

"I believe I'm up to tea."

Alec had won. His heartbeat was extremely rapid, but he had learned through years of Enstein's probing and his own revelations that no one could see into his heart. The nearsightedness of human perception was shocking. The only person in the world who had loved Achille van Golk could not recognize him at arm's length. Not that he hadn't wanted to fool her, not that he was surprised he had, but deep down, where the ghost of Achille still haunted him, he was disappointed.

"We're ready to order," he said, raising his hand and stopping the waiter. "Where do you get your smoked salmon these days?"

The young waiter looked up and smiled. "I beg your pardon?"

"Norway? Scotland? What part of the North Atlantic?"

"I don't know, sir. But it's very good. Everyone likes it."

"What reassuring news. But I still wish to know where it comes from."

The waiter was flustered. "From the kitchen, sir?"

Beauchamp stood up and pointed a finger at Alec. "What is this game you're playing?"

Alec turned to the waiter. "Madam is about to faint. Bring some water."

"Still water, sir, or sparkling?" the waiter asked nervously.

"Definitely still," Alec said as Beauchamp began to tremble.

"If you're a reporter, you'll get nothing out of me!" she shouted.

"Evian or Malvern?" the waiter whispered.

"For God's sake, not Malvern!" Alec snapped. "The only person who drinks that slop is the Queen."

The waiter hesitated. "With lemon, sir?"

"No."

"Ice?"

"And just what is the point of bottled water with ice?"

"I don't know, sir!" He raced over to the bar.

Beauchamp clenched a handkerchief between her teeth to keep from screaming. "How did you get my name?"

"It was scratched on the pyramid at Giza. For a Good Time, Call Beauchamp."

"Are you having a good time?" she sobbed. "Oh, please. Tell me about him. How does he look? Is he getting enough to eat? Tell me something. Tell me anything."

"I am Achille."

Beauchamp closed her eyes and slid to the floor.


TWO HOURS LATER, in Alec's corner suite overlooking Green Park, after having heard the Achille-Alec story twice, Beauchamp sat on the bed, staring blankly at her sensible shoes. "And what if I won't?"

"Why in the world would you refuse? I thought you loved me."

"I loved Achille van Golk. I married Achille van Golk, not you."

"Achille was a three-hundred-and-fifty-pound homicidal maniac."

Beauchamp began to cry again. "I know. What have you done with him?"

"He no longer exists. Achille was a devil that I have cast out. All that remains is his memory. I am finally free of his psychotic emotions and his self-destructive tendencies."

She sobbed loudly. "His rapier wit. His exuberance. His thirst for perfection at any cost. That uncontrollable Rabelaisian appetite. Gone. All gone." She was suddenly defiant. "Do you really believe it's possible? Can one simply pick a new personality off the shelf as one does a box of breakfast cereal? Yesterday you were Mr. van Golk. Today you are Mr. Muesli."

"Hardly. It took five years. A psychiatrist, two physical therapists, a dietician, a plastic surgeon, a speech therapist, a nutritionist . . ."

"And now you wish me to become Mrs. Muesli?"

"No. Mrs. Alec Gordon."

"Do you love me?"

"Beauchamp, do not count the ways. I am marrying you for my money."

"Love's plaything." She shrugged. There was no use fighting. "But there are medical tests . . . various applications."

Alec sat next to her. "The insurance agent last week?"

"Yet another setup?"

"Beauchamp, I have always taken care of you."

"Achille van Golk has always taken care of me."

"You shall continue to be a rich woman. Since you have no family and friends, you and your budgie, Henry the Fourth — "

She sniffed. "Poor Henry died."

"Oh, I am sorry. Did you get another?"

She nodded. "Henry the Fourth, Part Two."

"You and Henry will be taken care of for all your days. I've already given you my flat on Curzon Street, and you are due a substantial pension from the magazine."

"I do not intend to stop working at *Lucullus*."

"Nothing could be further from my mind. I shall require references from you. For Alec Gordon."

"So. I am to give you your past and your future."

"Yes."

"In return for my lonely old age."

"Beauchamp, you were lonely as a child. You were lonely as an adult. You have had a lonely middle age. I am offering you warmth in winter, food, dignity, and hand-embroidered linen."

"Where will you go?"

"To America."

"Of course."

Alec stood up and offered her his hand. "The vicar is in the next room. My plane leaves in two hours."

"I boarded the number 31 bus as Mrs. van Golk, and I am to go home as Mrs. Gordon."

"Beauchamp, I am hardly a savage. I hired a car and planned to drop you off on my way to the airport. Or, since the suite is already paid for, you may spend your wedding night here. Take an extra day or two. What does it matter?"

She began to cry again. "You will fool everyone, you know. It's quite a clever disguise. There is barely anything of Achille left."

"I shall tell the vicar we are ready."

Beauchamp grabbed his hand. "No! We are not ready yet!"

"I have been very generous."

"With everything but yourself."

"Beauchamp!"

"I shall have been twice married and still a virgin."

"You cannot be serious."

"Did the plastic surgeons touch your lips?"

"No."

"I thought not." She pulled him close. "Kiss me. I shall close my eyes and remember you just as you were."

Alec hesitated. But after all, he too could close his eyes. He glanced at his watch. He was determined to make that plane. He leaned over and kissed her.

"Achille," she whispered.

Natasha, he thought.

**LUCULLUS**

95 Curzon Street

London WCI 45G9

To Whom It May Concern:

It gives me great pleasure to introduce Mr. Alec Gordon.

For the past six years, Mr. Gordon has been employed by this magazine as Executive Assistant to both the late A. van Golk and his successor, Ms. B. Fairchild. We regret his decision to resign in order to return to his native country, the United States of America.

Mr. Gordon was responsible for maintaining Mr. van Golk's impeccable standards of culinary reportage during the calamitous period after the latter's unexpected departure. It is a tribute to Mr. Gordon that he performed this task seamlessly. Indeed, his words, and deeds, flowed with such piercing accuracy that it was impossible to identify where Mr. van Golk left off and Mr. Gordon began.

How we shall miss Alec Gordon! He is a modern Brillat-Savarin, and the entire food world is indebted to his breakthrough investigations into the renaissance of root vegetables, the origins of gluttony, and the synergy between Yorkshire pudding and the Battle of Hastings.

We wish him well in applying his unique talents to the great chefs of America.

Respectfully yours,

M. E. Beauchamp

MAXIMILIAN (MILLIE) OGDEN winced as he watched the black-kimonoed Japanese waitress with a painted white face and painted black lips tear the head from a live prawn. She held its writhing body between the perfectly parallel thumb and forefinger of one hand while she picked off each leg. Then, as the prawn went into spasms, she placed it on a sizzling hot rock, using two long chopsticks to hold down the convulsing corpse. Millie turned in horror to his hostess, Mrs. Nakamura, seated on the hard wooden bench next to him.

Areiko Nakamura had appeared at Fuji Food headquarters immediately after her husband's funeral and taken his seat as head of the board. No one had dared risk offending her by calling for a vote. She was at least fifty, possibly sixty, and still dazzlingly sensual, with the promise of erotic pleasures offered by women in Shunga prints. Catching Millie's glance, she enunciated carefully through blood-red lips, "*Ishiyaki.*"

"*Ishiyaki,*" he repeated, wondering whether it had something to do with the prawns or whether she was coming on to him.

"*Ishiyaki* means shrimp on stone."

"Some presentation. How the hell did Martha Stewart miss this one?"

Mrs. Nakamura began to smile and instinctively put a hand over her mouth. She cleared her throat and, as she continued laughing, removed her hand in a bold gesture of liberation. "I buy her books. I believe they are published by Random House." Mrs. Nakamura opened her mouth wide to show her perfectly capped teeth.

"You've read Martha Stewart?"

29

"She is funnier than Erma Bombeck." A pause. "McGraw-Hill, I believe."

Millie, vice president of American Good Foods, was in Tokyo. Specifically, he was in the $450-a-head Shumegawa restaurant, on the tenth floor of a greenish building across from the Sony building — the exact translation of the address given to his driver. Shumegawa, like the Sony building, was basically a samurai compound. One entered through a low doorway that led to a narrow, dark, pebbled passageway studded with rings cut from trees. The sounds heard along the shadowy path were those of water dripping into a small pond filled with bearded black fish, the grunts of shoeless businessmen drinking premium Scotch in their private bamboo dining rooms, and the whine of an ancient koto as headless prawns danced on hot rocks.

The waitress speared the *ishiyaki* with wooden skewers, tucked them into maple leaves, bowed, and backed out of the room. Mrs. Nakamura picked up her leaf and bit into the prawn. "Aaaah!"

Millie looked around. At four hundred and fifty bucks, they could give you a piece of lemon or a little tartar sauce. Where the hell was Mrs. Paul when you needed her? "You eat it plain?"

Mrs. Nakamura picked up Millie's leaf-wrapped prawn and held it to his mouth. "Ocean and land. What more do you want?"

He bit into the naked prawn while staring at her surgically rounded eyes. "A little ketchup?"

Mrs. Nakamura smiled and opened her purse. She took out a solid gold Dunhill cigarette case. Millie reached for his lighter and held the flame close. While inhaling, she ran her finger across the enamel. "Dupont. The Regency series?"

"It was a gift."

"Only life is a gift, Ogden-san. The rest is shopping." She held the lighter close to read the inscription. "Who is Natasha?"

"My ex-wife."

"How ex?"

"About as ex as she can get."

She reached for his tie. "Hermès?"

"Who else?"

Mrs. Nakamura pulled gently on the tie, bringing him close. She kissed Millie on the lips, inhaled deeply, and whispered, "Monsieur Givenchy?"

"Himself."

She let go, took a deep puff on her cigarette, and blew smoke into his face. "Gauloise."

Millie coughed. "The best." He cleared his throat. "I can't tell you how honored I am that you would see me, considering your husband's recent death."

Mrs. Nakamura glanced at her oyster Rolex. "Why don't we cut the shit? My husband was a short fat pig."

Before Millie could think of anything to say, the waitress reappeared with a large platter of tiny deep-fried fish with big black eyes. "Well, well, and what's this?" he asked, desperate to change the subject.

Mrs. Nakamura picked up a whitebait by the tail and dropped it into her mouth. "Southern-fried sperm," she said.

Millie sat back. "My favorite."

Smiling, she held a whitebait to Millie's mouth. "You don't want to insult the cook."

"They're not cooks, they're executioners."

She began to laugh again. A low, guttural, lewd laugh. "You are very amusing, for an American."

Millie bit into the whitebait and swallowed it. He didn't like being amusing for an American. He had too much at stake. Eight months of work on the Fuji Food deal when the fax came that the short fat pig had dropped dead before signing the papers. Millie's plan to refinance AGF was dependent upon the Fuji contract. He had a cargo plane full of deep-fried Pretzel People, chocolate bran muffins, and Space Tacos waiting to be flown to Tokyo, unloaded, and replaced with the frozen TV sushi dinners that he had convinced AGF would capture the U.S. market faster than salsa.

"Mrs. Nakamura . . ."

"Not that tone, Odgen-san. It is most unattractive, even for a hairy white man."

"I'm not all that hairy." Millie was in his middle forties, tall, clean-shaven, with a large aquiline nose and a full head of salt-and-pepper hair. His Cary Grant hair, he called it.

She took his hand as though it were an intensely intimate act. "I have recalculated the distribution figures based upon my buying a fleet of planes."

He pulled his hand back. "Are you kidding? Why would you buy your own planes?"

"Kazuo and my father were pilots during the war."

"The war is over."

"Not for those who lost."

"But buying a fleet of planes will change all the numbers."

"It is so difficult to do business with Americans. You make deals as though making a marriage." She rubbed her hand along his thigh. "Armani?"

He stopped her before she reached his crotch. "And how do you make a deal?"

"Like a divorce, Ogden-san. Does it matter how much you give up or how much you keep?"

Millie thought of his divorce, that he would have given up everything to stay with Natasha and that she wouldn't take anything from him.

The waitress returned with two wire frames each holding a conical shell. She put the frames atop the hot stone and reached for a pot of boiling broth. As the shells heated, the small creatures who lived inside extended their antennae. Millie groaned as the waitress ladled boiling broth into each shell and then, with her chopsticks, pulled the squirming mollusks from their homes. She dropped them into Imari cups filled with broth, a sliver of sour grass, and half a ginkgo nut. After presenting the dishes, she bowed and left.

Millie shuddered as Mrs. Nakamura picked up her chopsticks and lifted a creature from the broth. "You must swallow it whole, like an oyster."

"The problem is, I'm not an oyster." He put his bowl down. "I'm sorry. I can't let you control shipping costs. That puts AGF at your mercy."

"Open your mouth."

Millie hesitated and then gulped it down. "Delicious!"

"Now you drink the broth."

"Are you sure that thing was dead?" he asked, reaching for the cup.

"I will guarantee distribution costs for two years."

Millie looked around for something else to drink. He slugged down the sake. "Mrs. Nakamura, may I be candid? You have a refrigerated warehouse filled with frozen sushi dinners that you couldn't give away in Japan. You screw up this deal, and that's the one false move your honorable board of directors has been waiting for. Every one of those guys has been wined, dined, and fucked for eight months straight to get this deal into position. You come in now and play Dragon Lady, you're out on your ass."

"Back to being a geisha."

Millie put his hand to her breast. "Christian La Croix?"

She gasped. "Yes."

"Geishas don't buy, Mrs. Nakamura. They sell."

Without a word, she opened her purse and took out a pen. "Cartier."

Millie opened his jacket and took out the papers. "Your ass."

As soon as she had signed the contract, he stood up and shouted for the waitress. "*Uetoresu! Uetoresu!*"

"Ogden-san, what is wrong?"

"Let's get the hell out of here," he said, grabbing the contract from her. "I can still get us a table at Trader Vic's."

Hiram, ole kid, shalom!

Turn off your Panasonic, set the timer on your Hitachi, park your Mitsubishi, put a new disk in your Toshiba, change your Seiko to Tokyo time, and get on board the next JAL flight to the land of the rising Sony.

I don't care what they're teaching at the Nouveau School, just stand on any strasse in Munich or Tokyo and tell me that Hitler and Hirohito didn't know exactly what they were doing. The way I figure it, with failing economies, terminal unemployment, and too many crankies, a little unfriendly fire was just what they needed. Then all they had to do was stop shooting long enough to stuff their wallets with foreign aid and put everyone back to work. How come the Yalta boys weren't smart enough to lose the war?

Well, at least we're losing the peace. You should see the Fuji Foodies at work. No one but the Mikado rates a private office. (You don't want to go into the doorknob business in Japan.) All the worker bees swarm around in a big open communal space that doesn't do much for reading the paper, private phone conversations, or tushie pinching. Then, after a fast ten- or twelve-hour day, middle management schlepps off to entertain clients at McSushi's and then on to the nearest karaoke bar, where everyone gets drunk, throws up in the street, and crawls home for a few zzzzzz's before the morning crush hour. Now don't get me wrong: this is probably more fun than being boiled in oil.

But the Japanese concept of T&E loses something in the translation. It's like a kid shaving with a razor that has no

34

blades. It makes him feel all grown up, but he doesn't have the faintest idea what it's all about. Another example: everyone here claims to know English. But what they really know is how to read English and say "Good morning." You could walk up to one of the secretaries and say, "Miss Yamamoto, your hair is on fire," and she'd smile and say, "Good morning."

I tell you, Hiram, even with high-definition TV, a branch of Maxim's, and more neon than Vegas, this place is a goddamn Kurasawa movie. They're all still samurais, and beneath their very pacific exteriors, there's an emotional time bomb ticking. Mark my words, Japan is on a more dangerous fault line than southern California. One day these people are going to explode, and I don't want to be around when the yakitori hits the fan.

All of which is my way of saying that having s-layed the Dragon Lady, let's have someone else take over this account. Preferably someone who wears Calvin Klein underwear. You know the type. I think we have some left over from the '80s in genetic splicing or aroma packaging. Sniff around. I have decided to take the plunge. If she'll have me.

Max

THE LUNCH CRUSH was on at Neal Short's trendy new Los Angeles bistro, Le La. Iced tea, bottled water, and diet colas dotted the tables as though it were the cocktail lounge at Betty Ford. The "surf's up!" waitstaff whizzed by on roller skates, delivering thin-crusted frisbees dotted with duck sausage, goat cheese, and leeks; prosciutto, radicchio, and fig; shredded lettuce, truffle, and foie gras confetti.

Natasha was having lunch with food critic Roy Drake, whose most distinguishing features were his permanent sneer and a grease-stained Filofax. Slender, with thinning blond hair, Roy wore his half-glasses midway down his nose. He looked up as he stopped writing.

"I hear Mimi Sheraton gained another pound," he said with a smile.

"Give it a rest, Roy."

He pushed aside his swordfish with sorrel gnocchi and reached for a forkful of Natasha's grilled porcini salsa. "You sound like my agent," he said, sticking out his tongue at both the salsa and Bobby Silverstein.

"Roy, I didn't invite you for lunch to hear about your screenplay."

"You and everybody else. My screenplay is almost old enough to have a bar mitzvah." He picked up the bread and sniffed it before ripping off a piece. Then he stuck his knife into the butter and licked it clean. "You want to know how much the Frugal weighs?"

"I want to know if you're going to do a piece on the Culinary Olympics for me."

"I hate Paris."

"You don't hate Paris. You hate the Parisians, which is perfectly natural." She smiled. "Not that I'm accusing you of being perfectly natural. Come on, be a pal. We'll eat from dawn till dusk."

"Is that your way of telling me I don't need a five-star hotel?"

"Bitch, bitch, bitch."

The waiter skated over to the table holding two plates. "Neal is dying to have you taste these. Smoked duck spring roll salad with snap peas, apples, and fennel in a honey and raspberry-vinegar dressing," he said, putting a dish in front of Natasha. "And this is his latest, Mr. Drake, grilled Santa Barbara shrimp with chili-peach polenta and fresh mint pesto."

"His latest," Roy muttered. "Number twenty-seven."

Natasha smiled at the waiter and said, "Thank you." As soon as his ponytail was out of sight, she turned to Roy. "What do you mean, number twenty-seven?"

"What I mean is that there is one master menu for the entire city of Los Angeles. It's on file in the municipal building. You get a license to open a restaurant, you get a copy of an equal-opportunity menu on which you're permitted to change one ingredient per dish. You also get the official register of hearing-impaired and color-phobic restaurant designers, a list of movie stars who do not yet have permanent tables and are open for in-vestment, plus a catalog from Frieda's with a coupon for an in-troductory kiwi."

Natasha had taken a taste of everything on her plate. She switched dishes with Roy. "The duck is so aromatic. I wonder what he smoked it over."

"From what I hear, a couple of joints."

"Wait until you taste the spring roll. He must have used carda-mom."

"The hell he did. Cardamom is far too ethnic for the dark ages of culinary *perestroika*. Italian restaurants serve pasta with broccoli, the Chinese are back in Cantonese hell, and the French have surren-dered to the Japanese. Australians bottle their own Riesling, and Moët makes something called California champagne. Just who do you have to fuck to get a pizza with tomato sauce and mozzarella on it?"

"Don't look at me," she said.

"You least of all."

"Why me least of all?"

"Thanks to you, anyone who can undercook broccoli thinks he's a superstar."

"Thanks to me, young men who once dreamed of being auto mechanics enroll in cooking school. Kids all across the country graduate from culinary colleges as proudly as if they were Harvard MBAs. What's wrong with that?"

"Listen, you six-burner Cinderella, the more you glorify the chef, the more you kill off the restaurant business. Thanks to you, when a chef leaves a restaurant after you've skyrocketed him to fame, it closes! You can't get anyone to invest today unless the chef is part owner. Used to be, you needed a new cook, you hung around the track or the drunk tank. You went to a restaurant because the restaurant was famous, not the chef. What you've done is put the à la carte before the horse." Roy speared a piece of spring roll and held it up. "It's not cardamom!" he said triumphantly. "It's turmeric!"

"Cardamom!"

He waved his hand to get the waiter's attention. "Oh, skater!"

"Roy, don't make a scene! I'll put you up at the Plaza."

The waiter glided over. "Mr. Drake?"

Roy held up his half-eaten piece of spring roll. "Turmeric or cardamom?"

The waiter looked uneasy. "I'll ask Neal," he said, skating toward the kitchen.

Natasha started to laugh. "Why don't we make a little bet?"

"You're on," Roy said. "Cardamom, I go to Paris — "

"Turmeric, I also get someone else to go to Dallas and interview Parker."

Roy picked up a shrimp and sniffed it. "Don't eat them. At least not until I get an autopsy. God knows what they died of."

"The shrimp are perfect. Supernal. The chili-peach polenta is nothing short of brilliant. It's hot and sweet with a very sexy rush of cool mint pesto."

"Spare me. You sound like Gael Greene after too much radicchio."

"Go to hell. I love Gael."

The waiter returned with two more plates while the busboy cleared. "I didn't want these to get cold. Okay," he said, placing a dish in front of Natasha. "This is a napoleon of roast pork layered with Pernod potatoes and Napa Valley cabbage mousse in a sur-round of clementine-infused oil. And this," he said, putting the other plate in front of Roy and lowering his voice respectfully, "is one of Dustin's favorites. Pot roast braised with sweet vermouth and Michigan yellow cherries, Georgia sweet-potato wonton, and grilled Colorado baby beets."

Roy stared up at him. "Turmeric or cardamom?"

The waiter glanced from Roy to Natasha, obviously trying to figure out who had guessed which. Grimacing, as though bringing the message to Garcia, he said, with a sharp intake of breath, "Car-damom?"

Natasha and Roy both sat steely-faced until he left. "For the record," Roy said flatly, "I won't stay anywhere but the Crillon."

"For the record, you overpaid appetite depressant, you'll rough it with the rest of us at the Plaza-Athenée."

"Power-mad food bitch."

Natasha took his hand. "Roy, it's going to be fun."

"It's going to be cardamom. Pure cardamom." He shook his head. "I can't believe it's time for another marzipan marathon."

The waiter brought a phone to the table and plugged it in. "Long-distance, Miss O'Brien."

She raised her eyebrows in surprise and picked up the receiver. "Natasha O'Brien."

"Nat."

Natasha's heart stopped. She recognized Millie's voice immedi-ately. "I didn't read anything about hell freezing over."

"It's been a long time."

"Not long enough, chum. Listen, I'm busy right now . . ." Roy shrugged. He put his fingers into his ears and focused on his notes.

"Roy can wait."

"How do you know I'm with Roy?" As she looked up, Natasha caught sight of Millie seated across the room, a telephone in his hand. "They told me it was long-distance," she said softly, unable to stop staring at him.

"It is."

"You bet your ass it is," she said.

"I saw you this morning on the tube."

"Lots of people saw me. All kinds of people."

"Not the way I did. I know you. Everything's going great. Ev-

39

eryone's talking about you. The magazine. The Olympics. The White House. It must be driving you nuts."

Natasha's instincts short-circuited. She wanted desperately to hang up. He was the last person in the world she wanted to know how she really felt. "Millie," she whispered, staring at him, "I keep waiting for the ax to fall, the other shoe to drop."

"Maybe that's why you left me. You can't stand being happy."

"Don't be ridiculous. We were never happy. Besides, this is different. This is business." She paused. "Oh, Millie. It all started out so well."

"Are you talking about our marriage or your career?"

"Nothing ever goes this smoothly. Something has to go wrong." Natasha leaned forward, confiding in Millie as she allowed the Great Wave of Apprehension to engulf her. "Everyone is expecting me to pull it off."

"So what if they are?"

"So what if I don't?" Her tone changed suddenly. "Dear God, I'm talking to you as though you were a real person." And then another change in her voice. "You never used to go to restaurants alone."

"I'm not alone. She went to the ladies'."

"Bingo!" Natasha clenched her fist. "Forget everything I just said. My magazine and my life are headed straight for the top." She hissed, "No sequels!" and hung up.

Roy slumped back in his chair. "Bite your tongue. I have a meeting with Bobby this afternoon."

"You know, I really hate it when people start feeling sorry for themselves." Tears began to form in her eyes. "Why the hell don't you get on with your life like I did? You know what your problem is, Roy? You can't divorce yourself from projects that don't work out. Well, I can. I learned. No one can make a fool out of me unless I let them. I'm the only person who controls my life. No gremlins or ghosts lurking around the corner for me. Don't you get it, Roy? The joke is that God only has *one* shoe. Now shut up and eat your grilled Colorado baby beets!"

Suddenly Natasha was aware of how loud her voice had become. She glanced self-consciously at the next table. A man was reading a book. He didn't seem to be disturbed. He didn't even seem to be listening.

40

But he was.

He was Alec Gordon.


ROY STEPPED OFF the elevator and walked down the corridor toward Bobby Silverstein's office. The side with windows was for agents. Across the aisle, separated by shoulder-high partitions, were the secretaries and their fluorescent lamps. Bobby had the corner office. He also had Mae Sung. And Mae Sung had a big dish of fortune cookies, to which she was hopelessly addicted.

" 'Rising to the top sometimes means standing on someone's shoulders,' " she said, offering him a cookie. "That was some razz you gave Chasen's!"

Roy nodded, reaching over to pick a cookie. He opened it and read the message aloud: " 'Have patience. You will soon learn the truth.' "

Mae shook her head in amazement. "Son of a gun! Works every time. Go ahead in. He's on the phone with Killer Diller." She rolled her eyes. " 'The silent tongue lives in the wise head.' "

Roy felt himself tense. Bobby had promised to send the screenplay to Diller. "Who called who?" Roy asked.

"Barry called. Twice. Very excited. They've been on the phone for half an hour."

Bobby Silverstein wore cashmere sweaters the way Oliver Stone wore sincere. No matter where he was going or what the weather, Bobby draped a sweater over his shoulders and tied the sleeves across his chest. His hair cut short, his handsome face tan and clean-shaven, Bobby was California trim — except for the pot belly he had sprouted, which made him look pregnant.

His bookshelves were filled with sweaters, cans of tennis balls, videotapes, boxes of athletic supporters, bottles of cologne, and an alphabetized collection of mail-order catalogs. As he saw Roy, Bobby waved him in, then put his hand over the receiver as he asked, "What happened? Chasen's made you pay?"

Roy pushed aside the boxes of tennis sneakers on the leather sofa and sat down. Half a dozen mini–television sets in the bookcase were tuned to six different channels. No sound. There were no scripts in Bobby's bookcase, none piled on the desk or on the floor. There were no letters or memos to be seen. Not even a pen in sight.

The rumor had been circulating for years that Bobby could neither read nor write.

"Barry, are you crazy? She's got cancer. How can she play doubles? So who? No, she just had her tits done. The only thing she plays is Sidney's cock, and if I know Sidney, she plays it through a straw. Wait a minute, I got the expert right here." Bobby turned to Roy. "Where should we go for lunch?"

"Le La."

"Le La? Barry, you heard of it? Yeah? Another kingdom of the fagalas?" Bobby shrugged, then turned back to Roy. "Where should we sit?"

Roy whispered, "Did he say anything about the screenplay?" Bobby held up his hand to signal Roy to be patient. Roy said, "Don't let them sit you near the windows." Then he shouted, "Hi, Barry! Sit near the bar."

"You hear that? Sure, I'll tell him. Barry says he agrees with you about Chasen's."

Roy smiled nervously and shouted, "Great minds — "

"Barry wants to know what kind of pizza they have."

"Forget the pizza," Roy said. "Dustin loves the pot roast."

Bobby shook his head from side to side. "Dustin loves the pot roast," he repeated solemnly into the receiver.

"It's made with Cinzano and cherries and comes with sweet-potato wonton."

"Dustin also loved *Ishtar*. What else?"

"Santa Barbara shrimp with chili-peach polenta."

"You heard?" Bobby asked.

"Does he like it?" Roy whispered.

"No," Bobby said angrily. "You better come up with something else, and fast."

Roy felt the sweat run down the side of his face. He got up and walked over to the phone, shouting, "Smoked duck spring roll salad!"

Bobby nodded. "He likes it."

Roy began to giggle nervously. "It's got snap peas, apples, and fennel in a great honey–raspberry vinegar dressing."

"He loves it!" Bobby said, breaking into a broad grin. "This is a done deal!"

Roy mimed the words "Ask him about the screenplay." He sat down, accidentally knocking over the sneaker boxes.

"Barry, listen, before I forget, you didn't like that thing of Roy's I sent you, did you? No, I didn't think you would. Okay, so I'll see you."

Roy suddenly felt the sharp edges of the boxes. He leaned back, hoping the physical pain would detract from the sick feeling in his stomach. He looked up at Bobby.

"So?" Bobby asked. "What about dessert?"

Roy could barely breathe, much less speak. "What about dessert?" he coughed out. "What about me?"

Bobby rolled his eyes and slapped his belly. "Listen. Is it my fault you decided that everyone had to know what happened after Ingrid Bergman got on the plane with Paul Henreid?"

"I've been working on it for three years."

"But you just saw what they really want. They want to know what to eat for lunch. You tell Diller about lunch. That's your job. Bubbala, I understand. You live in L.A., and you caught the screenplay disease. There's no telethon for it, but then again it's not fatal. You'll get over it."

"*Casablanca II* is a damn good script!" Roy shouted.

" 'Good'? What the fuck has 'good' got to do with this business? You want good, go to shul."

"I don't want you to send it to any more producers. Send it to a director."

"All right, I'll send it to a director."

"Who?"

"David Lean."

"David Lean is dead!"

Bobby shrugged. "So he doesn't get too many submissions."

"Don't do this to me, Bobby," Roy shouted, getting up from the sneaker boxes. "I'm not some nobody. I've got edge. People can't wait to see who I'll destroy next. They read my column all over the country."

"Because you write about food. Do me the life of Sara Lee and maybe I could sell it to television. Roy, write about what you know. Give me something like that movie about killing the great chefs. That I know I could sell."

"You want me to write a sequel to *Someone Is Killing the Great Chefs of Europe*?"

"You're from New York, right?"

"Yes."

"Okay. So you must have a library card. Go look up newspaper headlines. That's all they're buying anyway. Take my advice, boychik, and I'll turn you into another Shana Alexander."

"But I hate writing about food. I hate going to restaurants, and most of all, I hate chefs!"

"Listen to you! Listen to that passion! That's what Barry and I have been waiting for. That's what makes Emmys and Oscars. Roy, I'm talking to you like Geraldo. Give me a true story. A docudrama. Go! Kill me a chef!"

FAX TO: Natasha O'Brien
FROM: Roy (Pussycat) Drake

After getting all my Third World shots and assuring my doctor
and my liver that I won't drink the water, I'm off to Dallas to
interview your toy boy Parker. My tastebuds quiver at the
prospect of eating dead animals as prepared by a subscriber to
the single-bullet theory.

Thanks for a tedious lunch the other day. Just to be certain
you don't believe everything you eat, I've thoughtfully enclosed
a copy of my piece on Le La. Fear not, Lady in the Dim, it won't
run until after I come back and interview Neal for your filthy
rag. Heh heh.


MOUTHING OFF
by Roy Drake


A Wolf in Sheep's Clothing

Just what L.A. needed: a restaurant with waiters on roller
skates. Oops, did I say restaurant? Neal Short's aptly named Le
La is as tongue-tied as the Three Stooges playing Shakespeare.
For starters, you need an A in Geography just to read the
menu: Plymouth Cranberry Soup, Niagara Farms Goat Cheese,
Idaho Red Lentil Salad with Iowa Corn-Fed Pork Cracklings. Is
this place an atlas or a restaurant? It looks like a restaurant
("Isn't that Don and Melanie?"), it smells like a restaurant
("Darling, your perfume is to die!"), it sounds like a restaurant
("Waiter, bring me a phone!"), and it even charges Restaurant

45

prices ($32.50 for six dead shrimp), but if you're looking for taste in this "damn the tournedos" bistro, you won't even find it in the decor.

Pulling up to Le La, located smack-bang on L.A.'s culinary skid row (aka La Cienega), one is immediately put on guard by having to surrender the car keys to a coven of Rocky Horror Show dropouts who look like the only thing they can drive is their mothers crazy. The room itself is a design disaster: all four walls are glass panels behind which flow anemic, drippy waterfalls that give one the impression of dining in utero. Or in a toilet bowl.

Which brings us to the food. While Le La ought to receive an award from the Environmental Protection Agency for recycling everyone else's menu, it's unlikely to survive the wrath of savvy Spagoites. What fools these chefs be to keep Pucking around with pizza. Smoked duck spring roll salad started out promisingly enough despite reclining on a schizo spread of snap peas, apple, and fennel. Unfortunately, once the unmistakable aftertaste of cardamom reared its redolent head, the spring roll promptly OD'd into an ugh roll. Grilled Santa Barbara shrimp with chili-peach polenta and fresh mint pesto was an exercise in overkill, from shrimp tougher than Bogart to a tragically inedible complex of pepper, sugar, and mint.

For his main courses, Chef Neal Short rounded up all the nouveau suspects: mahi-mahi, roughy, and skate; rabbit, venison, and duck. But as in a casting call for Pet Sematary III, everything arrived overdressed and underprepared. What ever happened to hot food? Or at least cooked food? Meats were bloody enough to have been just picked up off the rifle range. The fish was older than George Burns and salvageable only as bait. While focusing, however myopically, on veggies, the kitchen did manage to turn out a credible quartet of turnip chips, deep-fried spinach, tomato-stuffed potatoes, and an acceptable celery custard.

Also on the plus side was a napoleon of roast pork layered with rectangles of crisp Pernod potatoes and velvety cabbage mousse; and a tangy pot roast braised with Cinzano and showered with cherries. Shareholders in L.A. Power and Light take note: both dishes were actually heated higher than body temperature. Hurrah! One need not starve to death at Le La -- at least not until the FDA decides that it's safe to eat rare pork.

You can't go wrong with dessert. There's only one choice: a platter filled with more tarts than a Nevada brothel.

Le La keeps coming up Short due to lack of imagination coupled with fear of frying. If the chef got his act together, redecorated, hired a new staff, and changed the menu, this could well become a four-star, instead of just a movie-star, hangout.

But is that going to happen?

Not.

NATASHA PRESSED THE INTERCOM for her secretary. "Get me the Hemlock Society!"

"It's that bad?" Ester asked.

Natasha looked down at her desk. The layout for the premier issue of *American Cuisine* was covered with shreds of nail polish. "You're right. I'm overreacting." Her voice grew tight. "Make it the National Rifle Association."

"That tone," Ester sighed. "You must have torn every cuticle."

Natasha sat back with mixed feelings of horror and relief. IT had finally happened. She spread her fingers and stared at the jagged cuticles, bitten nails, and chipped polish. Her neurotic fear that something terrible was about to happen had finally taken shape and reared its ugly layout. Having conceived, piloted, and approved the editorial content of the issue, she had given it to the art director before leaving for L.A.

The door to Natasha's triangular office at the apex of the Flatiron building swung open to reveal Ester, an almost perfectly square woman. The ex–KGB agent wore flowered two-piece dresses and enormous blobs of costume jewelry. After the dissolution of the KGB, she had divorced her third husband and come to New York, where she put herself through secretarial school by working as a manicurist at Louis Licari's posh hair salon. The combination of talents had made her irresistible to Natasha. She had hired Ester, who brought her chihuahua, Pushkin, to work every day. He slept like a paperweight atop the IN basket.

Ester adjusted her shoulder pads and put her manicure kit down on Natasha's glass-topped desk. "And I thought there was pressure working in the Kremlin." Natasha pulled back her hands, but Ester

48

grabbed a wrist and smiled menacingly. *"Nyet* so fast, comrade."

"I am not your comrade! I am your boss!" And then suddenly melting as she showed Ester her hands, she said, "Save me before I bite again."

Ester shook her head at the sight of Natasha's nails. "It would take the entire cast of *Bambi* to save you."

"Please, Ester. Man has entered the forest."

Ester rolled her eyes. "Fucking up the forest is what man does best." She pulled up a Bauhaus chair that had belonged to Louis Kohner, the first of Achille's victims. "You Americans never learn. It's always forgive and forget. What this country needs is a good salt mine!" Louis's books lined the wall opposite the framed menus from dinners at which Natasha had cooked dessert. "I always liked the little skunk in that movie."

Natasha took a deep breath and closed her eyes as Ester went to work on her nails. The skunk's name was Wylie Phelps Norton.


NATASHA MARCHED through the art department radiating determination from her fingers to her Fioruccis, despite not having a clue as to who could replace Wylie. Never one to take a maître d's suggestions seriously, she had refused to hire a personnel manager. She did know one thing: she wasn't about to replace Wiley with his longtime assistant. Bad chefs rarely had good sous-chefs. The person to check out was the one furthest from the top — the prep man.

"What do you think of this layout?" she asked, waving it at Arnold Berkowitz, the new kid in pasteup.

"I think it's great," he said quickly.

Natasha smiled. "Thanks." So much for that theory. She walked away, scanning the room for the next candidate.

"You really want to know what I think?"

Natasha turned back.

Arnold was very nervous. "Listen, I'm from Newark, and I'm also not gay. You know how hard it is for me to find work as an artist?"

"I guarantee immunity. Tell me about the issue."

"It stinks. Almost as much as Jersey." Arnold grabbed the layout from her. "Listen, even the cover is lousy. This is a food magazine, right?"

"I used to think so."

"No offense, since you are one of the seven fancy-shmancy chefs on the cover, but I think a zaftig hunk of chocolate cake would sell a lot more copies."

She opened to the article on winter soups. "Keep going."

"This is still confidential?"

"As far as I know, you hang out in leather bars."

"What are you selling here? Antique soup bowls or soup? Like they don't have women wearing overcoats in *Playboy*. If you catch my drift." He hesitated and lowered his voice. "I'd appreciate it if you didn't let it get around that I actually read *Playboy*."

"What's your favorite restaurant?"

"You know Dominick's in the Bronx?"

She began to laugh. "In the what?"

"Their pork chops and peppers are like a Renaissance painting. You get this gigantic platter filled with thick grilled chops and big fat slabs of red pepper dripping with oil and vinegar."

"Describe the platter."

Arnold looked at her as though she'd gone crazy. "Who knows? I only remember the food."

"Lay it out. A full page. Bring it to my office in half an hour. With a redo on the winter soups piece."

"In half an hour? That's a joke, right?"

"I've got a short attention span. You've got thirty minutes to cross the state line."

Natasha continued down the corridor toward Wylie's office. She knocked sharply on the glass door. He looked up from a desk strewn with photos. Wylie was in his late forties, with white hair cut short. He wore broad-striped shirts and different-colored suspenders every day, but always a yellow tie.

"How long have I known you, Wylie?" she asked, tossing the pages onto his desk.

"Uh-oh. I guess we didn't like Mr. Layout."

"We hate it."

Wylie cleared his throat and took a deep breath. "Well, then, to answer your question, you've known me since before Bill ran *Bon Appetit*, since before Gail ran *Gourmet*, since before Mary . . ." He narrowed his eyes and sighed wearily. "I guess I've been around through all the prima donnas who came and went."

Natasha nodded. "Wylie, what's your favorite restaurant?"

"Grenouille."

"Why?"

"So many reasons. The flowers, the lighting — I just love those ricky-tick little lamps. . . ."

"What about the food?"

His face screwed up as though she'd asked an absurd question. "The food?"

Natasha slapped the palm of her hand on his desk. "The food, goddamn it!" She opened the layout to a full page of a chef standing in the middle of an empty restaurant. "Where the hell is the leg of lamb? I don't want Scavullo mood shots!" She turned the pages angrily. "Why aren't the cakes sliced so you can see what they look like inside?" Another page. "This typeface is unreadable." Next page. "Is this an ad or editorial?" More pages. "And these Ming soup tureens look like something out of a Sotheby's catalog!"

"You don't think they're beautiful?"

"That's the problem! They're too beautiful! We're selling food, not silverware or paisley tablecloths or Ming bowls!"

"I am simply trying to broaden the horizons of our devoted readership of neurotics with eating disorders. And I'll have you know, that silver came from James Robinson!"

"I don't care if it came from Edward G. Robinson! This hen is stuffed with figs, goat cheese, and spinach. And that's what I want to see!"

Wylie's face grew tight. "Then perhaps you should look up its ass."

"I think I just did." Natasha picked up the layout. "How long will it take you to get yours out of here?"

"Stop playing Hepburn. You'll never get this issue done without me."

"Correction, pal: I'll never get it done *with* you." She opened the door. "Tell accounting to give you a fourteen-karat parachute. But don't ask me for a recommendation. I'm a lousy liar."

She opened the door and walked past Arnold as he worked feverishly. "Last train to Manhattan, kiddo."

\*    \*    \*

WITHIN THE HALF HOUR, Ester rushed into Natasha's office and leaned back against the closed door. "You like the way Ester Berkowitz sounds, or should I hyphenate?"

"Ester, just send Arnold in."

"You'll keep your hands off?"

Natasha laughed. "I'll force myself."

Arnold strode into Natasha's office and stood at her desk. "What did you do to Wylie?"

"I fired him."

"For what?"

"For medical reasons. He had a massive art attack."

Arnold slapped his palm against his cheek. "You mean, you fire people around here just because you don't like the way they do their jobs?"

"Bizarre, isn't it?" She held out her hand for the pages.

Arnold sat down. "You will notice I took out all the soup bowls and used copper pots. Except for one. Symmetrical is too Connecticut."

Natasha leaned back. Arnold had managed to translate his own hunger onto the page. He was right: it wasn't symmetrical. He had drawn a spillover onto one of the pots. It was real. She looked at the page with the pork chops and peppers. Torn pieces of bread on the edge of the plate and crumbs on the tablecloth had brought it to life. "You know, I can pick up the phone and get a hundred Wylies in here within the hour."

"Don't try to bargain with me. I want to be paid what Mr. Suspenders was paid."

"In your dreams! Wylie's had years of experience on every food magazine published since — "

"You need me," Arnold said.

"And you need me. Take the rest of the layout home. I want it on my desk, completed, tomorrow morning."

"Hey, you expect me to stay up all night?"

"Yes. That's very New York."

"I can do it." He hesitated. "Listen . . ."

Natasha smiled. "We'll talk money tomorrow."

"Considering you run the place, you're all right."

She nodded. "I am now."

BUT ONLY TWO HOURS LATER, Natasha felt all wrong. Something had unnerved her. She put down the résumé and looked straight into the eyes of the man applying for the job of executive assistant. "I have the strangest feeling we've met before."

Alec Gordon smiled. "You may have seen me at *Lucullus*. We were never introduced formally, but I recall your passing through a number of times."

Natasha hesitated. "It's been years since . . ." Not wanting to finish the sentence, she picked up the letter of recommendation and smiled. "I always liked Beauchamp." Natasha decided to thank him for coming. She'd let him know. Not that her mind wasn't already made up. It was insane to even consider hiring someone linked to Achille. Achille, Beauchamp, *Lucullus* — the part of her life she'd worked so hard to put behind her, and here it was staring her in the face. For that very reason, she hesitated. She still had to prove something to herself.

"Alec, why did you leave *Lucullus*?"

"The truth, Miss O'Brien?"

"The truth, Natasha."

"Too many ghosts. I don't know if you can understand this, but I had to put that part of my life behind me. I'd spent enough time in Europe. I needed the one thing you can get only in America — a fresh start." He paused, looking deep into her eyes. "I had to prove something to myself."

Natasha sat back. What the hell was it about Alec? It was more than his being an attractive man. There was something oddly compelling about him. Almost dangerous.

"What did you have to prove?" she asked.

He leaned forward. "The same thing you did. That there was life after Achille."

A bell rang. They both looked up, startled. Natasha forced a smile. "It's the test kitchen. They're ready for the eleven-thirty tasting." She pressed the intercom for Ester. "Please tell Grace I'm busy. Ask her to bring in two plates." There was a long silence as she tried to fathom why she hadn't used the tasting as an excuse to get away from Alec rather than prolong the interview.

"I no longer believed in my work," Alec said, settling back on the sofa. "That slavish devotion to an outmoded concept of food. All those calories. The cream, the butter, the fat. Issue after issue. Such a calamitous way to eat. I know this sounds ridiculous, but the longer I stayed at *Lucullus*, the more I began to feel that I was killing people."

Grace Daniel, the test kitchen director, wore a white lab coat and a permanent expression of intensity. She carried a tray with two plates.

"Thanks, Grace. This is Alec Gordon. A visitor from the land of *Lucullus*."

"A pleasure to meet you, Mr. Gordon. You'll be tasting a dish we developed ourselves: Lobster Shortcake with Grilled California Chanterelles and Whipped Tomato Cream." She was careful to turn each serving for the full effect of the presentation. Before leaving, she gave them copies of the recipe.

Alec held his plate at eye level while Natasha scanned the recipe. Then she tasted a mushroom and frowned. "The chanterelle needs more of a char." She picked up her pencil and made a note.

Alec cleared his throat. "If I may, there's too much air in the tomato cream. It's a bit stiff. And I believe someone used brandy instead of cognac."

"Did you taste the lobster?"

"Somewhat overcooked."

"And sliced too thick," she said.

"By half. It doesn't cut neatly."

Natasha was still writing. "Perhaps we should use lobster tails. They're easier to portion."

"And control cooking time."

She looked up. Alec was no tourist. He knew the territory. Natasha felt as though she had just met an old friend in a foreign country. "Like the biscuit?"

"Not really."

"I still say the best biscuits are made with lard."

Alec leaned forward intently. "Don't even joke about it. You're already using too much butter for the nineties. How about canola oil with a little cayenne to pep it up?"

Natasha smiled. "Don't tell me you're a health nut."

"I'm a fugitive from the world of lemon curd, clotted cream, and bypass surgery."

"We could use someone like you around here," she said, suddenly stopping herself. "I mean, that is, if we could use someone like you around here." She felt her face flush and went back to the recipe. "How about raising the oven temperature to four hundred — "

"And baking them in a deep pan for added crispness?"

Natasha was stuck. She didn't want him to stay, and she didn't want him to go. He was too good. It must have been the day for A's. First Arnold. Then Alec. Perhaps she was on a roll. Even her nail polish was still intact. The ring from her private line shattered the silence. Saved by the bell.

"Hello?"

"Don't hang up." It was Millie.

"I knew things were too good to last!"

"This is not about you and me."

"Who are you kidding? It's always about you and me!"

"Nat, it's about Parker."

Natasha turned away and cupped her hand over the receiver. "Listen, you son of a bitch, you and I are divorced. I can see Parker whenever I want."

"Not anymore, you can't."

She put a hand to her forehead. "What the hell are you talking about?"

"Parker is dead."

"You wish. Sorry, chum. I saw Parker last week," she said, reaching for her calendar, "and I've got a date with him for — "

"Dead, Nat. Dead like the other chefs."

Natasha slumped back into her chair. All she could picture was Parker in his red, white, and blue shorts. She felt as if her voice were coming from another body. "What other chefs?"

Millie hesitated. "The police think he drowned."

"But Parker could swim."

"Not at the bottom of a barrel of molasses and ketchup."

"Oh, my God." Natasha felt her heart stop. "No, that's not possible. It must have been an accident." She was trying to buy time. "Parker never used ketchup."

"Someone did. And oil and brown sugar."

"No. I can't believe it. Nobody cooks like that anymore." There was a long pause. "What do you mean, they 'think' he drowned?"

"They're waiting for the coroner's report. They're not sure what killed him."

"You mean the molasses or the ketchup?"

"Nat, I don't know how to tell you this, but Parker was deboned, marinated, and skewered. They found him roasting over the barbecue."

Tears filled her eyes. "In that sauce?" Natasha dropped the phone on the floor. "He'd die if he knew."

Alec reached over and hung up the receiver. "Bad news?"

THE HOTEL DES ARTISTES, around the corner from Central Park West on Sixty-seventh Street, was built in 1918 to provide studios for working artists. The lavish wood-paneled apartments had two-story living rooms with spectacular walls of glass, fireplaces, bedrooms on the upstairs balcony, and no kitchen facilities whatsoever. The ground-floor café serviced the culinary requirements of tenants such as Isadora Duncan, Norman Rockwell, Noël Coward, and Fannie Hurst.

George and Jenifer Lang, who re-created Café des Artistes into the most romantic restaurant in town, had found an apartment for Natasha on the sixth floor. On hearing of Parker's death, they sent up chicken soup and a slice of Ilona torte, her favorite dessert.

Both sat uneaten as Natasha lay on the sofa, wearing a black sweatsuit and twirling the Stetson that Parker had given her. She stared past the brim to the two-story opaque windows, watching them change color as the clouds passed overhead.

There was a knock at the door. Natasha closed her eyes. She was in no mood to answer.

"Nat! It's me! Open up!"

"Go away," she shouted.

"Let me in!"

"Or you'll huff and puff and blow my house down?" she muttered. "How did you get up here?" she asked, leaning against the closed door. "Why didn't the doorman stop you?"

"He's a hopeless romantic."

"Millie, for God's sake, it's over." She knew that was a lie. It had just begun.

"Come on, babe. Let me in."

"How do I know it's you?"

There was a pause. "Last year the pizza industry sold eleven billion slices."

She unlocked the door. "Please go away."

"I can't." He pushed the door open. "It's tradition, babe. We always get together after a chef's been killed."

Natasha had no resistance left. She turned, walked back into the living room, and lay down, dropping Parker's hat over her face. Millie locked the door and followed her.

"You moved the sofas."

"Parker moved the sofas."

"Did he stay here with you?" Millie asked, looking up at the balcony that led to the bedroom.

"Not often," she said. "He hated this apartment."

"It's a great apartment."

"It has no kitchen."

Millie smiled. "That's why I love it. I'm glad you kept it."

"I merely divorced you. I didn't declare myself insane." She paused. "It's not as though I put myself into a clinic in Switzerland."

He sat down on the floor next to her. "Nat, I know what you're thinking, but Achille is dead. That's all in the past."

She took the hat from her face. "Tell it to Parker." She put her arms around him and held tight. "Oh, Millie, can you die of déjà vu?"

"Yes. That's why everything has to be different this time."

" 'This time'?"

"We're going to get married again."

"Now why didn't I think of that?" she sobbed. "Of course! Getting married solves everything!"

Millie pulled back in surprise. "Nat?"

"Let's not waste a moment. How soon can we set a date?" She got up and began pacing the room. "Well, there are a few things I have to do. For openers, I have to get rid of my brains and cut out my heart. And then I have to decide what color dress to wear. Vanilla? Chocolate? Strawberry? You decide, darling. You know all about that sort of thing," she said, her voice growing shrill. "What the hell is America's favorite flavor?"

"I'll tell you upstairs."

*      *      *

NATASHA AND MILLIE lay in bed holding each other for a very long time. Neither spoke. Their eyes were open, and they stared up at the ceiling. "You still have hair on your chest," she said.

"I know."

"It must be very popular in American households."

"My chest?"

"Hair."

"Not with me. I'd hate it if you had a hairy chest."

"*You'd* hate it?"

"I see you still paint your toenails," he said.

"Obsessively."

"You wouldn't believe the time I've spent thinking about your toenails."

"Millie, be a pal. Don't tell me."

"You hungry?"

"Ravenous."

"Still the same Natasha."

"Damn it," she whispered.

"I think we're having two conversations."

"We always did."

"Maybe it's time for a change."

"*Plus ça change*. The moving hand writes and, having writ, writes the same fucking thing all over again."

"Nat, it's time to lose something in the translation."

"Why do you think I didn't marry you in London?"

"You want to know what my shrink told me?"

"You went to a shrink? Oh, Millie, I'm so proud of you! Of course I want to know."

"He said you were a ballbuster."

"Is that what you think?"

"No. That's why I quit after one session. I knew that you'd been through hell. You just needed some time."

She leaned over and kissed him. "Thank you."

"But I didn't think you'd need five years." He held her face in his hands. "Nat, tell me I'm not crazy. We just had the best sex since Paris."

"*Oui.*"

He held her close. "You and I fit together. Even the parts that don't fit, don't fit better than with anyone else. And God knows, we have better fights."

"I can't argue that. We have great fights."

"So how often does that happen in a lifetime?"

"Millie, you want to know what *my* shrink said?"

"You want the God's honest truth?"

"Remember when you were a kid?"

"Uh-oh. You went to a Freudian."

"Remember Sunday night? The panic? You hadn't done your homework. You didn't study for the big test. And right after Ed Sullivan, it was Monday morning."

"You must have spent a fucking fortune."

"You promised yourself it would never happen again. All week you promised yourself. And suddenly it was Sunday again. Señor Wences was on and you still hadn't done your homework."

Millie made a fist, moved his thumb, and spoke with an accent. "Easy for you."

"Know what that's called?"

Millie shook his head. "What did you do? Go every day?"

"It's called repetition compulsion. The way some people live their lives making the same mistakes over and over again. Battered wives get divorced and then fall in love with someone who beats them up again."

"I never laid a hand on you!"

"I knew you wouldn't understand. That's why I was afraid to marry you in London."

He stared at Natasha. "But this is New York."

"And suddenly it's Sunday night again." The phone rang. She didn't take her eyes from him. "The machine is on. I'm not answering."

Millie reached over and picked up the phone. "Ask not for whom the bell tolls. That's what Conan the Analyst taught me." He held it out.

Natasha took the receiver. "Hello?"

It was Roy. "Are you sitting down?"

"I'm lying down. I'm in bed. Making mad, passionate love."

"Then you haven't heard."

"I've heard. Roy, what do you want?"

"You're not going to believe this, but I was the last person to see Parker alive. Except for the killer. Is that incredible timing or what?"

"Incredible."

"Just between you, me, and your vibrator, I wouldn't be surprised if those fucking cowboys think I murdered Parker! Anyway, I called my agent immediately and he set up a meeting with Warner's for Monday morning. It's the break I've been looking for! Sequel heaven! I'm going to pitch a screenplay called *Someone Is Killing the Great Chefs of America!*"

39. EXT. ESTABLISHING SHOT -- DALLAS RANCH --
AFTERNOON

A scene as placid as chicken soup -- rustic but very Ralph
Lauren. A bright egg yolk of a sun slips toward the horizon
behind an overhead sign that reads THREE TYNE FORK
RANCH, L. DEVEREAUX, CHIEF COOK AND BOTTLE WASHER.
We HEAR the voice of Tammy Wynette singing "Stand By Your
Man." As CAMERA PANS around to the back porch, we HEAR
the voice of LUKE DEVEREAUX as he sings along.

LUKE (VO)
(singing out of tune)
Staaaaaand baaaah yoooooo maaaaaaaan!

40. EXT. DALLAS RANCH -- BACK PORCH

Luke, mid-thirties, is devastatingly attractive. He's sprawled on
an old rocking chair, a guitar on his lap. He is dressed in very
expensive cowboy togs, including a fringed jacket, $2,500 de-
signer boots, and a pheasant-feathered Stetson. DOG, his old
bloodhound, HOWLS along with the music.

41. INT. DALLAS RANCH -- KITCHEN

CAMERA moves toward counter from KILLER'S POV. Killer's
gloved hand reaches out and turns on the Cuisinart. SOUND of
motor.

## 42. EXT. DALLAS RANCH -- BACK PORCH

Dog stops howling and listens to sound of motor. Dog BARKS. Luke stops singing. He turns off the music and listens to the sound of the motor.

> LUKE
> (whispers to Dog)
> It's the Kyoozeenart!

Suddenly, Luke HEARS another machine go on.

> LUKE
> It's mah blendah!

Another motor.

> LUKE
> (getting angry)
> Mah gelato makuh!!

Luke gets up and heads toward kitchen.

## 43. INT. DALLAS RANCH -- KITCHEN

Luke swings open the door and stares wide-eyed at a counter filled with empty, vibrating machines. A VCR has been turned on with a tape of Julia Child explaining where brisket comes from.

> LUKE
> Whut the hell is goin' on here? Who's cookin'
> in mah kitchen? And whut is they cookin'?

Dog starts to BARK. We HEAR ANOTHER MOTOR go on. Luke turns around.
CLOSE SHOT of Killer's gloved hands on a vibrating portable chain saw.

LUKE
Who the hell ah you?

INTERCUT Julia Child trimming a roast with a struggle between Luke and the Killer. We see the horror in Luke's wildly handsome face and HEAR the barking. Suddenly there is a spray of blood. Luke gasps and falls to the floor. His throat has been slashed with the chain saw. Dog WHINES. Julia merrily cuts away fat and bone on the roast as the Killer rips off Luke's clothing and exposes the hard, muscular body of a Greek god. As Julia pats the roast to show what a good piece of meat it is, Killer slaps Luke's taut pink buttocks before turning him on his back and slicing down his middle with the chain saw. Dog BARKS as Killer snaps open Luke's rib cage, picks up a knife, and begins to debone him.

JULIA (VO)
Of course, you could always ask your butcher
to bone the meat, but I think it's much more fun
to do it myself.

44. EXT. DALLAS RANCH -- HILLTOP -- SUNSET

We HEAR Tammy Wynette singing "Stand by Your Man" as CAMERA PANS up the hill to feature a Scarecrow dressed in Luke's clothing and then over to a large barbecue on which Luke's spineless, trussed flesh turns slowly on a spit. His arms and legs have been skewered to his shapeless body. As the spit turns, we see his face -- eyes wide open, an apple in his mouth.

Killer's gloved hand pours on more barbecue sauce and bastes Luke.

TAMMY (VO)
(singing)
Stand by your man...

CAMERA features Dog lying near Scarecrow -- gnawing on a huge bone.

WHILE MOST OF THE OTHER RUNNERS circling the reservoir in Central Park at six-thirty in the morning listened to personal stereos, Alec listened only to himself. Nothing was more important or more reassuring than statistics. At his current weight of 150 pounds, a ten-minute mile consumed 94 calories, and running five miles burned off 470 calories per day. As the week progressed and he passed the twenty-mile mark cited in the Pfaffenbarger study, he had the added bonus of providing himself with maximum protection from heart disease.

Repeating the numbers over and over had been a crucial part of his training ever since he began running the small path surrounding Enstein's clinic. Mathematics kept his mind from wandering, from losing control. During those crucial early years, the math had blocked out the angry voice inside, the voice he was so impatient to silence forever. " 'Too swift arrives as tardy as too slow,' " Enstein would say, quoting in German from *Das Tragödie auf Romeo und Juliet*.

Alec smiled, wondering what Enstein would say if he knew about his working for Natasha. Too swift? Too slow? Tragedy or comedy? None of the above. Alec was determined that it would become a love story.

Sex was the one passion he had not shared with Natasha. In the old days, they had argued vehemently about money, menus, and magazines. They had tasted everything from *aioli* to *zuppa inglese*, but never each other. Making love to Natasha was something Achille hadn't dared to think about. But Alec thought of little else. Alec was still a virgin.

He ran and he ran and he ran, confident that every lap would bring him closer to his beloved Natasha.


BY SEVEN-THIRTY, he was bounding up the four flights of the East Nineties brownstone, unlocking the door to his apartment. While he could have afforded a more luxurious address, he couldn't risk living above his "supposed" means or subjecting himself to the scrutiny of a co-op board. Most of all, he didn't want his mail examined by the prying eyes of building personnel, and so his first prerequisite for an apartment had been a lobby mailbox to which only he and the postman had keys.

He saw no problem, however, in spending a great deal of money redecorating. Alec could always claim that it had been left to him by some eccentric. Who would argue the point? Anyone would have to be crazy to spend nearly a quarter of a million dollars to bring in new electrical lines for central air conditioning and new plumbing to turn the bathroom into a fully equipped spa, and to replace the kitchen with a professional gym. But Alec was not crazy. To protect his investment, he had bought the building.

Upon returning to the apartment, he headed for the shower, watching himself in the mirror as he undressed. The hair on his chest and stomach had been shaped and thinned out by months of painful electrolysis. He ran the palm of his hand down his perfectly sculpted torso. Half a lifetime, he thought. Half a lifetime trapped in Achille's grotesque body.

Alec turned on the water and picked up the soap, almost reluctant to lose the rewarding scent of sweat for which he had worked so hard. He lathered himself under the steamy spray, taking muscle-by-muscle solace from the hardness of his new form. By the time he reached his groin, he was erect. He sat back on the slatted teak ledge, rubbing what his mother had called his private parts. He lathered them gently, then, leaning his head against the marble wall, tightened his grip and began to groan, allowing himself the full pleasure of what were more accurately his only original parts.

More than two dozen hand-tailored suits hung in his closet, and twice as many shirts. His briefs had been custom-made to ensure a perfect fit. He selected his clothes carefully, then brewed a pot of herbal tea. For the sake of appearance, he had installed a small kitchenette. But the only things he consumed on the premises were tea and soda water. He made certain there was nothing to eat.

By the time Alec walked downstairs, Stamos, the Greek cabbie he had hired to pick him up each morning, was there. He waved at Alec. "Don't worry. I didn't forget."

Alec opened the cab door, stepped inside, and sat down. "Forget what?"

Stamos held up a brown paper bag. "The dozen French crullers and the chocolate malted."

Alec was stunned. "What are you talking about?" He refused to take the bag that Stamos was offering.

"Hey, you gonna tell me you didn't call at four o'clock in the morning?"

"I most certainly did not!"

Stamos stared into the rearview mirror. "You said, 'This is Mr. Gordon. Bring me a dozen French crullers and a chocolate malted.' Actually, you said a 'chocolate frosted,' but I figured you must have been over the edge to call me in the middle of the night."

"It couldn't have been me. I was asleep at four o'clock!"

By the time they reached the Flatiron building, Stamos had finished three crullers and was draining the last of the malted. He burped loudly and smiled. "Maybe it wasn't you. Maybe it was a dream."

Alec got out quickly. "I didn't call."

"So maybe I called myself," Stamos said, laughing. "What does it matter?"

"It *does* matter," Alec said, leaning down and speaking intently. "If you eat those things you'll get fat!"

"Not me!" Stamos made a fist and began punching the air. "After the phone rang, me and my old lady got in a little exercise."


AS ALEC HEADED for Natasha's office, Pushkin looked up from the in basket and growled. Ester turned quickly from her computer and said, "Halt! Who goes there?"

Alec stopped. He was in no mood to play games. "Good morning. Is she in?"

"For the right people."

"And what does that mean?"

"It means, let me see your nails." Ester took his hands and nodded. "You can tell a lot about a man from his hands." She looked up and smiled. "You have very sexy moons."

Alec pulled away. "I want to see Natasha."

"Do you bring good news or bad?"

"None of your business."

Ester picked up her nail file as though it were a weapon. "Listen, cossack, everything is my business. Don't let this gorgeous exterior fool you. You can take the girl out of the KGB, but you can't — "

"I have good news. The eagle has landed."

"You may pass." Ester buzzed Natasha's office. "Mr. Executive Editor is reporting for duty."

Natasha sat behind her desk. She looked up and smiled, but Alec could see that her eyes were empty. She had just returned from Parker's funeral in Dallas.

"It must have been very difficult," he said, wanting to take her in his arms and comfort her. He was the only person in the world who knew just what she was thinking and feeling.

The news of Parker's death — or more specifically, how Parker had been killed — had thrown Alec into a panic. His first thought was to call Enstein. But no, he had to deal with it on his own. Life was filled with meaningless, bizarre coincidences. Twists of fate. Irrelevant echoes from an obscure past. Nevertheless, he had to take a pill in order to sleep. That was why he knew he couldn't possibly have called Stamos.

Natasha pointed to Arnold's new layout. "Isn't this great?"

"It's beautiful," he said, never taking his eyes from her. He was really saying, "You're beautiful."

"Check it through for me. I'm . . ." Natasha got lost. She began turning the pages on her calendar backward. "Five days ago he was alive. I was right here. Sitting at this desk while . . ." She looked up at Alec. "It was the first time I'd met Parker's family, people he always joked about, people I never expected to see."

"Why don't you go home? You're exhausted."

"There they all were. Aunt Goosie, who made green chili possum stew, and his sister, Sister, who made deep-fried pecan bread, and his mother, Lady, who bottled her own jalapeño bourbon." Natasha looked up, fighting back the tears. "You know what really pisses me off? With all the food they had, I didn't come home with one god-damn recipe."

He felt as though she were accusing him. But why? Parker had been killed before he was hired.

"I spent most of my time reassuring his mother that he wasn't 'queer' just because he liked to cook. I felt honor-bound to bear witness to his virility, and she wore me like a badge." Natasha smiled. "I think Parker would have liked my telling her that he was an incredible lover."

Alec was perplexed by the ease with which Natasha spoke to him about Parker. He'd been there only a week, yet she was already confiding in him as if he were an old friend. "What about having dinner tonight?"

"With whom?" she asked quickly.

"Me."

"And spend the entire evening obsessing over my troubles?"

"No. I have to talk to you about something."

"What?"

I'm in love with you, he thought. Instead, he answered, "The piece on Mom Cuisine."

Natasha began fidgeting with her calendar. "What about tomorrow? First thing?"

"What about tonight?"

She hesitated. "Thanks for not taking no the first time. But I don't pay you enough to baby-sit me through this."

"You don't pay me enough for anything I do."

She began to laugh. "You'd have liked Parker. He was a fitness nut, just the way you are."

Another threat. "How do you know?"

Natasha spoke in her best Garbo. "Is not for nothing, comrade, that I have the Queen of the KGB outside my door." Then, admiringly, "Besides, all anyone has to do is look at you."

"I wasn't sure you'd noticed."

"What do you think, Alec? I hired you for your typing?"


ACTUALLY, she could have hired him for his typing. One of the things he had done at the clinic, in order to stay in touch with the outside world, was to become computer-literate. He learned to

70

touch-type and then joined electronic bulletin boards to "converse" with people devoted to food, fitness, and psychology. He contacted young chefs throughout the world, identifying himself as a retired restaurateur. The name he used was Mort Canard.

But most often he sat staring at the screen like a voyeur while others chatted back and forth about the great meals they'd just had or the new recipes they had created. He logged onto international information services and scanned the food pages of major papers throughout the world for news of the only people about whom he cared: Natasha and Millie.

He had met Natasha while she was still in her teens, the adopted daughter of Louis Kohner, chef at the Savoy Hotel. A shame about Louis. Attracted to Natasha even then, Achille had focused his paternal instincts on Millie, who became the child he had never had. Achille had guided his career from the moment he arrived in London, confident that Millie would open the world's greatest restaurant. But then Millie had betrayed him. Not only had he fallen in love with Natasha, but he had taken a job with American Good Foods. Worse than sleeping with the enemy, he had decided to eat with them.

Alec sat down at his computer and turned it on. His mind was still with Natasha as he called up the editorial she had asked him to check: "Taming the Wild Sommelier." As her text appeared on the monitor, he began switching sentences and changing a few words.

Suddenly he pulled his fingers away from the keyboard as though he had just touched a hot stove. His eyes widened in disbelief as he stared at the last paragraph.

> The only unbreakable rule in town: don't take the sommelier's advice if he suggests a wine from the most expensive half of the list. Unlessxnnnncncbvncncn
> unless you get me something to eat, I will tear out your mind!!!

Alec jumped as the bell sounded for the eleven-thirty tasting. He cleared the screen and exited from the document. He did not save it.

*   *   *

GRACE DANIEL groaned as Alec entered the test kitchen. "Uh-oh. It's Mr. Mouth. Bermuda, you're in for it."

Bermuda Schwartz, a former *Vogue* model who had been fired for being too thin, raised an eyebrow without disturbing one additional muscle in her consummately anorexic body. She was the Recipes Editor.

"Good morning, everyone," Alec said, taking his seat. "I'm afraid Natasha won't be joining us."

"Oh, swell," Bermuda said in a deep, raspy voice more suited to a Damon Runyon character. "No Natasha. Now I really am dead. Another turd in the cat pan of life."

Christine, the Articles Editor, hurried in, still talking on her cellular phone. She waved hello at everyone and put her hand over the receiver as she sat down. "It's that fucking fact checker we just hired. The one who used to work at *Le New Yorker*." She winked at the others as she released the hold button. "Listen, Rajid, loosen up. You can't change the name of the magazine. I don't care what you've uncovered in the notes of A. J. Liebling, the word *cuisine* has been Anglicized. Totally assimilated into the vocab. A shortcut for 'style of cooking.' Get a life, kid!" She hung up the phone and started barking like a dog. "I'm starving!" she said, picking up the copy of the recipe near her plate. "Oh, great!" she said sarcastically. Then she glanced quickly at Bermuda. "Not that I don't adore chocolate pudding."

"Well, we can't live on the Pacific Rim forever, cookie."

Grace, who had taught home economics at the Georgia State Correctional Facility for Women before being hired to run the test kitchen, smiled as she walked around the table showing off her tray of balloon-shaped wine goblets heaped with chocolate pudding. "Now Alec, doesn't this look good enough for a centerfold?"

Alec had been staring at the huge crystal bowl in the middle of the table. It was filled with whipped cream. He cleared his throat and nodded quickly.

Bermuda leaned over toward Christine. "For the record, thunder thighs, it wasn't my idea."

"Who ever accused you of having an idea?" Christine asked.

"Let's not riot, ladies," Grace ordered, slipping into her prison-matron tone.

Alec felt his pulse quicken as Grace served them each a goblet of chocolate pudding. By force of habit, she put one at Natasha's place. Right next to him. "The idea was Natasha's. A highly creative response to the trend toward introspective dining."

"Some whipped cream, Alec?" Grace picked up the bowl. "You only live once."

He pushed away his glass. But she interpreted his action as a yes and spooned on a mound of cream. He watched her every move and broke into a cold sweat. As though someone else were guiding his hand, he reached out for the goblet.

Christine sighed theatrically as she picked up her spoon. "Whatever happened to good old chocolate mousse?"

"Backlash," Alec sputtered, realizing that his mouth was full of pudding.

Bermuda pointed a long skeletal finger at him. "Baby, you just hit the snail right on the head! All those itsy-bitsy portions used to drive me nuts. I'd leave the factory and meet the gang for dinner at Café Outrageous-Expensive, where the blue-plate special was one omega-three fish ravioli in clear clam broth with a few stale snips of chive that had been organically grown in some aging hippie's window box." A translucent layer of tight skin stretched across the sharp contours of her face as she laughed without making a sound.

"I don't know why we need eggs in here," Christine said, reading the recipe. "I never heard of using an egg."

"*Mon Dieu!*" Bermuda snarled. "Now I know how Lautrec felt! Fix her chin, Toulouse, and you'll have a masterpiece. Well, I'm sorry. I'd sooner you cut out my heart than the egg!"

"Up to you," Christine said. "Alec, what do you think?"

He looked up, trapped. He was holding Natasha's empty goblet. "About cutting out her heart?"

Christine smiled. "I'm sure it could be done on an outpatient basis."

"Ladies!" Grace waved her copy of the recipe for emphasis. "I for one would like to congratulate Bermuda for not falling into the Callebaut or Valrhona chocolate trap. I think it took real guts to use Hershey's."

"You didn't!" Christine shrieked, slamming down her spoon.

Bermuda slouched back in her chair. "So call the pudding police."

"Oh, my God!" Alec stood up and ran out of the room. He
remembered. He heard Enstein's voice saying over and over, "The
proof of the pudding." Heading toward the bathroom, he raced into
a stall. As he leaned over to throw up, his head began to pound. He
felt a sharp, searing pain. As though someone were tearing out his
mind.

(Note to Alec: Let's see if we can run with this in the issue with the feature on Lydia Shire at Biba, Alice Waters at Chez Panisse, and Anne Rosenzweig at Arcadia -- perhaps you can get Barbara Ensrud, David Rosengarten, or Andy Dias Blue. In a pinch, Frank Prial. I want a big fat box with recommendations for American wines only to go with regional dishes from their restaurants. Speak to Arnold: I'd rather run some wine labels than the obvious glasses of white and red -- not that you'd do anything obvious. For the teaser, use THE ONLY PERSON TO IMPRESS IS YOURSELF. It wouldn't be bad in larger type than my deathless title.)

## Taming the Wild Sommelier

The sommelier (wine steward) makes our previous villains, the maitre d' and the waiter, look like Saint Francis and Albert Schweitzer. While maitre d's and waiters have grown accustomed to people's being savvy about what they eat, most sommeliers still won't admit that we can also drink with discrimination. All you have to remember is three simple things before you can confidently tell them where to put their corks.

One: Never order the cheapest bottle on the list. Not because you're trying to impress anyone, but because every restaurant has a minimum price for wine. Therefore the lowest-priced bottle, like most "house" wine, generally has the biggest markup or is often the least distinguished choice. Your best value is a wine that costs a few dollars more.

Two: Never order the most expensive wine on the list. It's often there simply to be the Most Expensive for those who need to spend a fortune to know it's good. Not that there's anything wrong with the best. But <u>buy</u> the best at a wine shop and serve it under more controlled conditions at home. The sad truth is that few wines brought to the table are served properly: invariably the white wines are served too cold and the red wines too warm.

THE ONE UNBREAKABLE RULE IN TOWN: DON'T DARE TAKE THE SOMMELIER'S ADVICE IF THE ONLY WINE SUGGESTED IS FROM THE MOST EXPENSIVE HALF OF THE LIST. Unless he comes up with a vineyard from the low-rent district, he's trying to pad your bill or cover up the fact that he's been buying inferior wines. Either make your own educated guess or invest in research and order something you've always meant to try. Better still, cut out the middle man and ask the chef to recommend a bottle in your price range.

When the wine arrives (it should be brought to the table before your meal in order to give it a much-needed gulp of fresh air and to give you time to send it back), most people taste it, feign a look that's appropriately quizzical, then smile and nod their approval. If that sight has ever impressed you, READ THIS CAREFULLY.

The key factors in evaluating a wine are color, clarity, smell, and taste. Instead of reaching for the glass, pick up the cork that was taken out of the bottle. Sniff it. Does the cork smell fresh? Or is it sour? Check to see that the cork has been pulled out cleanly.

Then take the glass (by the stem, please) and hold it to the light. Good wine is always clear -- no cork, no sediment, no nothing. Swirl the glass and inhale the scent. Not to evaluate its degree of complexity or to compare it with other wines, but just to be sure it's sound.

Now for the moment of truth. Your last chance to send the

bottle back is your first sip. Protect your investment by knowing precisely why you're wetting your whistle. Whether you like the wine or not isn't the sommelier's problem. His only concern is to ensure that the wine you have hasn't turned sour, not that you like it. Tasting wine is not like tasting steak and then deciding you should have ordered chicken. You're tasting it only to make certain you got a good steak.

A final note: One of the best-kept secrets is the pleasure of a good dessert wine. Coffee is never the beverage of choice unless (heaven forfend!) you skip dessert altogether and munch absently on a generic cookie or two. Frankly, if you're that far into self-deprivation, pass up the almond tuile and put a quick splash of cognac in your espresso.

Let's face it, that great humanitarian Marie Antoinette didn't say, "Let them eat cookies."

"WILD FUNGI" PHIL, a professional food forager, had arrived for the shoot at *American Cuisine* in full safari garb, including a feathered hat whose broad brim was tucked up on both sides. But his long, unruly beard shattered the *bwana* image and made him look instead like the chief rabbi of Nairobi.

"Hey, like it's not written in stone," he said, holding up a morel he had picked in Central Park. "I mean, I could care less. If you want flowers and berries . . ." He half smiled as he shrugged his shoulders and shook his head. "I just thought we'd do mushrooms because, well . . . my name." Natasha looked at Alec and gave him the go-ahead. She was in no mood to play footsie with Phil. It had been only a week since Parker's funeral, and she was just beginning to get back in stride.

"Alas, Fungi old chum, the consideration is not your name but ours," Alec said.

"Like, it isn't important, but my friends usually call me Wild Fungi or just Phil."

"You're right. It isn't important. What matters is that this is a magazine, not a restaurant. We are dependent almost exclusively upon visual stimulation. A double-page spread of Mother Nature's edible tumors, however thrilling a montage for the *New England Journal of Medicine*, has far less eye-appeal than a cranberry-and-black-walnut pâté or a wildflower tart."

Phil held up his hands. "Hey!"

Natasha's purse rang. She rummaged through it until she found her cellular phone. "Yes?"

"I know you said not to call." It was Ester. "But that happily married man in advertising . . ."

"Bud Reilly?"

"I think so. All happily married men sound alike. He wants to bring someone up to see you."

"Who?"

"Some commissar wants to take ads but first he wants to see Arnold's layout. Him and me both."

Natasha made a fist at the phone. "Ester! When are you going to learn to get people's names?"

"Such a tone. We could have used you in Interrogation. If it's important that I humiliate myself, I'll call back and ask."

"Tell Bud to bring him in. Fast."

"I already did. They're in your office."

Natasha put her hand on Alec's shoulder. "If I'm not back in five minutes, come and rescue me."


NATASHA MARCHED down the corridor, annoyed that she'd have to do her dog-and-pony show for yet another advertiser, but at the same time, she was adding up the pages. And the number of times Alec had come to the rescue.

Ester jumped up from her desk as Natasha approached. "He's gorgeous. Like the morning sun on Saint Basil's." Pushkin looked up from the IN basket and yawned. "Wait until you see his manicure."

"Pervert!" Natasha walked past her and swung the door open. It took a moment for her heart to catch up with her brain.

Bud smiled as she walked in. "I'd like you to meet Max Ogden of American Good Foods."

Natasha didn't miss a beat. She extended her hand. "Haven't we met before, Mr. Ogden?"

"I don't think so, Mrs. O'Brien."

What the hell was Millie pulling? She was furious with him. No, she wasn't. She was furious with herself for being so glad to see him. "I'm not married."

"Sorry. I thought you were," Millie said, sitting down.

Bud tried to interrupt. "I've told Max all about — "

"I *was* married," she said, ignoring Bud.

"Widowed?"

Natasha smiled. "No such luck."

79

"I know just what you mean. My ex-wife is driving me crazy."

Bud reached for the dummy issue. "Max, just take a look at this — "

"Really?" Natasha asked. "And how does she drive you crazy?"

"Oh, you know the type."

"It's the first time anyone's done the White House kitchen!" Bud exclaimed, turning pages rapidly. "We even got a shot of the cat!"

"Do I?"

"She was so beautiful that every time I looked at her my heart would stop."

Natasha felt herself turn to jelly. How could he still make her feel that way? Didn't she have any moral fibre? "Bud, I hate to bother you, but I'd like to show Mr. Ogden your projection."

"Sure. I'll bring it right in."

Natasha and Millie stared at one another until Bud left. Without breaking eye contact, she picked up the phone and buzzed Ester. "Mr. Ogden and I don't want to be disturbed." She hung up. "Actually, I find myself very disturbed."

"Actually, I know a cure for that." He walked to the desk.

"Actually, I'm not sure I want to be cured." She stood up.

Millie put his arms around her. "Actually, it doesn't always work." He kissed her.

"Actually, you're wrong," she whispered. "That's my problem. It always works." They kissed again.

"It didn't work in court," he said, holding her close.

Natasha put her arms around his neck. "You mind telling me why you're here?"

"I want to advertise in your magazine."

"And?"

"And nothing. It's exactly what Bud told you. I just wanted to see the dummy."

"And now that you've seen her?"

"I swear on a stack of Aunt Jemima's, I came to see the layout."

Was that good news or bad news? She stared at Millie as though he had a caption beneath him that read, *What's wrong with this picture?* "Oh."

"There's no law against that, is there?"

"No. You're entitled to see it. All the advertisers have asked to see it."

"Well, there you are." He shrugged. "I only want what I'm entitled to."

"And that's all you're going to get!" She pushed Millie into a chair and threw the layout at him.

He stared at her. There was a long silence. "I lied."

Natasha stood angrily in front of him. A moment later, she sank down into his lap and put her arms around him. "You bastard." Natasha froze as she heard a voice bellow out from behind her.

"Ah, the cupcake king!"

Natasha and Millie stared at one another, the same thought crossing both their minds. They turned around. Alec stood in the doorway, looking every bit as shocked as they were.

"Who the hell are you?" Millie asked.

Natasha got up quickly. She began to laugh from the tension. "Alec, you should have heard yourself. You sounded just like — " Natasha shook her head as though to shake the thought from her mind. "Didn't Ester tell you . . ."

"Ester wasn't there." He started to close the door. "I'm sorry. I didn't mean to interrupt — "

"Wait a minute," Millie said angrily. "Why did you call me the cupcake king?"

Natasha took a deep breath. "Alec Gordon, this is Max Ogden."

"I didn't mean to be rude," Alec said, offering his hand. "I remembered overhearing Mr. van Golk at *Lucullus*. It just slipped out. I didn't expect to see you here . . . with Natasha in your arms."

"Alec worked at *Lucullus*." Why the hell did she feel she was on the witness stand?

Millie stared at Alec. "I don't recall meeting you."

"Neither did I," Natasha said defensively. "But lots of people worked for Achille. Even *I* worked for Achille."

Tentatively, Millie shook Alec's hand. "I didn't ever expect anyone to call me that again."

"Mr. van Golk was very fond of you."

"The hell he was," Millie said.

"He may have had difficulty expressing his true feelings . . ."

"My spittoon runneth over," Millie said. "Look, I'm sure you mean well, but — "

"Where is Ester?" Natasha asked, pressing the buzzer.

Alec edged toward the door. "Pushkin had an accident on the Roy Drake article."

"Everybody's a critic!"

Millie turned to Natasha. "Roy Drake? You hired that nut too?"

Natasha saw red. She slipped her arm through Alec's. "Perhaps you should get back to Mr. Mushroom."

Alec whispered, "I came to save you."

Natasha led him gently toward the door. "Alas, Galahad, you're too late. Besides, there's nothing going on here that I can't handle." She opened the door and found herself face to face with a stranger wearing a pair of high-intensity glasses that magnified his watery blue eyes. "Why do I even bother to have a secretary?" she asked, looking around for Ester.

"I don't know," the man said, flashing a badge at her. "Detective Davis, NYPD."

Natasha tightened her grip on Alec's arm, a move duly noted by Davis. "I think we ought to be alone."

Natasha motioned for Alec to stay. "It's all right, Detective."

Alec introduced himself. "Alec Gordon."

"You her lawyer?"

Before Alec could answer, Natasha snapped, "Why? Does she need a lawyer?"

"May I?" Davis walked into the office before Natasha could answer. He saw Millie. "Am I interrupting something?"

"Unfortunately not," Millie said, extending his hand. "Max Ogden. The cupcake king."

"Oh, yes. The ex-husband." Davis turned back to Natasha. "Are you sure . . ."

"No. I'm not sure of anything," she said, closing the door. "Except that you mean trouble."

"I was contacted by the Dallas police . . ."

Natasha sat on the arm of Millie's chair. "I told them all I knew when I was down there."

". . . and then I was contacted by the LAPD. They suggested I speak to you."

"Why? Someone hold up a Seven-Eleven?"

"There's been another murder."

Natasha slid down onto Millie's lap and stared at him. "Yes. I knew there would be."

"You knew?" Davis asked.

"I tried to convince myself that it wasn't all happening again," she said, still staring at Millie. "But here I am." She looked over at Alec. "You were my ace in the hole. I hired you to prove I was wrong."

Davis pointed his finger at Alec. "Who is he?"

"Is that the only reason?" Alec asked.

"Alec, don't look at me that way. Hiring you made me feel I had finally put the past behind me."

"I know a better way," Millie said.

Davis was impatient. "I don't have all day here. Can the group therapy wait?"

Alec cleared his throat. "Perhaps I should leave."

Natasha began to sob. "And miss the best part? We're about to find out who's been murdered. You know, Agatha Christie was all wrong. She told you who the victim was right away. As though the only thing that mattered was who done it." She leaned her head on Millie's shoulder.

Detective Davis shook his head in disbelief. "This is the nuttiest thing I've ever seen. Don't you want to know who was killed?"

Natasha, Millie, and Alec all said "No" at the same time. As her eyes filled with tears, Natasha held up her pinky. "Make a wish."

Davis couldn't take it any longer. "Neal Short was murdered. Decapitated."

Natasha clutched Millie as though he were a life preserver.

Reading from his notes, Davis continued without emotion. "The killer sliced off his nose and lips and dug out his eyeballs. He arranged them on a sausage, onion, and tomato pizza dripping with cheese and oil."

Millie winced. "I don't remember seeing that on the menu."

"According to the report, the killer wanted it to look like a giant face."

Natasha put her arms around her stomach. "I think I'm going to be sick." As Millie helped her up, she looked at Alec. "You're shaking," she said.

"I thought *you* were shaking," he stammered.

Natasha held out her trembling hand. "No, I'm steady as a rock. It's you."

Davis stood over them accusingly. "We're sure there's a connection between the murders."

Millie shrugged. "For that you went to detective school?"

Davis didn't smile. "No. You three are what I went for."

Alec moved away from Natasha. "You're wrong. What you're thinking is wrong."

"How do you know what I'm thinking?" she asked.

"It's written all over your face. You're convinced that we're doomed to relive the past. That Achille is out there somewhere. But he isn't. Achille van Golk is dead!" Alec shouted.

Davis narrowed his eyes. "The department thinks this is the work of a copycat killer. Possibly someone who knew van Golk. What we're looking for is someone with limited imagination. Someone bereft of an original idea. Your basic parasite."

"A critic!" Natasha blurted out.

"Roy?" Alec whispered.

She became flustered. "No, I don't mean Roy. Roy would never kill anyone." Natasha and Davis glanced at one another.

Davis flipped the pages in his pad. "Roy Drake?"

"For heaven's sake, Detective, forget about Roy. He's nothing but your everyday restaurant reviewer: an angry, bitter, vengeful man who hates chefs. I hired him to do some interviews for me."

"Parker Lacy?"

"Yes, but — "

"Neal Short?"

"The only way Roy kills is with words! He has a poison pen, not a cleaver." Natasha was very tense. "Besides, he's too busy to kill people. He spends all of his time working on a sequel to — "

"A sequel to what?" Davis asked.

She hesitated. "I can't remember," she said. "*Moby Dick*!"

Davis sighed and turned to Alec. "Immigration tells me you've been abroad, Mr. Gordon."

"Yes."

"We don't seem to have very much information about you."

"My thought exactly," Millie said.

"I worked in London."

"You worked for this van Golk."

"Yes."

"How closely?"

"Pretty damn close, from what I hear," Millie said.

Davis turned to Millie. "Do you mind?"

"My office was just across the corridor."

Davis smiled. "And you never knew he was running around killing chefs?"

"You took the words right out of my mouth," Millie said.

"Achille van Golk confessed, was sentenced, and later died," Alec said. "That part of my life is over."

"Maybe that's the problem. Must have been a pretty exciting time for you."

"Don't be absurd," Natasha said. "I worked for Achille too. You don't suspect me."

Davis was silent.

She was outraged. "You might as well suspect Millie!"

Davis nodded. "We do. He was around for all those other murders. Not that I'm trying to reopen the van Golk case. But I've got a hunch someone else is." He took out his notebook. "Now, why don't you tell me a little more about your relationship with Mr. Ogden?"

"There's nothing to tell. We were married. We were divorced."

Millie raised his hand. "But we were almost married again."

Natasha shrugged. "Almost doesn't count. I was out of my mind with worry. First Louis was murdered, then Nutti . . ."

"That was when you and Mr. Ogden had a reconciliation."

"Yes."

"Murder always brings us together," Millie said.

"But once the case was solved, you split up again."

"And so, in order to win her back, I've started killing chefs!" Millie held out his wrists to be handcuffed. "Brilliant!"

"And now you have started seeing each other again."

"Seeing isn't believing," Natasha said guiltily.

"You'd be surprised. The nicest people get the craziest ideas. They see something happen once, and they decide to do it all over again. We call it the sequel factor."

Natasha stared at Davis. "It's as though Achille were reaching out from the grave."

"No!" Alec took a handkerchief from his pocket and wiped the beads of perspiration from his brow. "That's not possible."

"Nat, give up the ghost," Millie said. "Forget about Achille. You've made a fresh start. Don't take two giant steps back."

But the sinking feeling in her stomach had nothing to do with Alec or Achille or another murder. Everything Millie said she had already said to herself. It wasn't a ghost that she couldn't give up; it was Millie. She had fallen in love with him all over again.

Davis put the notebook back into his pocket. "You going to be around for the next few days, Miss O'Brien?"

"Yes."

"Good. I'd appreciate it if you didn't leave town."

"Detective, you don't really think I — "

"I don't know what to think. I've got Roy Drake turning up everywhere. I've got you and Mr. Ogden playing footsie again. And now I've got Mr. Gordon. The only thing I know is that this is somebody's sequel. The problem is, I can't tell yet whose sequel it is."


AS NATASHA WALKED to the ticket counter, Detective Davis's words echoed in her mind: "I'd appreciate it if you didn't leave town." She looked up at the sign: FLIGHT 904: NEW YORK TO ROME.

The young woman behind the counter smiled. "May I help you?"

Natasha glanced around, afraid of being recognized. "A ticket to Rome, please," she said softly.

"What class? Meat Sauce or Marinara?"

"I don't care!"

"The fare is $10.95, and that includes a soft drink, pizza bits, antipasto salad with Italian dressing, cheese lasagna, and Italian bread. Today's dessert is frozen chocolate cannoli pie. If you join our frequent flier program, I can upgrade you to a large soda."

While Natasha rode the escalator up to the departure gate, she glanced back at the other check-in counters. NEW YORK TO LONDON: fish and chips. NEW YORK TO BERLIN: hot dogs, sauerkraut, and potato salad. NEW YORK TO ACAPULCO: tacos and enchiladas. Pie in the Sky was Millie's newest fast-food brainstorm after the "cholesterol cops" closed his H. Dumpty omelet chain.

The stewardess greeted Natasha. "Thank you for flying with us to Rome today. Would you like a window seat?"

"I'm meeting Mr. Ogden."

The stewardess's eyes brightened. "Oh, yes. Marinara class. Just follow me." She led the way through a "cabin" where people sat in airline seats with fold-down trays. The "windows" showed low-flying aerial views of Rome. Stewards delivered regulation airline meals and rolled carts up and down the aisle with soft drinks. "Here she is, Mr. Ogden. Safe and sound."

Millie stood up and embraced Natasha. "Babe, tell me what you think. Right off the top of your head. From the moment you stepped in."

"I feel as though I stepped in something, all right." Natasha sat in the window seat and automatically started to fasten her seat belt. "What the hell am I doing?"

"You see, it worked. It got to you."

"It got to me that you must be the Richard Nixon of food. There's nothing you won't stop at, and there's no way to convict you! Where the hell do you get the gall to serve airline food at this altitude?"

"You ought to know. You've held them."

Natasha turned away. "Don't talk dirty. You know how it distracts me."

"From what?"

"Millie, however much I've tried to convince myself that Parker's death was just a bizarre coincidence that had nothing to do with remembrances of murders past, I can't. Not after the way poor Neal died."

"And so?"

"And so, unlucky Lindy, I've narrowed the field down to two prime suspects."

Millie tugged at his earlobe. "Sounds like?"

"You and me!"

"That sounds like us."

"The truth is, if I were Davis, I'd arrest me in a minute. Here I am on the verge of a great new career. I've sold more ad pages than our projections, the layout is spectacular, the recipes are perfect, and subscriptions are rolling in. What better way to sabotage myself?"

"Is this a multiple-choice question?"

"I'm serious, Millie. You know I'm the most self-destructive human being since Little Black Sambo."

"Our divorce certainly proves that."

"It also proves something else. Your motive."

"Oh, yes. Your theory about my turning homicidal killer in order to frighten you back into my arms."

"Why else would I be in your arms?"

"Because you —"

Natasha put her hand to his lips. "Don't. Not the L-word."

He kissed her fingertips. "Babe, I asked you here for a reason."

"Of course you did. To poison me."

"Before things get any more out of hand, I wanted you to know that I remembered."

"Remembered what?"

Millie pointed out the window. "Let's go back to Rome. For real."

She smiled. "Is that why you asked me to meet you here? The last time we were in Rome together was on our . . ."

"Let's go on a . . . again."

She held her breath. "Millie, you're not asking me to —"

A man's head popped up over the seat in front of them. It was Detective Davis. "No. I'm asking you to." He stepped into the aisle. "Miss O'Brien, I'm taking you in for questioning in the murder of Neal Short."

Millie sat back smiling. "Isn't this the part where you tell her she has the right to remain silent?"

"I have no intention of remaining silent! And as for an attorney, the only reason I'll need one is to sue you for false arrest."

Millie took her hand. "Nat . . ."

"You see, Detective, as it happens, I spent the entire weekend in my apartment with Mr. Ogden. We never went out once."

"And so no one saw you?"

"No one had to see me! Millie, tell him!"

Millie looked at Davis and shrugged. "I told you."

"You told him what?"

Davis slipped handcuffs on Natasha. "He told me you'd say that."

"Because it's true!" Natasha struggled with the handcuffs. "Millie!"

A crowd had gathered in the aisle by the time the stewardess spoke over the PA. "Ladies and gentlemen, I'm afraid we're experiencing a little turbulence. The captain has asked that you return to your seats."

"Nat, trust me. I'm doing this for your own good."

"My God! You're going to let him lock me up. Don't you know what this is going to do to me once it hits the papers? Natasha O'Brien collared in the restaurant from hell!" Davis took hold of Natasha's arm and led her up the aisle as she screamed at Millie. "If you were going to double-cross me, you bastard, you could have at least done it at Lutèce!"


ALEC SAT deep in thought at his usual corner table at Chez René, a small bistro around the corner from his apartment. He had barely touched the Perrier. His fingers moved nervously in small circles on the white cloth, just as his mind turned the same thought over and over again: *If I'm not doing it, who is?*

He looked up, suddenly aware that Ravi, the waiter, had approached the table. "Sir, for your dining pleasure." Ravi announced each dish as he put it on the table. "*Coquilles Saint Jacques. Escargot Bourguignonne. Morilles au Gratin. Saucisson en Croute. Ravioli du Homard.* And *Foie Gras en Brioche.*"

Alec stared at the table in horror. "What are you talking about?"

The waiter smiled. "Your hors d'oeuvres. We thought it best to wait with the pigeon tart and sweetbread crepe."

"Are you crazy?"

"Well, if you wish, I can bring them out right away. René felt you might start with these six." Ravi smiled. "Otherwise, the rest will get cold."

"I didn't order this!"

"Which one didn't you order?"

"I didn't order any of them!"

"But sir," Ravi said, holding up his pad. "So it is written."

"I ordered the spa dinner. I've been ordering it all week."

Ravi looked puzzled. "Yes, sir. But you did not order it tonight." Ravi showed him the pad. "Look, sir. You also ordered vichyssoise, bouillabaisse, and the cream of pumpkin soup."

Alec grabbed the pad from Ravi and tore the pages out. "You're mistaken. I never ordered those things!" He stood up and threw a hundred-dollar bill on the table.

"But sir," Ravi called out as Alec walked quickly to the door. "If you didn't order them, who did?"

Alec's heart was beating rapidly, but not from running out of the restaurant and down the street to his apartment. His hand shook as he unlocked the front door.

Once upstairs, Alec ripped off his clothes and threw them onto the floor. He untied his shoes, pulled off his socks and underwear, and held his breath as he stepped onto the scale.

He had gained a pound.

Alec looked up quickly. He heard laughter. He put his hands over his ears. But the voice grew louder. Then, as suddenly as it had begun, the laughter stopped.

There was total silence. He was afraid to move.

And then he heard Achille whisper, "At last!"

# NEW YORK POLICE DEPARTMENT
Division of Homicide

## CASE REPORT NO. 18-5764-8976-3225-AB-218G-445

FROM: D. I. Davis, NYPD
TO: Det. Billy Bob Scooner, Dallas PD/Parker Lacy homicide
    Det. Chad Stone, Los Angeles PD/Neal Short homicide
RE: Natasha O'Brien

After a very thorough interrogation of Ms. O'Brien, I find myself harboring the uncomfortable suspicion that despite all evidence to the contrary, including her impeccable reputation, this woman wouldn't know a good chopped liver sandwich if it fell on top of her.

The bad news is that she's not the only one.

No offense, but you guys are barking up the wrong tree. O'Brien is no killer.

The problem is that you've been looking for answers instead of questions. You want to cut to the chase before you even know which way to run. You don't have one clue. Not one fingerprint. Not a hair or a key ring or a matchbook. You don't have a witness and you don't have a motive.

So how about using what you got instead of what you wish you had?

1) Big-time Dallas chef is barbecued. The poor bastard is covered in molasses and ketchup. How many briskets you seen cooked that way instead of letting the wood flavor the meat? Would a chef like Parker Lacy ever use molasses and ketchup?

2) Famous Hollywood chef gets his head cut off and re-arranged on a pizza. What kind of pizza? Deep-dish Chicago type? Or that paper-thin Yuppie crust? One of those fancy all-white pizzas that he's famous for? No. He's looking up in horror from an old-fashioned tomato pie slathered with a sloppy red sauce that he'd sooner die than serve.

Seems to me anybody can pull a trigger. But these were real performances. You're talking more than homicide. You're talking revenge. Someone with a real grudge against chefs.

Who? The critic? The fast-food king? The frustrated magazine editor? Or maybe some poor son of a bitch like me who doesn't understand extra-virgin olive oil, gravlax, or goat-piss cheese.

AMERICAN GOOD FOODS had its headquarters on the eightieth floor of the World Trade Center. Natasha was furious as she pushed her way off a crowded elevator and stormed past the receptionist. She had to find Millie as quickly as possible. And then she had to kill him.

"Excuse me, miss. You can't go in there! Stop! I'll call Security."

"To hell with Security. Call the coroner."

Not that Natasha knew where to find Millie, but she strode down the hall with the determination of a Romanian gymnast. She went into the coffee room and poured a cup. Then she headed toward one of the desks, noting the name plate. "Hi, Beth. Mr. Ogden's secretary stepped away, and he asked me to get him some coffee."

"Nice try, honey. *I'm* his secretary." Beth picked up the phone. "Is Iron John still in photo?" She hung up the receiver and pointed to the end of the corridor. "However, since we are an equal-opportunity firm and you did go to the trouble of getting all dressed up, go ahead. Only don't expect too much. He only bonds with men these days. Seems he's got a bad case of wife on the brain."

"Any particular wife?"

"The worst. His ex." Beth leaned forward. "Although from what I hear, she's really old."

Natasha leaned forward, purposely spilling her coffee over the papers on Beth's desk. "No kidding? From what I hear she's really clumsy!"

"The Fuji contracts!" Beth screamed.

Natasha continued down the corridor, pushing aside the security guard.

"Hey, you! Stop! You in the red."

"It's tomato!" Natasha shouted as she broke into a run and threw open the door marked PHOTO STUDIO. SESSION IN PROGRESS. DO NOT ENTER. The lights were blinding. She stopped dead in her tracks and put a hand to her eyes.

"Oh, triple shit!" someone yelled.

"Who the hell is that?"

"The shot is ruined!"

"Nat?"

She looked in the direction of Millie's voice and picked up the first thing she could find. It looked like a bowl of cereal with milk. But it was too heavy. "What the hell is this?"

"Put it down. It's Frooties in Elmer's Glue!"

As Natasha's eyes adjusted to the glare in the white-walled studio, she saw dozens of spotlights focused on tabletops filled with food. Or at least what appeared to be food. There were two camera setups, numerous stainless steel bank lights, and a small army of people with notebooks, spray cans, and trays of cosmetics.

"Nat, don't do it! You'll get glue all over everyone!" As Millie pleaded, the crew backed away.

Natasha smiled. She aimed the bowl at Millie, but instead it hit one of the floor lamps, which fell over and, in domino style, knocked over all the other lamps before shattering on the floor.

"Oh, my God!" a woman screamed. "The Frooties!"

"And this?" Natasha asked, picking up what looked like a pie but was actually merely a crust supported by tissue paper.

"It's nothing!"

"Good." She threw it to the floor. "And this?" she yelled, holding up what felt like pumice stone.

"Don't break my toast!" the food stylist pleaded. "It took days to paint in the right shading."

The security guard ran into the room. "I'll get her, Mr. Ogden."

"No!" Millie shouted. "I'll take care of it."

"Go ahead," Natasha shouted. "Have me arrested again. Maybe this time they'll hang me!" She hurled the toast like a discus and raised her fist victoriously as it splintered apart on hitting the wall. "Yes!" Then she reached for the turkey.

The food stylist rushed over. "Lady, please, not the turkey! I had to cook forty turkeys to get one to look like that."

94

Natasha looked down at her hands. They had turned brown. "What the hell is this thing covered with?"

"Angostura bitters and Vaseline," the stylist said. "With a touch of Max Factor Tropic Tan."

"Yuck!" Natasha held the turkey away from her clothes. She smiled meanly and hurled it at Millie.

The stylist cried out, "Catch it, Max!"

But the guard intercepted and shoved it under his arm like a football. Millie rushed toward Natasha. She picked up a platter.

The stylist began to cry. "Not the platter! It's my mother's!"

"Babe, are you trying to tell me something?" Millie asked as he came closer.

Natasha held the platter high. "Stand back. Ain't nobody gonna take Killer O'Brien alive!"

"Lady, please. I don't give a damn about the Frooties or the turkey."

"Nat, I did it to protect you!"

"*Protect* me?"

Millie started toward her. "Babe, you weren't just a suspect last time. You were almost a victim. I had to do something to draw attention to you."

"Oh, you did that all right. First they locked me up, and now I'm being followed as though I were Leona Helmsley!"

"She didn't want to lend me the platter because it was a wedding present!" the stylist sobbed.

"Who cares why they're following you," he said. "I had to be sure you were safe."

Natasha didn't take her eyes from Millie as she handed the platter to the stylist. "I think we ought to be alone." The room emptied immediately. Natasha walked to the next table. She picked up what was supposed to be a dish of pistachio ice cream.

"Green mashed potatoes and shaving cream," Millie said.

"I thought there were rules about truth in advertising."

"Not for the Japanese market. My megadeal with Fuji Food."

"What about the Natasha market?"

"All's fair."

"In what? Damn it, Millie. I can never tell whether it's love or war we're in."

"Let's talk about it at dinner."

"No thanks. I hate the wine list at McDonald's."

He put his arm around her. "I've got other plans."

She moved back. "So do I. I'm having dinner with Alec."

"Alec? Give me a break!"

"No. You give *me* a break. Do me a favor and don't try to help me. Don't protect me." Her voice softened. "Most of all, don't love me. Millie, we both know what's happening. First Parker. Then Neal. You think I have to call Nick the Greek to find out what the odds are? Don't you see? The only chance I've got is if you stay out of my life."

"I can't do that, Nat. Someone is killing . . ."

"Someone is always killing . . ." She leaned over and wiped the Vaseline from his lapel, fighting back the urge to throw her arms around him. "Sayonara, slugger."


THE ELEVATOR DOWN was the longest ride of her life. A group of tourists counted each floor like the chorus in a Greek tragedy. Natasha walked into the bright daylight of the lobby and out the front entrance, searching every car on the street until she found what she was looking for: the detective who had followed her.

Heading toward him with a look of resignation on her face, she waved and then knocked on the windshield. The young man, his face turning red with embarrassment, opened the door. Natasha sat down next to him and slammed it shut. "Listen, Sherlock, we might as well be civilized about this. Here's my schedule for today. I have a lunch date at one, then back to the office, maybe a quick stop at Bergdorf's — you can park on the Fifty-eighth Street side — and then home to change before dinner. Now step on it."

Without a word, he started the car.


THE WHITE CHIC was the East Side's hottest new restaurant. Whitey Harris, an albino, had been fired from some of the city's most innovative kitchens as, one by one, they lowered their prices and embraced bistro cooking. En route to oblivion, Whitey had begun a small catering business distinguished by the highest prices in town and the conceit that he would serve only white food on white plates. He hired male models, dyed their hair blond, and dressed them all in white. He was an overnight sensation. Within six months, he had two Academy Award–winners prepared to back him.

The all-white restaurant ushered in a new trend in "dinner-wear" thanks to a fashion editor who had two pages to fill and no budget for travel. A *blancmange* Mortimer's, reservations were agonized over before being approved. To be seated in the front room, where everyone wanted to be, no more than three degrees of separation were allowed. Diners were sorted not by area code, former marriages, or defense attorneys, but by color. Once the word was out, smart matrons who wanted to lunch near the front door arrived in packs of pastels.

Isidore, the maître d', put a hand to his forehead as Natasha walked in wearing her red St. Laurent miniskirt and red wool tunic. "I didn't know today was the Puerto Rican Day parade."

"Actually, I was on my way to Grandmother's house."

"Droll as ever," he said without smiling. "Fear not, Miss O'Brien, I know that beneath all that blinding primary schmutz there beats a heart of white."

"Don't count on it, blondie. I'm here to meet Mr. Hawthorne. Has he arrived?"

"I seriously doubt it. But he has been seated." Isidore hesitated. "Listen, I didn't know he was meeting you."

Natasha smiled. "What happened? You put him in Siberia?"

"In Siberia they still need sunblock." Isidore led Natasha along the white floor of a white lacquered room filled with white tables and chairs covered in white linen. As they crossed the threshold to the back room, the patrons' apparel grew more colorful. Isidore muttered, "Welcome to our Crayola Corner."

Roy, who fancied himself a master of disguise when reviewing restaurants, wore a curly wig, sunglasses, and a false beard. He had been seated between the men's room and the service area. As Natasha approached, he stood up and kissed her.

Isidore folded. "I beg you. Let me move you up front."

"And miss all the farting?" Roy snapped.

Natasha waited for Isidore to leave. "It's your own fault. No one would seat Roy Drake where they put Mr. Hawthorne. If you insist upon appearing incognito — "

"I'm doing it for my own protection. Not only did the cops in

Dallas bring me in, but after Neal was killed they questioned me in L.A. Apparently they think I'm Public Enema Number One."

She was startled for a moment. Davis had picked up fast on the fact that she had assigned Roy to profile both of them for the magazine. No wonder he had been so eager to bring her in for questioning. She was the missing link between the victims. But there was one thing Davis didn't know: she had also assigned Roy to profile Whitey.

"Poor darling," she said, "you must have been through hell."

"Let's just say I'm not hiding behind this beard because I'm afraid of the White Queen."

But more than Roy's appearance had changed. "Who *are* you afraid of?"

He hesitated, fingered the menu nervously, and then put it down. "You. Listen, the only reason I came to New York was because I'm late on this dumb piece."

"I don't recall contracting for a dumb piece."

"You want to bet?" He tapped his finger on the menu. "Veal with vanilla? Cornish hen stuffed with popped corn? Buttermilk pasta with white truffles? Almond-coated onions? Cream of wheat mussel chowder? What do you call that?"

"One of the most unique menus in town."

A muscular young waiter brought a tray of steamed bread and crisp thin sesame sticks. "Good afternoon. May I get you something from the bar? Perhaps a *champagne au lait*?"

"A what?" Roy asked.

"It's a glass of champagne with a jigger of Pernod that turns it all milky white."

"Two, please," Natasha said.

"And I'll have a Chivas on the rocks."

"We don't serve Scotch. We have white rum, vodka, gin . . ."

"Red wine?"

"White wine."

"Just bring me the water list," Roy said.

"We don't have a list."

"What do you have?"

"Saratoga and Deer Spring."

"Saratoga. Neat."

"And one *champagne au lait*?" Natasha nodded yes. "Would you like to hear our specials for today?"

"No."

"Yes," Natasha added quickly. She was stalling for time, not knowing how to pick up where Roy had left off. She wanted him to talk more about the murders. Although she was almost certain it was Roy, she needed a better motive than the profiles. It wasn't enough that she had always thought he was crazy because he lived in Los Angeles.

The waiter cleared his throat. "For starters, we have a brilliant Brie souffle."

"How much?" Roy asked.

The waiter looked stunned and put his hands together to approximate a portion. "About this much? Perfect for an appetizer."

"I mean, how much does it cost?"

Natasha hadn't seen Roy behave this way in years. Not since he couldn't get his novel published and he began reviewing books instead.

Roy leaned forward. "Surely you don't buy things without asking the price?"

"I think it's $12.95."

"You think?"

"I can check."

"You don't buy a car from a salesman who says, 'I think it's twenty thousand,' do you?"

"I can't afford a twenty-thousand-dollar car."

"Perhaps you could if you were a better waiter."

"I'll get the drinks." He paused. "The bread is free."

Roy watched the waiter walk away and then smiled at Natasha. "He's kind of cute, isn't he?"

"So that explains it."

"Don't be absurd. I never mix food with pleasure."

Natasha reached for his hand. "Roy, I'm worried about you." She was more worried about touching the hand that might have killed Parker and Neal. "You've been under such a terrible strain."

His fingers tightened around her wrist. "You don't know the half of it. The torture I've been through. Being dragged down to police stations. Sitting in dirty smoky little rooms with incredibly hairy detectives. I tell you, the hair was coming out of their collars and cuffs. It curled around their watches. I don't know how they could see the time. The same questions over and over again. Hour after hour of good cop/bad cop. And thinking that at any moment they were going to strip-search me."

"I'm so sorry."

He shook his head from side to side. "Why do you think they didn't strip-search me?"

The waiter returned before Natasha could answer. "Here's your *champagne au lait*." Then, putting a glass in front of Roy, he narrowed his eyes and said, "And your $3.50 two-cents plain in a complimentary stemmed glass. The Brie souffle, mea culpa, is $14.75."

Roy stared at the waiter. "If you give it to me for $13.50, I'll order it."

The waiter was expressionless. "Our entrees today are baked fish loaf with mashed potatoes and steamed white radishes . . . at a very reasonable $19.95, and white eggplant lasagna with goat cheese, smoked sturgeon, and jicama. $22.00 firm."

Natasha stepped in. "Darling, why not let me order?" Before Roy could object, she said, "Bring him the Brie souffle, and I'll have the mussel chowder. And then, to make things simple, let's have the two specials." She turned to Roy. "Is that all right?"

"Since you're paying, I'd like to taste the buttermilk pasta."

"Since I'm paying, we'll share an order."

The waiter nodded. "And may I bring you the wine list?"

"No," she said. "We'll each have a glass of sherry with our appetizers — "

"La Ina," Roy specified.

" — and then, as I recall, you have a very buttery Napa chardonnay."

"William Hill," the waiter said.

"Make sure it's not overchilled," Roy added. The waiter groaned and left.

Natasha was anything but overchilled. She was hot to stop Roy. "Darling, somehow I get the impression you don't really want to do a piece on Whitey."

"I'd really rather ask the waiter what time he gets off work."

"Maybe you're right."

"Good. Would you ask him for me?"

"I'm not talking about that. I'm having second thoughts. Perhaps The White Chic is too chic for Middle America."

Roy smiled. "Be still my heart. You're offering me a kill fee?"

His words gave Natasha goose bumps. Suddenly "kill fee" had an ominous ring. All it meant was paying a writer half his normal rate and canceling the article. "Yes."

"Have you told Victor Vanilla?"

"There's plenty of time for that. I'll take care of it."

"Done!" He looked at his watch. "I can make the seven-o'clock and be back on the Left Coast faster than Wolfgang can open a new restaurant."

Natasha had expected more of an argument from Roy. She had just pulled the pins out from under him. No Whitey, no profile. No profile, no murder.

Roy leaned across the table and whispered, "Bobby thinks my screenplay is the best thing I've ever written. More important, so do Fox, Paramount, and Columbia, who, even as we speak, are in a bidding war." He began to giggle. "And I haven't even killed my third chef yet."

There it was: Roy's motive. As clear as simple syrup. His screenplay. "Roy, being that we're such good friends, I've hesitated to say this . . ."

He stiffened. "Perhaps you should stay a good friend."

"No, I'd never forgive myself if I weren't absolutely honest. Don't you think your screenplay is somewhat . . . derivative?"

" 'Derivative'? What does that mean? Everything is derivative! Hollandaise and béarnaise are derivative, but no less individual or brilliant!" He sat back, his face flushed with anger.

They stared at one another as the waiter brought them each a glass of sherry. Natasha wasn't sure what she had accomplished. If Roy no longer had a motive to kill Whitey, who would he kill? Finally she raised her glass, hoping Roy wouldn't notice that her hand was shaking. "To your third murder."

*   *   *

ROY LEFT THE RESTAURANT before Natasha. She made excuses about having to powder her nose. In truth, she didn't want Roy to know that the police were parked outside. As she walked toward the car, she saw that there were two men waiting.

Natasha opened the back door and sat down. "Detective Davis, just the man I want to see." She handed the doggie bag to the driver. "Here, Sam Spade, this is for you. Rabbit poached in *eau-de-vie* with a superb cucumber cream. Of course, if I'd known you were here, Detective . . ."

Davis grabbed the bag from the other man. "Miss O'Brien, we are not running a free limo service."

"Well, then, what the hell are you running? Certainly not an investigation. You just let the key suspect walk away."

Davis didn't even look up from opening the bag. "What key suspect?"

"Roy Drake. The man in the beard. He left before I did."

Davis turned to the driver. "You eat rabbit?" The younger man stuck out his tongue. "Me neither. Miss O'Brien, is that what they serve in those places? Bunny rabbits?"

"Listen, Inspector Clouseau, you don't understand — "

"I understand that Roy Drake is writing a screenplay about the murders. So what? These days, that's what writers do. If it were a crime to write about murder, we'd have half the Authors' Guild locked up for life."

"But Roy Drake is crazy!" she shouted.

"Probably from eating bunnies. Yuck! What else did you bring?"

"Buttermilk pasta with shaved truffles."

"Those funguses pigs dig up?" He handed the bag back to Natasha. "No thanks. For the food and the suspect."

"But the Dallas police and the LAPD both questioned him."

"I know. He made a pass at one of the detectives."

"Look, I hired Roy to do a piece on Parker and he was killed. I hired Roy to do a piece on Neal and then *he* was killed."

Davis turned around and looked at Natasha. "So far you're batting a thousand."

"What does that mean?"

"It means we're following you and not Roy Drake."

"You think I'm the copycat killer?"

"I didn't say that. But Drake has airtight alibis and doesn't fit any known profiles. On the other hand, maybe you don't want your ex-lovers around while things are heating up with Mr. Ogden."

"I never went to bed with Neal Short. You can ask anyone."

"Anyone but Neal Short."

There was a long silence just crying out for the swell of background music. It was a moment from what they used to call a "woman's picture," in which the star was passionate, misunderstood, accused of a crime she didn't commit, fighting for survival against seemingly insurmountable odds. Or Claude Rains. "I have a good mind to get out of this car and take a taxi."

Davis softened. "Seems like a real waste of money. You want us to take you home?"

Natasha didn't want Davis to see her crying. She took out her handkerchief and pretended to blow her nose. "In the middle of the day? Back downtown, Philo. I've got a Christmas-cookie tasting I can't afford to miss."

(Alec, I'm terribly sorry the editorial is so late. I can't seem to catch up with myself. Hopefully, you'll be able to close out the issue today. Thanks to you, it's going to be truly wonderful. You seem to be able to read my mind. All of your suggestions have been right on target! Ironic, isn't it? It was my idea to tout comfort food. But between you, me, and the tapioca, everything but Rose's Christmas cookies conjures up such horrible images these days. I suppose if food is love -- then why not murder?)

## Mental Health Food

I love food, and I'm tired of feeling guilty about it.

I love reading cookbooks and eating birthday cake and setting my mouth on fire in yet another valiant attempt to find the best chili this side of the Pecos. I check my sun signs for compatibility with the Union Square greenmarket, Jeremiah Tower, and Orwasher's bread. I talk to my butcher as intensely as patients confer with their cardiologists. When friends arrive from distant ports, my second question is always about restaurants.

By clinging to the old chestnut that if it makes you feel good, it must be bad, high-cal hysterics have given food a bum rap. If Oliver Twist were alive today, they'd toss him into rehab because he asked for more. Given half a chance, those nervous Little Nells would put the tyke in stir-fry for the rest of his life.

No one is ever going to talk me out of food for comfort. When I find that my broker didn't sell short, or the VCR breaks just as Bette Davis says, "Fasten your seat belts...," or someone down at the Unisex suggests I might try a rinse for those gray hairs -- I'm in no mood for tofu. No siree, boys and girls. This is a job for chocolate pudding!

After all, we're in the nineties, and if there's one thing we should have learned it's how to skate on thin ice cream. The key to better mental-health food is being in control of being out of control. Know what you want before you want it. The minute you find yourself staring open-mouthed at the candy counter as though reading the Kama Sutra for the first time, you've lost it.

Do not wait until the quenelle tolls for thee. When you turn to food for solace, it doesn't matter whether your idea of nosh nirvana is a Big Mac or a Big Macrobiotic. Don't hate yourself if Tuna Crunch makes the earth move for you. So what if happiness is a knish in the dark? Remember: The founding foodies gave you the right to whatever turns you on within the privacy of your own mouth. And that's what this issue is all about.

In the beginning, there was mother's milk. Aside from its triumph of packaging, it was the quintessential nourishment for body and soul. It still is. We've stirred up some of America's great chefs for a new spin on good old Mom Cuisine.

Not surprisingly, they all had one ingredient in common: nostalgia. Each recipe serves six as well as the emotions, proving that we've come full circle. Food as power. Food as currency. Food as theater. Food as love. No one can resist its obsessive allure. When the going gets tough, even the tough eat.

NATASHA HAD INVITED ALEC to dinner to discuss the Culinary Olympics. But her agenda had changed somewhat since Davis told her Roy was no longer a prime suspect. The case against Alec built in her mind all afternoon. Alec had worked in the shadow of Achille, admiring him, perhaps even secretly wanting to be him, until finally Alec snapped and his life became a giant sheet of tracing paper. She took a deep breath before opening her apartment door to the man who had murdered Parker and Neal.

"Oh, my God!" She gasped. Alec was wearing a blue suit, a pencil-thin red and white striped shirt, and a red silk tie.

"Do I have the wrong day?"

"No," she said, starting to laugh. "The wrong suit." Natasha was wearing a double-breasted blue pants suit with a white shirt and a red bow tie. "Copycat!" she blurted out.

He smiled. "Perhaps *you're* the copycat."

"Are you accusing me of . . ."

"Looking beautiful. Aren't you going to ask me in?"

Natasha stood aside, suddenly afraid that Alec was already too far in. "I should change."

"I don't think you should change a thing."

"Except my head." She forced a smile, wondering how she was going to get through An Evening of Double Entendres with Alec and Natasha. Watch him make veiled passes! Watch her parry with suspicious indictments! "I forgot to make a reservation."

"I know." Alec held out his hands to show off his manicured nails. "I asked Ester." He smiled, almost boyishly. "So, I took the liberty. Actually, I made four reservations. I didn't know what you had in mind."

Neither did Natasha. It was one thing to suspect Alec in the abstract, but quite another to suspect him while he wore an impeccably tailored double-breasted suit. She had to keep reminding herself that the killings hadn't started until Alec showed up. But then again, they hadn't started until Roy began his screenplay. "Four reservations?"

"Le Cirque, the Russian Tea Room, 21, and The Four Seasons."

"You left out the Carnegie Deli."

Alec walked around the room as though taking inventory. He stopped in front of a small Rembrandt sketch. "I see you still have . . ." His voice trailed off.

"I still have what?"

He turned quickly. ". . . not succumbed to photography. The television of art. I always suspect people who collect black-and-white visions of the world."

"Of what crime do you suspect them?"

He walked slowly toward her. His face was expressionless. "Lack of forgiveness."

"I need a drink."

"Have you ever looked closely at a Picasso painting? The canvas is littered with drip marks. Why didn't he bother to clean them up? Because they weren't important. The human eye is powered by a brain and a heart. A camera has batteries. No compassion. No mercy."

Natasha shuddered. It was pure Achille.

Alec smiled and looked around. "Well, where is the bar?"

"In the lobby."


CAFÉ DES ARTISTES was the perfect place in which to fall in love. Alec allowed himself to be carried away, as did everyone, by the Howard Christy Chandler murals of cavorting buxom beauties, the sparkle of crystal and silver, the patina of old wood, and the gentle purr of a sophisticated clientele.

George Lang, the Mozart of the restaurant business, opened his arms as Natasha approached. "Tasha, my darling. I hear you've been through hell."

Natasha kissed him. "Worse than a Mandy Patinkin concert."

He looked quickly around the room. Nearly every table was

filled. "But it's too early for you to eat, anyway. Did you want the bar?"

"Desperately," she said.

The bar at des Artistes was uniquely situated. Nowhere near the front door or the coat room. Instead, it was nestled toward the back of the restaurant. Lang shrugged helplessly. "All I have is two seats at the end."

"Not anymore you don't." Natasha led the way. " 'Evening, Willy," she said to the bartender.

"I was worried. I thought maybe you'd moved out." He nodded to Alec. " 'Evening, sir." Then back to Natasha. "The usual?"

"Two."

"No champagne for me," Alec said.

"How do you know that's what I ordered?"

How indeed? His mind was falling captive to memory. Seeing the Rembrandt had shocked him. Not because he had remembered being with her when she bought it, but because a recollection had slipped past the sentry. "A lucky guess."

"America was a lucky guess. Besides, you're not an odds-on guy. Otherwise, why all the reservations?"

"The December issue. I checked the schedule. You haven't assigned the piece on power dining. I decided to overpower you." The bartender brought two flutes of champagne. Alec raised his glass, wanting to toast her with "I love you." Instead, he offered a quick "To drip marks."

A waiter brought a bowl of marrow bones and some crusty bread. "Compliments of Mr. Lang."

"New Age caviar," Natasha said, picking up the small spoon and scooping some marrow onto a piece of bread.

Alec watched closely. She was eating it just the way he had taught her. But that had been a lifetime ago. Literally.

She moved the bowl over to him. "Heavenly."

Alec stared at the soft fatty marrow and swallowed hard. His hand moved imperceptibly toward the bowl. He grabbed hold of his glass instead.

"Now, what are we to do with all those reservations?"

"It depends upon how hungry you are." He watched Natasha tear off another piece of bread and slather it with marrow.

"Listen, you must have some," she said, handing him the piece, "before I eat it all."

"But it's pure . . . fat." As Alec took it from her, his stomach began to rumble. Pretending to be distracted, he put the bread down on the bar. "I suppose I should call and cancel."

"Cancel which ones, Smart Alec?" She spooned out more marrow and then realized he was staring at her.

Alec kept watching the nervous expression on her face. The apprehension in her eyes. What was she afraid of saying? Or feeling? Was this Natasha on the verge of falling in love? Surely, it was Natasha at her most vulnerable.

"What name did you use?"

"Dr. Pangloss."

She laughed. "You *were* optimistic." She picked up the spoon. "Frankly, between you, me, and the marrow, I'd be very happy sipping champagne and clogging my major arteries with major hors d'oeuvres."

"Death by foreplay?" He had expected her to smile.

She narrowed her eyes. And lowered her voice. "I was hoping for something short of death."

Alec's heart began beating rapidly. His mouth was suddenly dry. "Hors d'oeuvre. Translated literally as 'outside the work.' But inseparable from the meal."

She reached behind the bar for the phone. "Cancel every reservation. I can't have four empty tables on my conscience, even if they're not in my name."

He picked up the receiver. "What number is information?"

"Who are you calling?" she asked.

"Le Cirque?"

"794-9292."

As Alec began to dial, he noticed that his hand was shaking. By the time he'd finished the third call, he had shooting pains in his stomach. He turned to Natasha. "The Four Seasons?"

"754-9494. But take a break. You look like you're suffering from withdrawal." She lifted the marrow spoon. "This will fix you up."

"No, no," he said, dialing. "I still have some over — "

"I think you ate it after 21. Here." She gave him another piece.

"Good evening. The Four Seasons," the operator answered.

"I'd like to — " Alec began to cough into the receiver. Something was stuck in his throat. "I'd like . . ."

Natasha took the phone from him. "Are you all right?"

He nodded yes. But he wasn't all right.

"This is Dr. Pangloss's secretary," Natasha said. "He has to cancel for tonight. An emergency brain bypass."

Alec sipped his champagne and, to be polite, reached for the bread Natasha had just given him. But it was gone. She must have eaten it.

"Okay, Dr. P," she said, hanging up the phone. "Now that we've canceled all the reservations, let's get going."

Alec reached for the check. Natasha grabbed it from him, their hands brushing for a split second. His memory might have failed him, but his sense of touch was still responsive. With the speed of a supercomputer, he had cloned, from the touch of her finger, the feel of her entire body.

"Don't be silly, Alec," she said while signing the check. "This is business."

Unfinished business. It was at that moment he decided he must have Natasha. Sex was the only appetite he didn't have to share with Achille.


AS THEY WALKED onto the street, Alec started to hail a taxi.

"No need," she said. "I have a driver." Natasha waved at the man sitting in a car across the street. "Hey, pal, are you the night shift?"

"What are you doing?" Alec asked.

A young Hispanic rolled down the window. "Ma'am?"

"Relax. I know you're tailing me."

The man nodded and smiled. "Detective Solares. No known food fetishes. I eat anything that doesn't eat me."

"Not tonight, Solares." She opened the door and hustled Alec in. "We're going to hold up a few bars. You'll be lucky to get a paper umbrella. First stop is Fifty-eight East Sixty-fifth."

Solares nodded approvingly.


THE RINGMASTER at Le Cirque was Sirio Maccioni. Although he packed tables closer than the Rockettes during a high kick, no one ever complained: it was *the* place to be. Le Cirque reflected the best of Sirio's personality, kept on its toes by the worst of his fears. "Natasha!" They embraced while he looked frantically over her shoulder for an empty table.

"Darling, you must meet Alec."

"Welcome." Sirio shook Alec's hand while his eyes continued to scan the room.

Natasha smiled. *"No agita, caro.* All I want is a couple of bar stools."

Sirio forced a smile. "What about a private room? You don't have to eat."

"Give the Eurotrash a private room. I want to sit at the bar with the grown-ups."

"What you want is to drive me crazy!"

Choreographing an exit suave enough for Fred Astaire, Sirio escorted a party of four away from the bar. Before leaving, he turned to Natasha and pointed to the empty space. Natasha led the way and sat down, patting the stool next to her for Alec.

The bartender bowed slightly. *"Buon' giorno,* Signorina O'Brien," he said. "The usual?"

*"Grazie."* Natasha smiled at Alec, determined to peel away the veneer and get some answers. Of course, she'd have to oil him up first. Or at least oil herself up first.

"You don't mind if I have a Pellegrino?" he asked.

"Oh, snore!" she said. "You barely drank half a glass at des Artistes." Of course, he had polished off the entire bowl of marrow. "What are you afraid of?"

"Three more bars."

Natasha shrugged. "Not to worry, I'm a very classy drunk."

"I don't want you drunk."

It was his emphasis on the word *want* that upset her. The son of a bitch! Not that Alec didn't have a certain appeal. Perhaps in some other incarnation — if they were stranded on the planet Alpha-Epicure, where life was as orderly as a strawberry tart and there was no need for memory because tomatoes grew all year round. But in New York-on-the-Ganges, where people lived in paper cartons and houses of cards, where good old Give-My-Regards-to-Broadway Broadway had become an independent Third World nation, where humanity and the Automat had died of apathy, she was not about to fuck around with her executive editor. No matter how attractive he was.

The bartender brought a glass of champagne and was about to pour the Pellegrino. "No!" Alec said sharply. "No ice! No lime!"

Natasha felt herself flinch. It was as if she had overheard the Devil himself.

"*Scusi, signore. Scusi.*" The bartender whisked away the offending glass, replaced it, and poured the sparkling water.

She had to get some answers. "You may wonder why I've asked you here tonight."

Alec clinked glasses with her. "I was hoping you'd forget."

She smiled. "I was hoping to get to know you better. 'Man lives not on what he eats but on what he digests.' "

"Dumas. Terribly indigestible. Especially in English. He translates as poorly as a madeleine."

Natasha nodded. "Pound cake in shell molds. I guess you had to be there."

"I wish *you* had been there."

"Where?"

"In Paris. With Proust and me."

"*Marcel* Proust?"

Alec leaned close. "Haven't you ever wanted to erase your past? Exchange your memories for someone else's?"

"No thank you. I'm having enough trouble being who I am."

"I'm not talking about who you are. I'm talking about who you were."

Natasha sipped her champagne and then smiled. "I used to be an absolute horror."

"Me too."

The waiter brought over a silver casserole dish. "Compliments of Sirio. *Fantasie de St. Jacques en Habit Noir.*"

Natasha groaned. "What a way to go. Laid out in black truffles, floating on a pool of white wine, butter, and truffle juice." Her mind flashed to images of Parker and Neal, and that was the end of her appetite. She moved a truffle-covered scallop onto the sauce spoon and scooped up some of the buttery vermouth. Forcing a smile, she held it to his mouth. "Now, tell me all about the big bad person you used to be."

Alec mumbled, "I can't talk with my mouth full."

But Natasha knew it wasn't Alec's mouth that stopped him from talking. Something else held him back. Something she saw in his eyes. If eyes were a window to the soul, Alec was one of those people who didn't do windows.

"Let's not talk about me," he said.

"First no business. Then no Alec. What's left?"

"You."

She shrugged. "My life is an open book. And a movie, yet."

"I never saw that movie."

"Neither did I."

"Then as far as we're concerned, it doesn't exist."

"My memories exist."

"Let them go!" he said.

Alec reeked of danger. And God help her, there was something compelling about the scent. "Even your pal Proust couldn't let go. He folded over a cheap little cookie."

"I don't consider you a cheap little cookie."

She smiled. "Such flattery." It was no use. He wasn't biting. At least not at her bait. Instead, Alec reached for the casserole and scooped up all the butter sauce as though he had just found the only oasis in the desert. One by one, he collected the truffles, stabbed them with his fork, and swallowed them. Without pausing for breath or even looking up, he ate scallop after scallop after scallop until the dish was empty.

There wasn't a doubt in Natasha's mind. Alec was the killer.


"WHAT WILL IT BE TONIGHT, Miss O'Brien, vodka or champagne?"

Although the Russian Tea Room was outrageously festive with its year-round decor of Christmas ornaments and gold tinsel, Alec was oblivious to everything but the sense of foreboding in his stomach.

Natasha spoke to his reflection in the mirror behind the bar. "You're not going to pull another Pellegrino on me?"

"No."

"Champagne," she told the bartender.

"And I'll have club soda," he said.

"Would you care for a slice of lime, sir?"

Alec sensed Natasha waiting for his reply. "Yes, I always like lime. And some ice, please."

She smiled. "Very funny."

"There's nothing I wouldn't do to cheer you up."

"Or to prove a point. But is this the 'let go of the past' point or the 'people change' point?"

Alec didn't know what to say. Suddenly everything fell into place. He supposed the thought had always been there, unexpressed, somewhere in his subconscious, ever since he heard the news about Parker. But it was no longer memory-resident. He could see it in her eyes. It must have been the pressure of starting up the magazine. Or the extraordinary parallel between her running *American Cuisine* and Achille's running *Lucullus*. Whatever it was, she had short-circuited. He didn't doubt it for a moment. Natasha was the killer.

"I don't suppose you're hungry?" she asked.

He was startled by the sarcasm in her voice. She must have been referring to the fact that he had scrupulously avoided eating anything all evening. "What did you have in mind?"

"A couple of hundred blini."

"With red caviar?"

"They have the best in town," she said, brightening. "It's unprocessed."

"But no sour cream."

"And no onions."

"And no capers."

"And no dill."

"Not even lemon."

"So far, so good." She grabbed hold of him. "But what about butter? God forgive me, I must have butter!"

"I won't tell." It didn't matter to Alec what she had done or why. His love was unconditional. Butter or murder.

"Barkeep!" she called out. "A bucket-o'-blini!"

Alec put his hand on hers. "Not all the memories are bad."

"That's the terrible part of it." Her eyes half filled with tears. "There's something I've never told anyone." She hesitated. "I couldn't help crying when I heard that Achille had died."

114

Alec stopped breathing. It was as though he no longer required air. Like some sensately amphibian creature, he gulped emotion to meet the demands of a new environment. Suddenly he realized that despite all he had been through to exorcise every trace of Achille, he was, at heart, the Phantom, the Beast, the Frog, yearning to be loved for himself.

She leaned her head on his shoulder. "He taught me everything I know about artichokes."

Alec nodded. "The large, round *Camus* of Brittany."

"The small violet *poivrade* of Provence," she said.

He whispered into her ear. "*Artichauts à la Diable.*"

"Garlic, capers, olive oil, and bread crumbs! Alec, stop!"

"*Artichauts Braisés Farcis au Gras.*"

"Oh, yes! Stuffed with sausage and wrapped in bacon. I warn you, Alec. The floodgates are open."

He took both her hands in his. "Did you really cry?"

"You must never tell anyone."

"Of course not."

"Instead of feeling vindicated, all I could think was, Poor Achille."

Alec hesitated. "I'm surprised you didn't go to the funeral."

Natasha drew back. "Are you crazy? He tried to kill me!"

"I mean, I was surprised so few people showed up."

"You were there?"

"No. But Beauchamp went. She told me all about it." He cleared his throat. "Actually, she was the only one present."

"*Quel surprise.*"

"No one even sent flowers."

"Alec, get real."

The waiter brought two plates, silverware, and napkins. Alec waited for him to leave. "Well, he was a rather extraordinary man. I mean, give the Devil his due. He had the keenest palate in England, perhaps in all of Europe. He was an astute observer of the arts, a brilliant conversationalist, and a shrewd businessman. Frankly, I have never met anyone with his unique range of expertise."

"You obviously found him quite a role model."

There was a noticeable change in the tone of her voice. Alec realized he had said too much.

"You know, Alec, let me be absolutely honest. From what I've seen, you could have taken over *Lucullus* and done it as well as Achille. Why didn't you?"

He took a deep breath. "Because I am not Achille van Golk. I despise the wretched excesses that ruined his life. I wanted the magazine, and the appetites it supported, to die, just as he did."

The waiter brought a silver tureen filled with hot blini. He put down a steaming pitcher of melted butter and a crystal bowl of salmon caviar.

Alec suddenly felt weak, nauseated, as though he hadn't eaten for a long time. He watched anxiously as she put blini onto their plates. His breathing grew labored as she poured melted butter over them, allowing each small pancake to absorb as much as it could. She took the crystal spoon from the bowl and topped them each with a large dollop of caviar.

Natasha nudged him as she opened her napkin. "A little wretched excess, in moderation, never hurt anyone."

He picked up his fork. "Well, perhaps just a taste."


THE DINING ROOM at 21 had a ceiling littered with the toys of the rich and famous: baseball bats, ballet slippers, model planes, trucks, boats, and football helmets. The bar ran nearly the length of the entire room.

"No, you may not have Joan Crawford's Dom Perignon '59," owner Ken Aretsky said smiling. He kissed Natasha's cheeks lightly. "Nor the '62 Pommard left by Onassis." He was referring to bottles stored for good customers in 21's legendary wine cellar.

"But they're not coming back for them," she pleaded.

"Probably not Onassis, but I wouldn't put it past Crawford." As he spoke, his eyes scanned the U-shaped all-star dining area that ended at "Bogie's Corner," the table at which it was said Bogart and Bacall had fallen in love. "Are you two interested in being alone?"

"No," Natasha said.

"Yes," Alec added quickly.

Natasha hesitated. "What about the bar?"

"Two stools coming up!"

"We'll stand. This is my seventh-inning stretch. Alec, do you mind?" she asked, without waiting for an answer.

116

"Yes, I do mind," he said, following her to the bar. "I'd like us to be alone. Most of all, I'd like you to say whatever it is you've been afraid to say all night."

She turned to look at him. "It's all over my face, isn't it?"

"Yes."

"That damn mouth of mine!"

He reached out and took her chin in the palm of his hand. "That damn mouth of yours."

Alec leaned over and kissed her on the lips. Natasha gasped for air. With any luck at all, she'd have a massive cerebral hemorrhage and slip to the floor. However, while waiting, she put her arms around his neck. "You're fired."

"Good. Then there's nothing to stop me from kissing you again."

The moment he embraced her, Natasha whispered, "You're hired."

"Make up your mind."

Still not letting go, she looked up at him, wondering why she didn't just tell herself to say "Goodnight, Gracie" and start running. She couldn't. She was playing straight man to her emotions.

"Tell me what you're thinking," he asked.

"Believe me, it's nothing personal. But if Roy didn't kill them and I didn't kill them and Millie didn't kill them, there's only one person left."

His voice was taut. "You think *I* killed Parker and Neal?"

Before she could answer, the bartender poured two glasses of champagne. "How about a little chicken hash or a burger?"

Natasha was starving. Alec had already eaten everything in sight. "I'm not very hungry," Alec said.

"You weren't hungry during the marrow or the scallops or the blini, either." Natasha looked at the bartender and shrugged. "Sounds to me like a double order of chicken hash." She waited for him to leave and then turned to Alec. "I'm sorry. I don't know what made me say that."

It must have been the champagne talking. No, it was the kiss. The fault, Dom Perignon '59, lies not in tasting stars but in ourselves. She picked up her glass and emptied it in a single gulp. "This stuff is worse than truth serum." It was no use. Who was she kidding? As much as she wanted to believe it, as much as she wanted to tie things up neatly, Alec was no killer. "I'm sorry. It's just that Detec-

117

tive Davis said we were looking for a copycat killer, and all I know about you is that you worked for Achille."

"So did you."

"Well, yes, but — "

"If we're talking about copycats," he said angrily, "you're the one who started your own food magazine."

"Alec, what the hell are you getting at?"

"People who live in *glace* houses . . ."

Natasha was stunned. "Are you accusing *me* of killing Parker and Neal?"

"Nothing personal."

"Thank you." Natasha wondered whether to laugh or cry or tear him apart limb from limb. Suddenly she was horrified. "I'm sorry, Alec. I meant to say 'thank you,' not 'fuck you.' "

"You didn't say 'fuck you.' You said 'thank you.' "

"Well, that's what I meant to say." She banged her glass on the bar. "Artenderbay, oremay ampagnechay!" Impatient, she reached for Alec's glass. "You know, you're right. I did kill Parker and Neal."

"What are you saying?"

"If it weren't for me, they'd be alive today." She emptied his glass. "I don't know how I did it, but I know it had something to do with me. Alec, let's get the hell out of here. I'm beginning to feel the champagne."

He reached out for her arm. "Does this mean we're finally getting past the hors d'oeuvres?"

"It means we're finally getting to The Four Seasons. My kingdom for a slice of Chocolate Velvet!"


AS THEY WALKED up the flight of stairs to the reception desk, all Alec could think about was their leaving. Going back to Natasha's apartment. He imagined himself standing at the door as she pulled him toward her.

Natasha stumbled and pulled him toward her. "I told you I was a classy drunk. I only trip in the best places."

Paul Kovi, co-owner of The Four Seasons, had a worried expression on his face as they walked toward him. He looked like a character from an old Lubitsch film — the man from whom Dietrich had stolen the diamonds. He embraced Natasha. "I just gave away your favorite table."

"Darling, as long as you didn't give away my favorite cake," she said, holding tight to Alec's arm. "We've been doing hors d'oeuvres all night and it's time to 'dessert' the ship. I'd like you to meet a friend of mine, Achille van . . ."

Alec's heart began to race. He extended his hand quickly. "Alec Gordon. I imagine you can find space for us at the bar?"

"Give me one moment," Kovi said, heading across the room.

As soon as they were alone, she whispered, "I don't know what I could have been thinking of."

Having Natasha suspect him of being a murderer was bad enough, but her calling him Achille, no matter how much champagne she'd had, was unbearable. He grabbed Natasha's hand and pressed it to his chest. "Can you feel my heart beating? That's *my* heart, not Achille's." Alec felt a sharp pain in his chest, just beneath her hand. "I've gone to lengths beyond anyone's wildest imagination to avoid comparisons with Achille. I'm nothing like him!" The spasm constricted his lungs. "I hated him, most of all, for what he did to you." Alec's throat tightened. He spoke in breathless gasps. "He tried to kill you."

Natasha took his hand. "Alec, you'd better sit down."

The Richard Lippold metal sculpture over the bar was an elegant shower of brass rods made all the more attractive by a hint of danger: it moved. Not the sensuous ripple of the brass swags in the windows — the Lippold was tense. The rods jumped nervously against the air current.

Kovi pulled out two stools as they approached. "I'll make a platter for you. A little bit of everything."

"My hero." As he hurried off, Natasha turned quickly to Alec. "Perhaps you should have something to drink."

Alec nodded at the bartender. "Roederer Crystal." Another mistake. It was Achille's favorite.

"You know, I always said that when I died, I wanted to be chocolate-covered. Maybe I shouldn't wait. It would shut me up."

"I can think of other ways to shut you up."

She leaned over and kissed him on the cheek. "So I've noticed."

"I thought you said no more kisses."

119

"I'm the boss. I can kiss you. It's just that you can't kiss me."

"Sounds like sexual harassment."

"Oh, I don't mean never."

"When?"

"When the first issue is on the stands. When the U.S. team wins at the Olympics in Paris."

"Paris?"

She smiled. "That's what this whole evening was supposed to be about. Alec, I'm going to need help on the article."

It hadn't occurred to Alec that he'd be going with her. His mind began racing in all directions. The first time he had met her was in Paris. And now, to return as lovers . . .

"We'll have a wonderful time," she said.

They both jumped as the bartender popped the cork. "Sorry," he said, pouring the champagne.

"Why don't you say what you're really thinking?" he asked.

"I'm not very good at that game." She forced a smile. "Millie and I were never more in love than in Paris, at the height of Achille's madness."

"Murder makes strange bedfellows. Perhaps that's why . . ."

"Why what?"

"Perhaps that's why you want me to go to Paris."

She emptied her glass as though drinking water.

The waiter brought two enormous platters with slices of cakes and tarts, scoops of mousse and sorbet, small pastries, chocolates, and cookies. Alec stared at them. His eyes began to water. As though from strain.

"Stop!" Natasha held out her hand. "Don't even put them down," she told the waiter. "Alec, I don't feel well. Please take me home."

Alec began to tremble. He winced at the sharp stabbing pains in his head. "Perhaps you need something sweet." He looked around. It was as though his voice had come from somewhere else.

"No!" Natasha grabbed his sleeve. "No Chocolate Velvet! No Roederer! No nothing! Just take me home."

Alec looked at the bartender. "Check, please." His head began to pound so loudly that he couldn't hear the bartender's reply. He couldn't hear what Natasha was saying as she tugged on his arm. All

Alec could hear was Achille's voice bellowing inside him, "Are you crazy? I have just begun to eat!"


NATASHA SAID NOTHING the entire ride home. She stared out the window, her thoughts racing ahead faster than Solares could drive. What if Alec was right? What if? What if? What if for once in her life she stopped trying to answer the riddle of the sphinx before crossing the road?

Alec caught her as Solares made a sharp turn and she lurched forward. She accepted his arms and his hand brushing the hair from her face. Natasha sank back against his chest. It wasn't as though she were still married to Millie. It wasn't as though she were cheating on him. The only person she was cheating on was herself.

"O great sphinx, the answer is, to get to the other side."

"What did you say?" Alec asked.

"I didn't say anything."

"Oh."

"O great sphinx . . ." She glanced guiltily at Alec. "I didn't say anything."

"I didn't hear anything."

"You didn't?"

"No."

"Alec, when we get to my apartment, are you going to take advantage of me?"

"Yes."

She leaned her head back against his chest and sighed deeply. "Good."

He took her key in the elevator, he took her shoes in the foyer, he took her clothes in the living room. Then he took Natasha in his arms and carried her upstairs as she wondered when the hell he was going to start taking advantage of her.

"Alec . . ."

"Yes?" he asked, putting her down on the bed.

"You do know that I'm looped."

"Yes."

"I thought men had rules about such things," she said, watching him unbutton his shirt.

"What things?"

"Drunks and bosses." She leaned over and looked closely as he took off his trousers. He was hard. "I guess not."

"Are you disappointed?"

"Oh, no! About what?"

Alec sat on the edge of the bed. "My total lack of morals."

She reached for his nipples and drew him close. "All you think about is yourself."

"All I think about is you!"

"But you don't even know me. Not the real me. We're like two shits passing in the night."

"Ships," he said.

"Whatever. Did I tell you that Millie and I always fall in love when there's a murder?"

Alec kissed her stomach. "Yes. But I think you're making too much of it."

"Oh, I don't think I'm making nearly enough of it. I feel as though I'm becoming a different person. I don't know how much of me is me anymore."

"It's easy," he said, kissing her nose. "That's you." He kissed her eyes, one at a time. "That's you." He kissed her lips. "And that's definitely you."

"How can you be sure?"

"Natasha, my darling." He whispered as he bit her on the shoulder, "I can tell you with my eyes closed whether I'm eating a piece of chocolate by Godiva, Teuscher, or Lenotre." He kissed each nipple. "I can taste the difference between Château Lafite-Rothschild and Château Mouton-Rothschild." He buried his face in her breasts. "I can inhale the difference between petit-suisse and mascarpone." He circled his arms around her. "I can see the difference between cognac aged in casks made from Tronçais or Limousin oak." He pressed his knee between her legs and pushed them apart as he entered slowly. "What makes you think I can't tell the real you?"

"Just asking."

She held tight to Alec as tears streamed out the corners of her eyes. Please, O great sphinx, let *service* be *compris*.

# AMERICAN CUISINE

MEMO FROM:   Natasha O'Brien, Editor in Chief
TO:   Alec Gordon, Executive Editor

I'm afraid we have a problem. I spent a great deal of time this morning going through your suggestions for upcoming articles, only to find they simply don't work. You've taken too much for granted in trying to second-guess my intended thrust for the magazine. This is particularly upsetting since only yesterday I agreed with absolutely everything you wanted to do. What can have happened between yesterday and today?

Let's see if we can't get back on the right track.

For starters, there's a world of difference between comfort food in the last issue and your proposed piece on Greek diners. As far as I'm concerned, the only Greek diners worth writing about are Aeschylus and Euripides.

"No, No Nouvelle" is a clever title, but I don't want to throw out the baby with the tomato water. Why don't you see if you can come up with something that 1) isn't French; 2) respects American chefs; and 3) starts a trend. Can you have it by tomorrow?

The cross-fertilization of ethnic recipes into a cross-cultural cuisine is an interesting concept, but it's far too cerebral for me. It's one thing to have an idea, but it has to be fleshed out. I guess that's the pattern I'm really objecting to: when you come up with an idea, you can't run away from it and expect someone else (me) to connect the dots. We both have enough experience to know there's many a slip between what seemed like a good idea at the time and one that doesn't work when push comes to shove.

I've come to shove. I run this magazine the way I run my life. That's why I need more than promises.

ROY ARRIVED AT THE WHITE CHIC promptly at ten the next morning as though nothing had happened. As though Natasha had not canceled the article. He had an appointment with Whitey that he was determined to keep. Article or no, Roy Drake had his own agenda.

All the lights were on in the restaurant as the busboys set tables and the bartenders removed traces of yellow rind from the lemon slices. Without his beard and wig from the day before, Roy was immediately recognizable to Isidore, the maître d'. "Oh, look, everyone. It's the Wicked Witch of the West!"

"Fuck you."

"The very thought sends chills up and down my spine."

"You have no spine. You work on tips."

"Moyles work on tips. I work on gratuities." Isidore pulled out a chair for Roy. "Why don't you rest your brains and I'll tell him you're here. Oh, Carlos," he shouted to the busboy. "A roll of toilet paper and a pencil for table six. The critic!"

Roy shook his head, wondering what the hell he had ever seen in Isidore. Or why Whitey had ever married him. It didn't matter. That was all in the past. He saw a future filled with sweaty young messenger boys and smooth-skinned Oriental chauffeurs as he took off for his own private Planet Hollywood. There was no critic at table 6. There was a screenwriter. A screenwriter about to become hotter than bistro food.

Whitey appeared in his chef's whites, holding a white cellular phone and rolling his pink eyes as he waved hello to Roy. A true albino, he had milky skin and white hair. He looked like the White Rabbit without long ears. "Oh, puh-leez, don't be brown," he said into the receiver. Then, putting his hand over the mouthpiece, he said "Hi, sweetie" and kissed Roy before flopping down into the chair next to him. "Arnold and Maria's lawyer," he whispered before taking his hand away. "Listen, you tell them Bruce and Demi never said anything about ketchup." Whitey put his hand on Roy's while continuing the conversation. "I don't care who grossed more, and frankly, I didn't think *Hudson Hawk* was all that bad. Talk to me when the overseas video figures are in. Oops, gotta go. Goldie's on the other line." Smiling, he put the phone down.

Roy shook his head. "My ass, she is."

"Your ass, she is what?" Whitey began to giggle as he patted Roy's hand. "Poor baby, miss the hard times, don't you? But enough about you. Here's a joke Bobby De Niro told me, and I just don't understand it. What's the difference between bad food and bad sex?"

It was all too much for Roy. Arnold and Maria. Bruce and Demi. Goldie. Bobby. Never mind what the difference was between bad food and bad sex, what was the difference between what Whitey was selling and what he was selling?

Isidore appeared and smiled at Roy. "Your throat must be parched with envy. Can I get you a nice glass of iced pee?"

Whitey tugged at Isidore's sleeve and pouted. "Bring me something."

"What would Mommy like?" Isidore asked.

"Surprise me."

"And for King Cobra?"

"Black coffee," Roy said.

"We don't serve black coffee."

"Then send out for it."

"It's all right, Daddy. Let him have it."

"Don't tempt me."

Roy looked at Whitey. "The difference between bad food and bad sex is . . . ?"

"Now this is supposed to be a joke. But I don't know what's funny about it." Whitey cleared his throat. "The difference between bad food and bad sex is that bad food sucks." A giant shrug of puzzlement.

Carlos rushed over to the table. "It's Liza. A table for eight at lunch?"

Whitey picked up the cellular phone. "Hi, sweetie. Tell me first what you're going to wear." He began to giggle.

Something was very wrong with the world as far as Roy was concerned. Basic American values had certainly gone to hell if Liza Minnelli, who was perfect for the woman in his screenplay but was virtually unreachable, was talking to someone who cooked dead animals for a living.

"You know," Whitey said, hanging up the phone with a sigh, "I've heard of two more Judy sightings in the past month alone. It's like a Menotti opera. God forbid Liza should find out. But enough about her." Whitey rapped his knuckles on the tablecloth. "Guess what I've decided to do?"

Die, Roy thought.

"I've decided to really push the envelope this time. I'm going to call in Adam Tihany or Milton Glaser and redo the whole fucking place. Something really new and fun. Spark up the room with some vanilla and ivory trim."

"Wow!"

Isidore reappeared. "A glass of coconut milk for Mommy, and a buh-lack coffee for the Prince of Darkness."

Roy took a sip from the steaming cup. "Mmmm. This is great coffee!" Wringing the last drop from his damnation with faint praise, Roy continued. "You really know how to make a good cup of coffee."

Isidore groaned and left.

Whitey sipped his coconut drink. "So. What kind of spin are you planning for the article? I should tell you, in all fairness, that *Architectural Digest* and *Elle Decor* have already been here."

"And what did they think of the coffee?"

"Oh, puh-leez! This isn't going to be one of those boring food things?"

"Heaven forbid. Give me credit for a little imagination. We both know no one comes here for the food. Especially not after Gael and Bryan spread the word about your new vanilla and ivory trim. No way," Roy said, sitting back. "I'm talking an in-depth profile, a real character study. A day in the life of — "

Isidore called from across the room. "Godzilla on two."

Whitey raised his eyebrows. "My book agent." He picked up the phone. "So what have you done for me lately? Uh-huh. Great. Sure

I can get quotes from everyone, but I want final jacket approval. What about the tour?" Whitey winked at Roy. "I don't want their publicist! Some Ivy League bimbo in a Peter Pan collar. Have them call Howard. He knows where I like to stay. And tell them to add one more city. I read somewhere that Dean Fearing had fifteen cities. I want twenty. And we keep foreign rights and first serial. 'Bye."

"That's the spin!" Roy said. "Arnold and Maria. Liza. The photo shoots. The book deal. Working with the lawyer, the agent, the publicist, the architect, and the designers. The chef of the nineties coming out of the kitchen!" Roy leaned forward almost threateningly. "I'm going to capture the real you!"

Whitey smiled and brushed back his hair. "Oh dear. You may have to kill me first."

FROM: Ogden-san

TO: Hiram Heartburn

Damn it, I'm in love! Fourteen hours in a plane going from right to left, with nothing more to look forward to than a relapse of chronic Fuji syndrome, I close my copy of <u>Huckleberry Finn</u>. I am only on page 5 when I suddenly realize that the twain has been met.

I am the twain. I am not a camera or a teenage werewolf. I am the east that is east and the west that is west. Me! Think about it. What I have always had trouble meeting is myself. This is deep stuff. Better put away your autographed picture of Ross Perot.

Have you ever looked out the window from 35,000 feet? The earth is not round. The horizon is not endless. The world begins and ends with my shoe size. One small step for man. The world is what I can hold in my arms, and Hiram, I have been embracing the wrong stuff. I guess I always knew. Down deep, in that teeny tiny part of me that has no preservatives or artificial flavoring, I knew she was right when she said I was wrong.

To explain. I get on board a plane that will take me all the way from New York to Tokyo, which is about as far as you can go without having to move your bowels. But when I get off United's <u>Nina II</u>, there is no land for me to claim for Spain. Testosterone shrugged. I am met at Customs by a nearsighted driver who holds the card with my name upside down. I step into the limo and pick up the phone. DNA propels the male forefinger toward a dial. The Y chromosome has been imprinted with an inexorable desire to claim this land for Spain. Arigato and gomen nasai, get me Queen Isabella!

Hiram Hockfleisch, let me tell you something: Like the earthquakes in California, the fault lies within ourselves. Beware of flying homonyms. Priorities pervert. The discoverer discovers himself.

In comparison to me, Columbus was an armchair traveler, Magellan was an agoraphobic, and Cortez had nothing but ants in his pantaloons. Add up my frequent-flier miles. Recalculate the cost of the Lady of Spain's money in terms of today's dollars. Amortize my expenses versus theirs. Price the returns on their discoveries versus mine. Nolo contendere, buddy. Tomatoes, potatoes, chocolate, and corn versus Natasha. I just met a girl named Natasha.

All of which is a roundabout way of saying that she loved me once, she loves me twice, and I'm not going to screw it up again. We don't often get the chance to rewrite our lives, and this time, goddamn it, it's going to have a happy ending.

NATASHA HAD KEPT the answering machine on all weekend. She had put herself under house arrest as she wondered how she was going to face Alec on Monday morning. He had called dozens of times. Even Millie had phoned twice from Tokyo. She let their messages pile up just as she did the newspapers outside her door. She didn't know what to do. It was going to be another Monday morning without her homework.

She needn't have worried.

Her confrontation with Alec took place at the police station. They caught sight of one another through the glass partitions while each was questioned in the death of Whitey Harris.

The torment in Natasha's mind had shifted from not knowing what to say to Alec after she slept with him to the horror of Whitey's murder. All during her session with Davis, she answered his questions with a shake of the head or a nod. Natasha finally spoke as she was ready to leave.

"Stuffed with what?" she asked, gripping the doorknob.

Davis consulted his notes. "A mousse of scallops, white truffles, beaten egg whites, and heavy cream."

"And then he was . . ."

"Poached," Davis said. "In a fish stock."

"White turnips?" she asked.

"And celery hearts."

"No amateur," Natasha said.

"I think not."

"Any clues?"

"We had you under surveillance all weekend, but you never left your apartment. And Mr. Ogden is in Tokyo."

"That leaves . . ."

"Mr. Gordon and Mr. Drake?"

"It can't be Alec," she whispered.

"Because he spent the night with you on Friday?"

Natasha had forgotten all about Solares. Of course. He had driven them to her apartment. He didn't see Alec leave until Saturday morning. "Because I know what makes people tick. I understand them as well as I understand myself." She turned back to Davis and shouted, "I could never have slept with a killer!"

"I didn't say you had."

"Then I was right. It is Roy!"

"No. We can't put him at the scene of the crime."

"Why? Because he gave you some flimsy alibi? Can't you see through that?"

"Not really, Miss O'Brien. His alibi is Mr. Gordon."


NATASHA SAT UP FRONT as the detective *du jour* drove her up-town to the office. She stared out the window. "What makes some-one kill people?" she asked.

The driver put his foot down on the brakes. "Given the circum-stances, I don't think I'm supposed to discuss company business."

"Why can't you tell just by looking at someone?"

"Because it's nothing you can see. People kill for money or power or love. I remember somebody telling me, 'You want to find a killer, first find someone who's hungry.' "


A POSSE HAD GATHERED outside Natasha's office. Bermuda, Christine, Bud, and Arnold snapped to attention as she stepped off the elevator.

"I've got to see you!"

"We have to talk!"

"There's a real problem here!"

"This can't wait!"

Natasha walked past them without a word and quickly closed the door behind her. She barely had enough time to mutter "Vultures!" before Ester came in with the mail.

Important letters were put in the middle of Natasha's desk, near the jelly donut Ester had brought from Brooklyn. Phone messages to the side. Ester held up the rest of the mail. "You don't have any money to buy stocks this month, you're too busy to subscribe to the Met, I've decided to go to most of the press dinners myself — except there are some you should consider — and I've already said no to all the free trips for the next two months, although believe me, I could use a few days at Sundance, God forbid I should meet someone named Robert Redford." She waved the mail. "Garbage?"

"Garbage." Natasha looked down at the donut. "Ester, I can't eat this."

"Eat half. Then technically it becomes a leftover and I can feed it to Pushkin with a clear conscience."

"I wish I had one of those."

"No you don't. He pees on everything."

"I meant a clear conscience."

Hesitating, Ester asked, "How bad was it?"

Natasha held out her hands. She had chipped off the polish and bitten her nails to the quick.

"So this time you really did it."

The tears began to stream from Natasha's eyes. Yes, this time she felt as though she had really done it.


AFTER A GOOD CRY and a manicure, Natasha was ready for the next round. Ester opened the door and everyone started talking at the same time.

"I can't believe there's been another murder."

"We're going to run out of chefs."

"The American Beef Council is getting nervous."

"I've got to tell you about Grenouille!"

Natasha looked at Arnold. "About where?"

"Me and Ester went for lunch. After she helped me move on Saturday. It was like the Botanical Gardens. I never saw so many flowers."

Natasha sensed danger. "What else?"

"The dishes. The service. Those funky little lamps on the tables."

"And what did you eat?" she asked ominously.

"Who remembers?"

Natasha banged her fist on the desk. "What the hell is going on here? I turn my back, get arrested for ten minutes, and you, Mr. Noo Joisey, you forget why I hired you."

Bermuda shook her head at Arnold. "You should have said the fish was overcooked. You'd have been a hero."

So much for Natasha's unfailing instinct about people. She had hired Arnold the same day she hired Alec. "Next!"

Bud took a deep breath. "The American Dairy Council is getting nervous about their twelve pages."

"You look like *you're* nervous about their twelve pages."

"Let's face it. These murders aren't doing us any good. The advertisers keep reading your name in the tabloids."

"What the hell is happening to you people?" Natasha asked. "You're folding faster than warm egg whites."

Christine interrupted. "I've got to replace those profiles with something."

"What about 'Mom Cuisine'?" Natasha asked.

Bermuda made a gagging sound. "Why do we have to jump on the bandwagon just because every cook in America has developed an Oedipus complex?"

"Kill me, but I didn't graduate from the Columbia School of Journalism to write about meat loaf with gloppy brown gravy and lumpy mashed potatoes," Christine said.

Natasha should never have hired Christine. How could she have made such a mistake? "What about the piece on Barbra Streisand's seder?"

Bermuda waved the recipes. "May my Bubbie rest in peace. Latkes with truffles? Tsimis with caviar? That little *brucha* is going to cost more than *Terminator 2!*"

"Listen," Bud said, "I sold pages based on great American chefs, not dead American chefs! They're beginning to connect you to the murders. What do I tell them? I've had calls from Publishers Clearinghouse."

Natasha stood up. "You tell them I'm leaving for Paris on Wednesday. You tell them I'm coming back with an entire issue dedicated to American culinary excellence as recognized around the world. You tell them we have lip-smacking recipes from the most innovative cooks in America. You tell them this is going to be the best damn food magazine in the country. And no half-baked lunatic is going to get in my way!"

The door was flung open. Everyone turned as Alec stood there, pale as a ghost. "Excuse me." His voice was tense. "Natasha, I must see you. Alone."

She couldn't look him in the eye. "Not now."

"Now!"

Bermuda rattled her papers, pretending to be frightened. With great exaggeration, she tiptoed out. The others followed. Natasha and Alec stared silently at one another.

Where was Emily Brontë when you needed her? Natasha stood there as though she were alone on the moors. The wind was chill, night was falling, and she was lost.

Alec locked the door. "Sit down."

"Not another chef."

"No. Not yet."

She sat down, praying that something would pop into her head. A sentence, a word, anything that would explain to Alec, and to herself, what had really happened on Friday night. But he didn't seem interested in what she had to say.

Alec's voice was flat. Devoid of emotion. "I met Roy at the police station this morning. He came back to the office with me. He wanted to speak to you."

"Roy is here?" she asked.

"No. He had to make a plane." Alec handed her a contract. "He came to return this."

"His Olympics contract? That bastard! I won this fair and square! What the hell do I do now?"

Alec ignored her question. "I sent him over to accounting to get his kill fee. While he was gone, I looked through his briefcase."

"You did what?"

"I found these." Alec offered her some papers. "I made a copy."

Natasha didn't want to take them. "What are they?"

"Pages from Roy's screenplay. That's why he couldn't go to the Olympics. He said he had to finish it." Alec paused. "There's a scene in which a chef is stuffed with scallops, white truffles, egg whites, and heavy cream."

"He must have heard it on the news. He writes fast."

"Too fast for his own good." He handed her the pages. "Read this."

"I don't want to read it. I don't even want to touch it."

135

"He wrote more than one scene. He wrote the next murder."

Natasha reached for the phone. "I'm calling the police."

Alec slammed down the receiver while her hand was still on it. Natasha backed away, as though she could retreat from the incredible thought that had just crossed her mind.

Alec spoke softly. "The victim is a famous dessert chef who runs a food magazine."

Natasha had just become a bonus question in the final round on *Jeopardy*.

As Alec put his arms around her, Natasha no longer wanted to disavow Friday night. Suddenly she felt safe. Not the way she did with Millie. Alec was so different. First, there was no back story. Second, Alec was very much like her. It wasn't a question of opposites attracting. And then, although he didn't really look it, she sensed that he was older, or at least more mature. At that moment, with all the evidence pointing to Roy, she relaxed into his arms.

"I've taken care of everything," Alec said. "We're booked on the next flight to Paris. There's a car waiting downstairs to drive us to the airport. Once we're in Paris, I'll notify Inspector Davis. He'll pick up Roy, and the nightmare will be over."

Natasha held tight to Alec. "Shouldn't we call him right away?"

Alec glanced at his watch. "It wouldn't do any good. Roy's plane just took off."

She pulled back. "It's really Roy?"

"Yes."

"It's Roy," she repeated.

"Roy."

Then, suddenly, "But Davis said you were Roy's alibi."

"Sunday was the Soltners' anniversary. They had a party. Everyone was there."

"I wasn't there."

"You weren't answering your phone. I called to remind you."

"Was that why you called?"

"What do you think?"

"I think Roy could have put in an appearance and left." She felt herself grow flush. "I think I'd better send André and Henriette some flowers." She smiled helplessly. "I think I was hoping that you had called for some other reason."

"I think you'd better kiss me."

136

"I thought you'd never ask."

"I didn't ask. I said you'd better kiss me."

"And if I don't?"

"You leave me no choice. I'll have to kiss you."

She leaned forward and brought her lips to his. "You know the rules about not kissing the boss." Alec kissed her with the hunger of an adolescent. It was a kind of excitement she hadn't felt in years. She sensed that he wanted to devour her. Natasha pulled back. "But I can't go to Paris without clothes. I have to go home and pack."

"You'll buy new clothes."

"What about my toothbrush?" she asked.

"I'll buy you a new toothbrush."

"It looks like you've thought of everything."

"I know how difficult it is to start over."

"But I can't go running off to Paris" — she shrugged her shoulders — "just to save my life."

Alec glanced at his watch. "We have to leave."

Before she could take refuge in the Kingdom of Alec, there was something Natasha had to know. It was the same question every convert asked.

"Alec, you read the pages. How do I die?"

He lowered his eyes. "I don't know. Roy didn't get to that part yet."


THE FIRST-CLASS CABIN of the Air France 747 was less than half full: four Japanese businessmen, a young man using a laptop, and Angela Lansbury. Alec had arranged for bulkhead seats, just as Achille always had, to avoid having anyone overhear his conversation or lean back into his air space.

"I feel so strange," Natasha said nervously. "Like a little girl. Free of all responsibility. I guess it's that I've never traveled without baggage."

He smiled. "It means you've finally let go of the past. Besides, I told you that I'll see to it you have everything."

"Alec . . ."

"I will. I can afford it."

"That's not the point. I'm not a little girl. Every time I mention something I need, you can't say you'll buy it for me."

"Don't you believe me?"

"The problem is that *you* believe you." Natasha was worried. Alec, simply because he had slept with her and saved her life, now thought he owned her. Not that she couldn't see his side of it — after all, what the hell more did most other women want from a man? Trying to get things back on track without hurting his feelings, she took his hand. "Dear Alec, your job description doesn't include providing a limo, buying plane tickets, or getting my passport back from the — " She stopped short. "How did you manage that?"

"I bribed someone at the French Consulate."

"Alec, that's dangerous!"

"About as dangerous as putting croutons in soup. The French won't give you the time of day without a *pourboire!*"

The steward leaned over, smiling. "Are we ready for some champagne now?"

Before Natasha could answer, Alec said, "No, we are not. Bring us two Perriers. No ice. No lime."

That tone again. Why was it that whenever she was with Alec, she thought of Achille? Except when he had made love to her. And now that was the one thing she didn't dare think about when she was with Alec.

"I could have used a drink," she said.

"Cheap champagne does terrible things to the digestion."

"So does murder. I'm starving!"

"Suppose I told you that I had in my possession the world's single most perfect pear?"

"Not an Oregon Comice?"

"Yellow with a slight red blush. And — "

Natasha began to feel uneasy as she finished the sentence for him. " — a wedge of Stilton and a split of d'Yquem?"

"Not overly chilled, either."

Her words were barely audible. "Of course not."

Alec pressed the call button and then took a thermal bag from the overhead compartment. The steward appeared immediately. "Tray tables, please. Also, two stemmed white-wine glasses." He opened the bag and took out two plates. "But first — "

"I know. Sturgeon smothered with Osetra."

Alec hesitated. "How did you know?"

"And Polish potato vodka."

"Precisely."

She watched as he took a frosted bottle from the freezer chest. Smoked sturgeon and a jar of fresh caviar coded 000 for its light color from one compartment, and two stemmed crystal vodka glasses from the other. How many flights had she been on with Achille? Whether to Istanbul, Majorca, or Kyoto — each time he had gone through the very same ritual.

"What is it?" Alec asked. "That look on your face."

"Nothing . . . really." Natasha felt a sudden chill, for the first time understanding what they meant about someone walking across your grave. Someone with a very heavy footstep.

Alec put his hand on hers. "I thought we agreed. No baggage on this trip."

No baggage? At that moment Natasha was flying a fucking cargo plane! Daring to look Alec straight in the eye, she asked, "What made Achille do it?"

"I don't know!"

"You were right there with him. You . . ."

Alec whispered, his words barely audible, as though he were afraid someone very close might overhear. "I was not right there with him. He isolated me from his life as though I'd never existed. He never let me into his world, much less his thoughts."

"I had no idea. I imagined that you and Achille . . . well, that he was your mentor."

"My jailer."

"But you're so much like him."

Alec smiled. It was a chilling smile. Self-satisfied. Triumphant.

Natasha sat back and held tight to the armrests, as if to reassure herself that she was not falling through space, catapulting into a forbidden time zone. She knew it was impossible, but she also knew that she was sitting next to Achille.

# AMERICAN CUISINE

MEMO FROM: Natasha O'Brien, Editor in Chief
TO: Max Ogden

Millie,

How difficult this is to write, especially since I've been sending out the wrong signals. Or at least I've been sending out old signals. Like old habits, they die hard.

Promise you'll be happy for me. For the first time in my life, I'm happy for me, and I wanted you to know that at least, in part, you've won.

I have decided to step down as editor in chief of <u>American Cuisine</u> and give that job to the person to whom it really belongs, just as I've decided to give myself to the person to whom I really belong -- Alec.

I know how you feel about Alec, but you're wrong. One of the most important things I've learned from him is to look deep within for the heart of the artichoke. I think of all the years I've spent judging the outer leaves -- it makes me feel like such a little fool*%# YOU ARE A FOOL TO BE WRITING THIS SOPHOMORIC LOVE LETTER TO YOURSELF, AND YOU ARE AN EVEN BIGGER FOOL TO BE PIDDLING AROUND WITH YOGURT WHEN I WANT SOME PATE AND BRIOCHE*ˆ% and yet, Millie, Alec speaks so fondly of you@#$ THAT'S A LAUGH*˜ # that I know we're all going to be great friends STOP STOP STOP ALL THIS BORING PROSE WHEN WE COULD BE WRITING ABOUT CORNICHON PICKLING IN THE LOIRE.

I'm going to marry Alec as soon as possible + )\ THE HELL

SHE IS<>[ and I wanted you to be the first to know = ˆ*
DON'T BE A TURNIP, I WAS THE FIRST TO KNOW%'@ By the
time you read this, Alec and I will be in Paris WHAT ARE YOU
WAITING FOR YOU MUST CALL AHEAD AND BOOK MY TABLE
AT TAILLEVANT and, can you imagine, I don't even care where
we eat!˜ + WELL, I DO CARE WHERE I EAT AND YOU HAVE
AS MUCH CHANCE OF MARRYING NATASHA AS SYLVIA
PLATH HAD OF COLLECTING SOCIAL SECURITY

**FAX**

FROM: A. Gordon
TO: Beauchamp

Get the lead out of your bird cage. I arrive in Paris tomorrow with Natasha under my wing. Have been up all night tidying loose ends, saving the best for last.

You may consider yourself divorced. I have alerted the solicitors to exercise all relevant codicils in the prenuptial agreement. Effective immediately, kindly revert to your previous persona as the Virgin Queen of Notting Hill Gate. All employee benefits shall continue according to contract.

Thank you very much for being my wife.

YUZURO, THE CHAUFFEUR, had been at JFK waiting for the plane from Tokyo to land. As Millie exited Customs, Yuzuro bowed three times and then hurried off to bring the car around. As he passed a newsstand, Millie saw the headlines about Whitey. He took out his cellular phone and dialed Natasha. Answering machine at home. Voice-mail at the office. No use calling Ester again. She had instructions to hang up on him and had been doing so for days.

Mrs. Nakamura was the only person actively trying to reach Millie. She had left twelve messages at his hotel in Tokyo, four at the airport, two on the plane, and one with the ground crew. Yuzuro had handed him six more.

Millie dialed his secretary, who told him that he could make the memorial service if he went directly to The White Chic. He'd be sure to catch up with Natasha there. Poor Nat, she must have been half out of her mind.

Millie stepped into the black Mitsubishi limo to find three packages from Mrs. Nakamura. A large bottle of cologne, a box of candy, and a life-size, anatomically correct blow-up balloon of a woman.

Once they were on the expressway, Millie began to undress. Yuzuro nearly went off the side of the road as he glanced into the rearview mirror. Millie could feel the shift in the car each time the chauffeur looked back. Always one to clean his dirty laundry in public, he opened his alligator Gucci carry-on filled with fresh shirts, underwear, and socks.

Millie was stark naked as he unzipped his matching alligator toiletries kit, took out the electric razor, shaved, and slapped his face resoundingly with Mrs. Nakamura's cologne. He opened the bar compartment, poured a quarter of a glass of white vermouth, and brushed his teeth with it. Next he took a linen napkin, doused it in vodka, and gave himself a quick, and very careful, rubdown.

While drying off, he looked in the fridge and found a jar of olives. He dipped the napkin into the jar, soaked up some olive oil, and shined his shoes. Then he washed his hands with the rest of the vodka. By the time Yuzuro reached the East Side Drive, Millie was fully dressed and ready to meet the Queen of England. Or Tina Brown.

Almost. One of the most important business tips he had learned at the Wharton School was to use the facilities before he had to. Familiar with all of the car's amenities, Millie opened the side compartment and took out the screw-top urine bottle as Yuzuro headed down Lexington Avenue toward The White Chic.

The glut of limos in front was more impressive than a Sondheim closing. Nothing but staged entrances as the legion of terribly bereaved but terribly chic and terribly hungry posed for the paparazzi.

Millie couldn't wait the last half block. He tapped Yuzuro on the shoulder and said, "Give me ten minutes. Then you'd better be right in front with the motor running, or else you lose your whole benefits package for six months, including your charge at Tiffany's."

Yuzuro jumped out of the car, opened the door for him, nodded, and bowed three times. Millie hurried down the block until he reached the line going into the restaurant. He was right behind Paloma Picasso. Her lips were so red she looked as though she'd just kissed Count Dracula.

"What is the delay?" she asked, applying more lipstick.

Millie shrugged. "You know how people dawdle over dessert."

She glanced at Millie, wondering for a moment whether she was supposed to know who he was. She shrugged.

The delay was due to the stunned reaction as each person walked into the restaurant. With the exception of the walls and floor, everything at The White Chic was black. Black chairs, black tablecloths, black napkins, black roses in black vases. The waiters wore black tunics and black tights. A tuxedoed string quartet played "Pavane for a Dead Princess."

Beth Morgan of Chickpea Morgan's, California's hottest organic-food restaurant, grabbed Millie's sleeve. "I need to network."

"Call CBS." He removed her hand as though it were a piece of lint. He had disliked Beth ever since she called a press conference to accuse American Good Foods of "poisoning" kids with Sparkle Cup-cakes — coincidentally, on the eve of opening her restaurant.

"Max, I'm worried."

"Have you seen Natasha?"

"She must be here. Listen, Max, it's time to put our cupcakes behind us."

"Why?"

"I hear AGF is looking for an executive chef. If you remember, I did work with Troisgros and Bocuse."

"Give me a break! It isn't possible that all the cooks who say they worked for Bocuse actually did. Or if they did, they couldn't have done more than empty the garbage for a week." He turned from her and began making his way through the crowd. Among the 24-carat celebs — Michael Caine, Glenn Close, Zubin Mehta — there was a roomful of nervous chefs. David Bouley, Jean-Georges Vongerich-ten, and Daniel Boulud stood in a circle joking about being safe because they were French, while Alfred Portale, Andrew d'Amico, and Michael Romano wondered whether ethnicity counted. Millie felt a hand on his shoulder.

"Max!" It was Dewey Arno from New Orleans. He was the chef at A Restaurant Named Desire.

"Have you seen Natasha?" Millie asked.

"No. I've got to talk to you."

"After I find Natasha."

"Max, I know who's going to be next."

Millie took a deep breath. "Who?"

Dewey pointed to himself.

Millie looked away, scanning the crowd. "Any particular reason, or just chef's intuition?"

Dewey grabbed Millie's shoulders, forcing eye contact. "Max, I was the one who invented tomato water. Oyster water. Cucumber sweat."

Millie nodded. "I myself could kill you for that."

"Don't you see the pattern? The chefs who were murdered all had high profiles for translating regional American dishes into healthy, modern cuisine. You must have seen the piece on me in the *New England Journal of Medicine*. I have a book coming out, a monthly spot on *Good Morning America*, and I've been hired by Spielberg to cater his next movie. Max, you are looking at a dead man!"

"You sure you haven't seen Natasha?"

Millie spotted a waiter carrying drinks and was about to reach for a glass when he realized they were serving champagne in black flutes. Who the hell had thought that one up? You couldn't see the color of the champagne or the bubbles, and where the hell was Natasha, anyway?

There was a mob around the buffet. People holding black plates as waiters served Beluga caviar, black bean soup, blackbirds stuffed with black truffles, blackberry pie, and black coffee. He turned to Connie Chung. "Wouldn't you just kill for a marshmallow?"

"I know you," she said. "You were married to — "

"Lana Turner," he said, moving away. "Or was it Tina Turner? One of them."

Isidore stood at the head of the receiving line. Like a czar in mourning, he was dressed in white. Next to him, in dark suits, were Whitey's key suppliers — his butcher, his poultry man, his fish man, the greengrocer, the baker, and his decorator. Isidore recognized Millie and his mouth dropped open. "Max? Is that you?"

"Izzy?" The two men embraced. "How long is it?"

"The same length it's always been," Isidore said as he began to cry.

Between semesters at Cornell, Millie and Isidore had spent a summer waiting tables on the *QE2*. Although they had bumped into one another a few times over the years, they had lost touch until Isidore wound up sobbing in his arms. The two men eased their way into an alcove.

"When I stepped on the glass, the chief rabbi of Cherry Grove said it would last forever. Lucky for him he wasn't in the calendar business. Max, what the hell am I going to do?" Isidore brushed the tears from his face. "I don't have a table for you."

Millie held on to him, taking the opportunity to scan the crowd over his shoulder. "It's all right. I'm looking for Natasha."

"You and who else."

"Who else?" Millie asked, pulling away.

"*Le gendarme*. Some wussy detective. I sat him next to Ivana. Max, I can't believe Natasha did it."

"She didn't!"

"Oh, please. I was here." Isidore shook his head. "She came in a couple of days ago and, God forgive me, I sat her near the men's room." Isidore gave a "case closed" shrug.

"Who was she with?"

"Roy Drake." He rolled his bloodshot eyes. "But he likes sitting near the men's room."

"Is Roy here?"

"He wouldn't dare show his face. Not after the fight he had with Whitey."

"About what?"

"Roy came back the next day to interview him. Blah blah blah. And then it all started again." Isidore sighed. "Over me. Whitey and Roy had a thing going until Whitey came east." Isidore raised his eyebrows. "In Roy's case, a very small thing."

"Did you tell the police?"

"Max, baby, Roy couldn't kill anything but a good time." Suddenly Isidore gasped. He was staring at the entrance to the restaurant. "Oh my God!" he groaned, heading toward the door. "It's Marla!"

Millie edged his way past Bobby Short and Diane von Furstenberg to reach Detective Davis, who was holding a plate of caviar and a cup of coffee. "Can't drink on duty."

"Where is she?" Millie asked.

"You don't know?"

"Is she all right?"

"I hope so." Davis spoke between hurried mouthfuls of caviar. "We never even saw her leave the office. Some getaway. A real pro."

"Where is she?"

"She left for Paris last night. Must have worn a disguise."

"Paris? Why the hell aren't you going after her?"

"What for?"

"To protect her!"

"I'm not in the protection business. I investigate crimes, I don't prevent them. At this point, I don't have anything to hold her on. Her secretary said she left because of a problem with the . . . Culinary Olympics? There is such a thing?"

Millie nodded. "Every four years. A high-class Pillsbury Bake-Off."

"According to the secretary, Miss O'Brien and Mr. Gordon — "

"Not Alec Gordon?"

"Not Flash Gordon."

"Son of a bitch! I knew there was something about him . . ." Millie handed Davis a napkin. "Your tie. A material witness leaves the country and you stand here dribbling Beluga on your Ralph Lauren knockoff."

"I've notified the Sûreté."

"That's as good as putting up a No Fucking notice in the Bois de Boulogne."

"What do you want me to do?"

"I want you to get her the hell away from Alec Gordon." Having said it, Millie knew that was something he had to do himself. Davis wasn't in love with Natasha; he was. Davis didn't think of Natasha every morning when he got up, every time he went to bed with another woman, or every time he ordered dessert. Impulsively, Millie grabbed hold of Davis and hugged him. "You're right! I'm leaving for Paris immediately."

Davis pulled back and looked around nervously. "Keep her away from Roy Drake."

"I knew it!" Millie said. "I knew it was Roy. Have you got him locked up?"

"LAPD has him under surveillance."

"What does that mean? Everybody is under surveillance in L.A. It's either the studios, the IRS, the *Enquirer* . . ."

"I have no proof."

"Who needs proof? L.A. lives on innuendo. It's the capital of half truths. Davis, trust me. Get the LAPD to pick this guy up for jaywalking and he's a shoo-in for the gas chamber!" Millie began edging his way through the crowd.

"Max?"

Millie was face to face with Benno St. Louis, owner of the exclusive Jean Valjean Bakery. "So who's minding the store?" Millie asked.

Benno's eyes were red. His cheeks were tear-stained. He put an arm around Millie. "A terrible thing to have happened." Then he leaned closer. "You hire anyone yet?"

"*Et tu*, Benno?"

"I've had it with the bakery business. It's too crazy for me. I might as well head production at Fox."

Millie had had it too. He was tired of everyone's using Whitey's memorial as an excuse to make a pitch for the job. Not that he'd lose any sleep over the loss of a one-trick pony like Whitey. But still. "So, Benno, I hear the police are looking for you."

"What?"

"It's probably just the old 'round up the usual suspects' business. I'm sure you have an airtight alibi for where you were when Whitey was killed." That ought to shut him up for a while, Millie thought, scanning the crowd for Isidore. He was only half listening as Benno spoke.

"Oh, I know where I was, all right. I was with Jeanette. Screaming at her for putting the cherries upside down on top of a *Saint-Honoré*. As though I had to bother. In walks this guy, and without even looking, he buys out all my cakes. *Voilà!*"

**CONFIDENTIAL**


Private Line Fax


TO: Bobby Silverstein
FROM: Roy Drake


I've got it! The last chef to be killed! It's going to be a woman!

ROY WAS ALMOST an hour late for his meeting with Bobby. As he rushed down the corridor, Mae Sung looked up from reading *The Good Earth*. Without a word, she offered him the dish of fortune cookies. " 'A wise rider selects a speedy horse.' "

Roy brushed it aside. "A wise canary knows when to shut up." He nodded toward Bobby's office.

"He's talking to Paramount. He's been frantic. I haven't seen him this worried since the day they gave away his table at Morton's."

Roy opened the door to find Bobby on the speakerphone, playing darts, a lemon-colored cashmere sweater tied around his neck. The couch was filled with open boxes of tennis shorts from Tommy Hilfiger. Each of the television sets in the bookcase had a different video game on screen.

Seeing Roy, Bobby clutched his heart and rolled his eyes. He offered him one of the remote controls while continuing his conversation. "No, I don't want Bisset again. I want someone more nineties, like Melanie, Michelle, or Demi, and what does Penny know anyway?"

Roy stood in front of Bobby's desk, which was littered with dozens of packages of sweat socks rather than scripts. "Get off the phone," he said.

Bobby looked up in surprise. Without taking his eyes from Roy, he shouted into the speakerphone, "Gotta go, bubbala. I'm late for my facial."

"You hear the one about the Polish starlet?" the voice on the other end asked. "She slept with the writer."

Bobby laughed, switched off the phone, and became serious as he motioned for Roy to sit down on the couch. "It's time this business got back on track. All this crap about film being a director's medium. Tell that to Selznick, Goldwyn, or Thalberg. You heard it here: Film is a producer's medium! The producer is the *auteur!* So. You got more pages?"

Roy didn't move. He motioned toward the couch. "Get rid of this garbage so I can sit down."

"Sure." Bobby hurried over, picked up the boxes, and threw them in the corner of the room. "Say, babe. How about something to drink? I got some brand new water. From Utah, yet."

"I want a Chivas. Neat."

"Coming up." Bobby turned on the intercom. "Get me a case of Chivas and a glass."

"A case?" Roy asked.

"Whatever you don't drink, you'll take home. So. You got more pages?"

"No, I don't got more pages."

Bobby sat down next to Roy. "Boychik, all you got to do is kill off the lady chef. One more measly little murder. You can do it." He reached for one of the boxes on the floor. "What size shorts do you take?"

Roy slid off the couch and began pacing. Things were heating up too fast. First he had the police breathing down his neck, and now Bobby was breathing down his shorts. "Who was on the phone?"

"Paramount."

"And you're talking casting with them?"

"Why not?"

"Because you told me they came in with the lowest offer!" Roy shouted.

"Only for the screenplay."

"What the hell else am I selling them?"

"Hey, babe. You gotta learn something. In this business, it doesn't pay to be greedy. You have to give a little. Everything isn't me, me, me. Film is a collaborative art."

"Apparently so is deal-making."

Bobby walked over to his desk and sat behind it. "You got enough socks?"

"I want to know what's going on."

"Sounds like writer's paranoia to me."

"I want to know why you're ready to take the lowest bid. How is that in my best interest? Do you have any idea what I've had to do to write this screenplay?" Roy covered his eyes for a moment. No, not even the police really knew. No matter how many times they had dragged him down for questioning. "I don't want my deal screwed up because the agency is packaging it."

"Where does it say that? Did Chuck Heston leave that one up on the mountain? Forget about the agency. They're not packaging it. I am. Yours truly is the bow on this little package. You and these beautiful dead chefs are my ticket out of the agency and onto the lot. So stop worrying and get back to writing. The whole world isn't screwing you. If anybody's screwing you, I am."

"You want me to make a deal with Paramount because they're going to let you produce."

"Hey! You're getting smart. You could be a waiter at Le Dôme."

"But you're supposed to be working for me! You're supposed to be looking out for *my* best interests!"

"Tell me, genius, how better can I look out for your interests than to be there all the time?"

"But producers hate writers!"

"Not as much as agents do! You people think we should bottle your every fart and get Elizabeth Taylor to endorse it."

"Does that include *Chefs*?"

"No. *Chefs* is a good idea."

"Bobby, you just don't know what I've gone through on this one. You don't know what it's cost me."

"And the reason it's a good idea is because it was my idea!"

Roy smiled bitterly. "You bet your ass it was your idea." He pointed his finger at Bobby. "You remember that. You tell that to the jury. You hear me?" Roy shouted. "You tell them it was all your idea!"

"What does the Writers Guild do? They make you take an oath to be ungrateful? You haven't even finished the script and already you're suing me?"

Roy held on to the wall for support. "Bobby, I'm in trouble." The evidence was mounting. Not that they had enough proof to charge him formally, but he was the last known person to have seen Parker. His review of Neal's pizza had been interpreted as a confession, and somehow the police had found out that the article on Whitey had been canceled the day before. Roy hadn't covered his tracks. But what the hell did he know about being a killer?

"Sit down," Bobby said. "We'll work it out. I told you. I'm on your side." He picked up a package from his desk. "Kiddo, are you sure? Nobody ever has enough socks."

Roy sat down. He knew he had to be careful. Bobby would turn him in faster than a Stroganov curdles.

"All right. So tell me how the lady chef gets killed."

"I don't know," Roy said, unable to stop his voice from trembling. "I haven't figured that one out yet."

# DRAKE / SCREENPLAY /
# SOMEONE IS KILLING THE GREAT CHEFS OF AMERICA

FIRST DRAFT / SCENES 101 - 109

101. INT. OLYMPIC STADIUM -- PARIS -- TEST KITCHEN -- DAY

CAMERA FOLLOWS Lucinda through the smoke and steam as
she runs tearfully past dozens of chefs toward Robby. She
wears an apron over her Givenchy gown.

                    LUCINDA
     Oh, Robby. You came. I was hoping against hope.

                    ROBBY
     What a fool I've been. Lucinda, you're the only
     thing in my life that makes eating worthwhile.

                    LUCINDA
     But darling, what about your lunch? The twelve-
     course tasting at Tour d'Argent?

                    ROBBY
     My place is here. Now that we've finally found one
     another, not even the most famous restaurant
     in Paris can keep me away from you.

                    LUCINDA
     I've no right to ask that of you. Your work is
     too important, my darling. All of America is wait-
     ing for your review.

155

ROBBY
(smiles)
Frankly, Lucinda, I don't give a damn!

102. INT. OLYMPIC STADIUM -- PARIS -- AWARD AREA

MUSIC UP as the PRESIDENT OF FRANCE kisses Lucinda on each cheek. He reaches for the GOLDEN TRUFFLE AWARD.

103. CLOSE SHOT -- GOLDEN TRUFFLE AWARD

We HEAR a ticking.

104. INT. OLYMPIC STADIUM -- PARIS -- AUDIENCE

Robby, eating a croque-monsieur as he watches, signals "thumbs up" to Lucinda.

105. CLOSE SHOT -- GOLDEN TRUFFLE AWARD

President's hand touches the award. More ticking.

106. CLOSE SHOT -- LUCINDA'S TEARFUL FACE

She is overwhelmed as president hands her the award.

107. INT. OLYMPIC STADIUM -- PARIS -- AWARD AREA

As ticking grows louder, Lucinda clutches the GOLDEN TRUF-FLE to her breast. She smiles at Robby.

108. INT. OLYMPIC STADIUM -- PARIS -- AUDIENCE

The killer's gloved hand holds a detonator. We see his fingers tighten and HEAR an explosion.

109. INT. OLYMPIC STADIUM -- PARIS -- AWARD AREA

SLOW MOTION as we see part of Lucinda's dress floating in the air.

"MISS O'BRIEN'S ROOM, please."

"*Merci, monsieur,*" the switchboard operator said.

Millie paced back and forth in his suite, staring out the window that overlooked the lake. Although he would have preferred the Hilton, he had switched reservations to the Beau Rivage. It had been Achille's favorite hotel in Geneva, and somehow that seemed fitting. If not fitting, at least appropriately vindictive.

"I am sorry, *monsieur*. Would you like to leave a message?"

Millie slammed down the phone. He had already left four messages and was beginning to think he should have gone straight to Paris instead of stopping in Geneva. But he was sure that Enstein, after years of treating Achille, would know what the copycat killer might do next. Presuming that he hadn't done it already. Damn! Where the hell was Natasha?

"*Bonjour.* Clinique Enstein," the operator answered.

"Dr. Enstein, please." There was a long pause. "Hello? Dr. Enstein?"

"One moment, *monsieur*."

Millie turned on his laptop computer and logged on to Infotel for the Geneva-Paris airline schedules. "Hello?" he shouted.

"Clinique Enstein," another voice said. "May I help you?"

"I want to talk to Dr. Enstein!"

"May I ask what it is in reference to?"

"Just tell him it's Maximilian Ogden. I'm sure he knows who I am."

"*Monsieur*, I must ask what this is about."

Millie growled as he said, "It is about Achille van Golk."

A pause. Then, "One moment, *monsieur*."

He should have gone to Paris, picked up Natasha, and brought her with him to Geneva. No one ever got killed in Geneva. People died of boredom, but no one ever got killed.

"*Guten Morgen*, this is Herr Doktor Konig."

"I didn't ask for Dr. Konig. I asked for Dr. Enstein."

"So I understand. But in life we do not always get what we ask for, *ja?*"

Millie took a deep breath. "May I please speak to Dr. Enstein?"

"You wish to speak with him about Herr van Golk?"

"Yes."

"That is too bad. I am afraid Herr van Golk is dead."

"I know he's dead! I still want to talk to Dr. Enstein."

"I am afraid Dr. Enstein is also dead."

Millie sat down. "What did you do? Get a discount at the cemetery?"

"Herr Doktor was killed."

"I'm sorry." Millie glanced at his laptop for the next plane to Paris. "What happened?"

"His head was bashed in."

"By whom?"

"We don't know."

"What do you mean you don't know?"

"Enstein collected strays and misfits the way a dachshund collects fleas. He had a crackpot theory that he could change behavior patterns. I told him it was impossible. But he wouldn't listen. It was his own fault. It wasn't my fault that he died, *ja?* I told him that even a *dummkopf* like Freud knew that people were driven to do the same things over and over again."

"Dr. Konig, there must be a clue of some kind."

"I tried my best. I warned him to be more careful."

"What about his files?"

"He kept no files. Everything was in his head."

"When did he die?"

"It is about two months now."

Then it couldn't have been Achille. But Millie was still convinced there was a link between the killings of the American chefs and those of the Europeans. And perhaps even Enstein. "Doctor, there must be a clue."

"I did everything I could," Konig repeated. "Was it my fault he wouldn't listen to me?"

"Doctor, think back to the day he died. Did anything unusual happen?"

"Nothing. I tell you what I told the *polizei*. Nothing happened. I saw no one. It was a very ordinary day. The most exciting thing that happened was that the town bakery sold out all its cakes."

Something flashed through Millie's mind. He closed his eyes, trying to recall where he had heard that before.

"Herr Ogden," Konig continued, "one more thing you must know."

"Yes?"

"To avoid any false conclusions, I was born in Zurich. I am not German."


AS MILLIE TURNED from the cashier's desk, he caught sight of a woman dressed in black. A large black hat covered most of her face. He stepped aside and watched as she crossed the lobby, almost certain that he knew her. He did.

It was Beauchamp.

Something was going on. He saw her get into a car and immediately waved over his driver.

"*L'aéroport, monsieur?*"

"No," Millie said, quickly getting into the limo. "I want you to follow that car. *Schnell!*"

The driver turned around and smiled. "*Pardon, monsieur*, but I was born in Lausanne."


BEAUCHAMP'S CAR wound its way through the outskirts of Geneva and stopped at a small cemetery. She got out carrying a Fortnum & Mason shopping bag in one hand and some gardening tools in the other. Millie was too far away to hear what she was saying, but her driver looked at his watch, nodded, and got back into the car.

Millie followed her path through a maze of old tombstones. And then he saw it, on the top of a hill, like the moon rising: a huge round slab of white marble shaped like a dinner plate. Emblazoned in gold was the name ACHILLE VAN GOLK, and the epitaph *Let us eat and drink; for tomorrow we shall die.*

Millie stepped back to recover from the sudden pounding in his chest. Although Achille had once treated him as the heir apparent to the *Lucullus* empire, Millie had sworn he would never forgive him, no matter how insane he had been, for trying to kill Natasha. Yet as he stood there, he felt nothing but sadness and regret. He had never made his peace with Achille. So much had been left unsaid. Not that he would dare admit it to anyone, but Millie missed Achille.

"It's too late now, Mr. Ogden." Beauchamp shouted over her shoulder as though reading his mind.

Millie walked slowly toward her. She was on her knees, digging up the soil in front of the headstone. "Still the keeper of the flame, Beauchamp?"

"You should have been at the funeral. You above all. It was a disgrace. No one came. Would you mind passing me the tarragon?" Beauchamp was planting an herb garden. Her bag was filled with shoots of dill, rosemary, coriander, thyme, and sage. "You had no right to abandon him."

"He tried to kill Natasha!"

"Mr. van Golk was . . . confused," she said, taking the tarragon from him. "You should have been there when he needed his friends."

"He needed his friends *dead*."

Beauchamp began to sob uncontrollably. "I still can't believe he's really gone. I don't know what to do, Mr. Ogden. I sometimes think I don't want to live if I can never see him again."

Millie reached toward her but then stopped. "Pull yourself together, Beauchamp. It's been three years since he died."

She opened her mouth as if to scream. Instead, she whispered, "He's not dead!"

"Oh, Beauchamp." Millie knelt down and put his arms around her. "You really did love him, didn't you?"

"Mrs. Gordon, are you all right?" It was Beauchamp's driver. She nodded yes. "Thank you, André."

"Mrs. who?" Millie was astonished.

"We'll be going back now, André," she said, quickly smoothing over the earth.

160

"Mrs. Gordon?" Millie asked. "Mrs. *Alec* Gordon?"

Beauchamp brushed off her skirt and took the driver's arm as he led her back to the car. "He was particularly fond of coriander," she said softly.


"NAT?"

"Oh, Millie, I'm so glad to hear your voice."

"Where the hell have you been?"

"I had an interview on *Bonjour Paris* and then I absolutely had to buy some clothes."

"At a time like this?"

"I'll explain it later. Where are you?"

"Never mind where I am. Where is Alec?"

"I sent him to cover the lighting of the torch. Millie, there's something I have to tell you. It's incredible, but —"

"Nat, I'm at the airport in Geneva. I'll be in Paris in an hour. Get the hell away from Alec. Don't let him know where you are. Meet me at Chez Auguste."

"But Millie —"

"I know who the killer is!" they both said at the same time.

**\* Concours Olympique des Cuisiniers \***
**Culinary Olympics**
**\* Olympiade der Köche \* Olimpiade dei Cuoci \***

10TH INTERNATIONAL CULINARY OLYMPICS
ROOM 210, GRAND PALAIS
Secretaire du presse: Eve St. Laurent
Office (555-88999); Residence (555-98211);
Lover (555-44326)

PRESS RELEASE/English

<u>GREAT CHEFS FROM 21 NATIONS</u>
<u>STIR UP SPECIAL EVENTS</u>

Over 1,000 cooks will take part in the culinary world's
greatest international competition, being held this week at the
Grand Palais. Merely to stroll through the test kitchens and
exhibit areas is to inhale a living library of aromas that have
seduced diners through the ages.

Chefs will compete in a variety of settings open to the public: national restaurants, catering kitchens, health-food restaurants, an armed forces' mess, a hospital kitchen, and a
children's restaurant. In addition, there will be hot- and cold-
platter displays and galleries for sugar, ice, butter, marzipan,
and chocolate sculpture. The best in each category will be
awarded bronze, silver, and gold medals, with the highest
award given by the sponsors -- the Golden Truffle -- presented
in recognition of innovative gastronomy.

The special events to be featured this year are:

162

THE WELL-LAID TABLE, sponsored by the Lichtenstein Association of Waiters and Skilled Restaurant Staff. This three-dimensional multimedia display has been mounted as a thought-provoking preview of what a well-laid table will look like in the year 2000;

GERMAN ARMY MESS, cosponsored by the Pipeline Pioneer Battalion 850 from Zweibrucken and the Supply and Transport Squadron of Bomber Group 38 from Schortens, will prepare 750 portions of food whose preparation costs less than U.S.$3.25 each;

GLOBAL WARMING BUFFET, sponsored by the Baltic Sea Fishermen's Association in keeping with their motto of "cold fish with warm thoughts," will present its award-winning Denizens of the Deep buffet;

INTERNATIONAL LACHS COMPETITION, sponsored by Peer Gynt Carbon Steel Blades, will focus on uniform slicing of smoked salmon;

INTRODUCTION TO DUTCH WINES, a seminar hosted by "the nose" of the Netherlands, Utwe van Snopp;

GREAT MEALS IN HISTORY, a new edition of the award-winning restaurant that has enchanted attendees. This year's presentations will include the Last Dinner of the Romanovs, Summertime Buffet on Catfish Row, and Brunch with Henry VIII.

THE CHILL, GRAY, OVERCAST SKY had drained all the color out of Paris. Members of the Organizing Committee for the Culinary Olympics, dressed in morning coats, striped trousers, and top hats, gathered in front of an old house in Montparnasse. Alec, his raincoat pockets stuffed with Pâtisserie Ladurée's *pain au chocolat*, watched from a doorway across the street. He was relieved that Natasha had decided not to attend the ceremony. It gave him time to feed Achille and silence the voice screaming inside him.

A young chef, his starched toque square atop his head, hurried down the narrow cobblestone street. After solemnly kissing each member of the organizing committee on both cheeks, he led the way into the old house that served as headquarters for the Académie Nationale des Pommes Frites. Alec brushed the buttery flakes of pastry from his lips and walked to the entrance. He took out his press pass.

*"American Cuisine,"* he announced to the young man who was checking credentials at the door.

*"Monsieur!"* the man said impatiently.

Alec showed him the press pass.

The young man stared at it. *"Cuisine Americaine?"* He shrugged his shoulders. *"Impossible!"* he muttered under his breath. He forced a smile and looked up at Alec. *"Monsieur,"* he said, motioning to Alec's mouth. *"Chocolat?"*

Alec quickly took out his handkerchief and rubbed his lips.

The man sighed wearily and handed back the press pass. *"Entrez, monsieur."*

Following the last of the officials and press, Alec walked through the foyer, across the dining room, and into the kitchen. Two gendarmes stood at attention on either side of a stove that had once belonged to Escoffier. The president of the Académie, wearing a bright red sash across his chest, looked around the room to be certain everyone was ready. The TV crew focused its camera. Lights were switched on. After receiving a nod, the president struck a long wooden match and lit the fire in the stove. Photographers began taking pictures.

The young chef made his way through the crowd holding Escoffier's chafing dish. While everyone's eyes were on the chef, Alec reached into his coat pocket, tore off a piece of croissant, and stuffed it into his mouth.

"I prefer the ones from Pâtisserie Millet," Achille said.

Alec closed his eyes, thinking that he hadn't had time to go to the Left Bank and that the ones from Ladurée were excellent.

"How dare you argue with me!" Achille shouted.

Alec gasped as he felt a sharp, stabbing pain in his head.

The chef stood next to the stove. He lifted the lid from the alcohol burner in the chafing dish. As the crowd edged closer in anticipation and flashbulbs began to pop, the president ignited a wooden skewer from the flame on Escoffier's stove and lit the alcohol burner in the chafing dish. The room burst into applause. As Alec started to clap, he realized that his hands were sticky.

The young chef, holding the dish aloft, marched toward the door. Everyone filed out behind him. Once on the street, he quickened his pace to a trot amid cheers from the spectators. He was to carry the flame from Escoffier's stove through the streets of Paris to the Grand Palais for the opening of the Culinary Olympics.

Alec hurried down the street. But no matter how fast he walked, there was no escape. Turning the corner, Alec found a bench and sat down. He took the bags from his pockets, both of which were stained with butter and chocolate. His eyes filled with tears of anguish as he began to stuff his mouth with croissants to silence Achille's cries for "More, more, more!"

Finally, he burped.

Afraid to think any thoughts that Achille might overhear, he folded his raincoat inside out so that the stains wouldn't show and carried it over his arm. He got up and walked slowly toward a flower stall. He would take back some flowers for Natasha. But as he approached the stall, he suddenly felt himself go limp. Like a marionette. His head began to bob. His arms swung loosely. The raincoat dropped onto the street. His feet searched for firm ground as he was pulled back from the stall. One foot in front of the other, as though on a tightrope, he was propelled into a small bistro next door.

*"Bonjour, monsieur,"* the waitress said quizzically as he fell back onto a chair. *"Voudrez-vous la carte?"* She handed him the menu.

Alec whispered, "No."

"What do you mean, 'No'?" Achille screamed.

*"Non?"* the waitress asked.

Taking a deep breath and gathering all his strength, Alec was determined to push himself away from the table. Straining against the pressure in his chest, he spoke to Achille for the first time. "This body is mine!"

*"Monsieur, ça va?"* The waitress stepped back.

Alec held on to the table with both hands, put his feet flat on the floor, and very slowly lifted himself up. Breathless, he paused for a moment and smiled victoriously. Before he had a chance to catch his breath, Achille pulled him back into the chair. Again, he held on to the table and struggled to stand on his feet. "It's not your body. It's mine. It belongs to me!"

His eyes glazed over from the blinding flashes of light. His ears nearly burst from the roaring in his head. He gasped for air as his throat tightened. He was being strangled from within.

*"Mon Dieu!"* The waitress ran to the back. "Pierre! Pierre!"

Alec's face was contorted in pain, the most intense he had ever felt. Unable to open his eyes, he grabbed the edge of the table and pushed against the wind-tunnel force of Achille. "I created this body. It's mine!"

Inch by inch, Alec made it to his feet again. He lifted one leg and then the other as he walked in slow motion toward the door. As his hand touched the knob, every organ seemed to erupt with pain. The hot lava of Achille's anger scorched his body as he fumbled with the handle. He couldn't turn it. His fingers kept slipping. He couldn't get out of the restaurant.

Alec stepped back and pulled his jacket over his face. He pushed his shoulder against the glass door and, as it shattered, stepped through. The moment his feet touched the pavement, the pain stopped. He opened his eyes and began to run.

Standing in the middle of the street, he waved his arms frantically at a taxi and lunged for the door even before the driver stopped. He fell against the seat cushion, quickly slammed the door shut, and then locked it. He rolled up the windows. *"Fermez la porte!"* he shouted to the driver, pointing to the front door.

The driver didn't budge. *"Où allez-vous, monsieur?"*

Alec opened his mouth, but no sound came out. He couldn't speak.

*"Monsieur? S'il vous plaît?"*

Achille's voice escaped from Alec's mind and captured his vocal cords. Loud and clear, Achille van Golk told the driver, "Tour d'Argent! And step on it!"

# MAXFAX

FROM: Holmes

TO: Watson

Hold the presses! Hold the phone! Hold on to your jock-strap! Alec Gordon gets the Xerox of the year award!

Hiram, baby, add this up on your trusty abacus:

1) Alec worked for Achille

2) Alec left Fergieville without passing Go or collecting $200 and made a beeline for Natasha (don't get me wrong: not that he'd have a hope in hell with my one and only)

and (DRUM ROLL!)

3) Alec married Achille's secretary!!!!

The only thing the son of a bitch didn't do was gain three hundred pounds, and I wouldn't put that past him.

Looks like the copycat is out of the bag!

"*SOIXANTE,*" Natasha announced as she turned out her sixtieth crepe. Sensing that she was being watched, Natasha looked up for the first time since she had begun. The chefs behind the line at Chez Auguste met her eyes, then glanced at one another as she turned out number sixty-one. "Not to worry, *mes amis*, they freeze very well."

Auguste was nearly eighty and wore large steel-framed glasses that made his eyes appear twice their actual size. He shook his finger at the piles of crepes in front of her. "But I do not have a freezer!"

He was one of the last of a dying breed who put in eighteen-hour days and was periodically arrested for beating up a member of his staff. Luckily, the local police chief was addicted to his *terrine de lapin* and wasn't about to see his favorite restaurant close because of a labor dispute. The most recent aggravated-assault charges against Auguste, for stabbing a waiter in the leg, had been reduced to self-defense after he explained that the son of a bitch had let an order of *poularde aux morilles* get cold.

Natasha was on her next crepe. "*Mon cher*, you can fill these with poached fruit or a mousse, even an Italian meringue. Or you can tie the tops and make pouches stuffed with champagne grapes and *crème Chantilly*. Oh, my darling Auguste, limited only by your imagination, you can go light-years beyond mere *Crêpes Suzette*." Then she muttered, "Who the hell was Suzette, anyway?"

"*Un moule!*" a waiter shouted as the lunch rush began. "*Un coquille, trois escargots!*"

"Natasha, *mon amour*," Auguste pleaded, "perhaps you would like to peel some potatoes or onions. . . ."

"If I'd wanted to smell of onions and garlic, I wouldn't have become a pastry chef. Oh, I have such a wonderful life, Auguste. There are days I fairly reek of vanilla beans or strawberries."

"Hi, stinky."

Natasha melted into Millie's arms. "Thank God you're here."

He turned her around and kissed her. "Thank God you're safe."

Another waiter. *"Un terrine, un pâté!"*

"I've been counting the crepes until you arrived," she whispered breathlessly as she brought her lips to his.

*"Un saumon, un homard roti!"*

Natasha drew back from Millie just far enough for her lips to form words. "We have to talk." He leaned forward slightly and their mouths touched. "We have to kiss," she said, pressing tight against him.

"You're right. First we have to kiss," Millie said, coming up for air. "Then we have to talk."

"I know," she said, kissing him. "There's so much I have to tell you."

"Me too." He kissed her again.

*"Huitres, huitres, jambon, timbale, terrine!"* a waiter shouted, limping away.

"It's a matter of life and death, Nat."

Auguste gently pushed them out of the way as the cooks became busy. *"Oui!* My life or death! The chief of police is out there!"

Millie turned to Auguste. "We've got to speak to him."

*"Non! Impossible!* Not while he eats my terrine!"

"But I know who's been killing the chefs!"

Auguste narrowed his eyes. "Max, you eat too many warm dogs. We all know who killed the chefs. And thank God Achille is dead."

"No," Natasha clarified. "Someone is killing American chefs!"

Auguste raised his hands to the heavens. "And for that you wish to interrupt the man's meal?"

"Natasha is in danger," Millie said.

*"Jambon, pâté, pâté, artichaut!"*

Auguste put a hand on Natasha's shoulder. He spoke softly. "Natasha was in danger when the European chefs were killed. And now she is in danger when the American chefs are being killed?"

"Darling, I was part of Achille's favorite dinner. It didn't matter whether I was European or American."

"And why is someone killing American chefs?" Auguste asked. "Other than for sport."

Millie pleaded with Auguste. "I have to speak to the police. I know who the killer is, and I've got to protect Natasha."

Natasha burst into tears and threw her arms around Millie. "It's no use. You can't protect me from myself. It's happening all over again. Here we are back in Paris. In the same oppressive, hot, filthy little kitchen where we worked."

Auguste's eyes widened in shock. "Hot?"

The limping waiter laughed as he picked up his oysters.

"My whole life is back just the way it was five years ago. Nothing has changed."

Millie opened his arms broadly. "Was Freud a genius or what? I'll bet he could do a whole chapter on your friend Alec."

Natasha was terrified. What did Millie know? More to the point, had Millie somehow found out that she had slept with Alec?

"I knew you shouldn't have hired him," Millie said.

"Why not?"

"You mean, just because he's a killer?"

Natasha breathed a sigh of relief. Millie didn't know. "Alec may be a lot of things," she said, thinking of all the things Alec was, "but he's not the killer. It's Roy."

"Oh, yeah? Davis said he was looking for a copycat."

"Just because Alec worked for Achille doesn't make him —"

"Babe, wake up and smell the *café au lait!* Friend Alec is married to Beauchamp. What the hell does that make him?"

Natasha's head began to swim. The real question was, What the hell did that make her?


AUGUSTE GAVE THEM a table from which they could watch the police chief as he ate lunch, on the condition that they didn't approach him until after *le fromage*. Natasha sat staring at the menu. She couldn't look Millie in the eye.

Suddenly all the players had changed roles. No one was who he or she appeared to be. Least of all Natasha O'Brien. But come hell or high water, she had to put things back in perspective. She had to tell him the truth. "Millie, there's something you don't know."

He took her hand. "Don't tell me. You married Beauchamp too?"

"What's the big deal about Alec's marrying Beauchamp? What possible difference could it make to me? It doesn't matter. Why should it? I hired Alec because he was the best person for the job. Period. My only concern is getting the magazine off the ground. And if I had to, I'd hire Achille himself!"

"That's what you had to tell me?"

"There's more. Roy is working on a sequel to *Someone Is Killing the Great Chefs of Europe.* All of the victims in his screenplay die the way Parker, Neal, and Whitey did."

"So?"

"So?" She was beginning to hyperventilate. "Roy is more of a copycat than Alec."

"The hell he is! He didn't marry Beauchamp!"

"There you go again. Beauchamp, Beauchamp, Beauchamp! As though that had any relevance to my life. I told you, I don't care. What I care about, Millie, darling, is that the next chef to die in Roy's screenplay is me!" She sat back triumphantly. "I rest my case."

The limping waiter stood ready to take their orders as they looked at the menu.

"I'm not hungry," Natasha sighed, putting the menu down. "Bring me a dozen oysters."

The waiter looked around to see if he was being watched. Then he shook his head no.

"Really?" Natasha picked up her menu. "Well, thank you. Then the pâté?"

The waiter shrugged and motioned *"mezzo-mezzo"* with his hand.

"What about the terrine?" Millie asked, nodding toward the police chief's table.

The waiter stuck out his tongue.

Natasha took both menus and gave them back to him. "You choose." Once the waiter left, she leaned forward. "You ever see me do that before? There's your evidence. My priorities have changed totally. All I care about is the success of *American Cuisine.* And anyway, how do you know for certain that he's married to Beauchamp? Maybe it's just an old maid's fantasy. I mean, you can't deny that Alec's an attractive man."

"I can't or you can't?" He took her hand. "You always were a lousy poker player."

172

She slumped back in her chair. "That list gets longer daily. All the things I'm lousy at."

"Well, let's face it. You sure as hell screwed up our divorce."

Natasha smiled. "I was up against impossible odds."

"Such as?"

"The statistics. Do you have any idea how many divorces end in marriage?"

"Next."

"Bastard. You're really going to make me crawl, aren't you?"

"On your belly." He tightened his grip on her hand. "What happened, Nat? Alec made a pass at you? Then you find out he's married?"

"Something like that." If she couldn't convince herself, how could she convince Millie? "Stay with me. I'm at the Plaza."

"I had my bag sent to your room."

Natasha sat back in her chair. "Damn. Am I that easy?"

"Not for everyone."

"Then why do I feel like such a sitting duck?"

"Nothing's going to happen to you," he said, squeezing her hand. "Not as long as I'm around."

Natasha shook her head. "Alec said he'd call Davis after we arrived in Paris and I was safely away from Roy. But you know me. I called Davis just to be sure. Apparently, so had Alec."

"That doesn't make sense."

"Of course it does. It proves that Alec isn't the killer. Otherwise why would he have called Davis? Not that the call did any good. No matter what Roy wrote in his screenplay, Davis said nothing could be done until he actually made an attempt on my life."

"What makes you so sure Roy was writing about you?"

"Beautiful, witty, wildly successful pastry chef? Not that he even began to do me justice."

"How did Roy . . . in his screenplay . . . how did he . . ."

"Kill me? He didn't get that far." She shrugged. "Not yet, any-way."

Millie glanced over at the chief of police. "I don't suppose the gendarmes are going to be too sympathetic either. Nat, I want you to go home."

"And walk straight into Roy's arms? No thank you. Roy tore up his contract for the article he was going to do on the Olympics. I'm safe in Paris. For the moment, we have nothing to worry about." She looked at her watch. "Except that I've already missed the opening ceremony, I'm supposed to meet Professor Wladiszceucz, and I have a judging at three o'clock." She forced a smile. "Besides, Roy doesn't kill the world's most gorgeous dessert chef here." She looked away quickly, afraid her eyes might betray her. "Now, where the hell is that waiter?"

As she looked around the room, the waiter walked in through the front door, making certain that everyone in the restaurant saw him. He proceeded solemnly to their table and, in front of each of them, dropped a bag from McDonald's.


ROY GOT OFF the plane in Paris after nearly eleven hours of unrelenting turbulence. He had spent the entire flight from L.A. in white-knuckled terror. It had been years since he'd flown in coach, and the thought that he might have to do it again filled him with dread. But he had come to Paris on his own agenda. There was no one else to foot the bill.

Before leaving, Roy had resigned from the paper. His screenplay had become too demanding a mistress — his Mrs. Simpson. And he, like Edward VIII, the Duke of Windsor, had abdicated his kingdom and his power. No limo to the airport. No first-class ticket. No stewardesses hovering over him. No messages for Mr. Drake to report to the Courtesy Desk. He was a commoner.

But not for long. Roy was determined that his life would change as soon as he had accomplished what he had come to Paris to do. If he did it right, as seamlessly as he had done the others, he would soon become part of another royal family.


INT. NIGHT. DOROTHY CHANDLER PAVILION. THE OSCARS.
Meryl Streep opens the envelope nervously and takes
out the card.


MERYL
(bursts into tears)
And the winner is ... Roy Drake!

174

In the meantime, there was no driver holding up a card with his name on it as he cleared Customs. Roy headed for a phone booth and dialed the number he had committed to memory.

"*Oui?*" the man's voice answered.

"*Etienne? C'est Roy.*"

"*Moment, s'il vous plaît.*" Then, "I wanted to turn on the scrambler. Where are you?"

"At the airport. I just arrived."

"*Bon.* I am working at the Grand Palais as an electrician. Go to the service entrance and ask for me. They are expecting you."

"Who do I say I am?"

"Louis Quatorze."

"Oh, for God's sake! Couldn't you come up with a better name?"

"You didn't pay for a better name."

"What about the — "

"I have everything. Except the money."

Roy hesitated for a moment. "You said it would be quick."

"*Monsieur*, she will never know."

Roy hung up the phone and hurried out of the terminal. He got into a taxi and told the driver, "Hotel Plaza-Athenée!"


"HOTEL PLAZA-ATHENÉE," Alec said breathlessly as he sat back in the taxi. The moment the driver pulled away from Tour d'Argent, Alec loosened his belt and opened his collar, grateful that the pounding in his head had stopped. Achille had been fed. Alec put a hand to his stomach. It was bloated and aching as it pushed against his shirt, pulling at each button to create horizontal fault lines in the broadcloth.

Again, his first thought was to call Enstein. But the old man would most likely insist that he return to the clinic for further treatment. No, he would fight Achille on his own. And somehow he would lose the weight he had gained. As they neared the hotel, Alec grimaced in pain as he battled his own flesh to fasten the collar button on his shirt.

Exhausted by the day's confrontations with Achille, he picked up his keys at the front desk, eager to go upstairs and rest. But then he saw Roy at the registration desk. Roy wasn't supposed to be in Paris. Why had he come? Alec's heart began to pound. He knew precisely why Roy had come. The question was how to prevent him from killing Natasha.

"Mr. Drake," Alec said brightly. "What a pleasant surprise."

Roy turned quickly, at first not recognizing him. "Oh, yes. Alec, isn't it?"

"Natasha will be so pleased to learn you're here. Is there anything I can help you with?"

Roy nodded. "Yes. I'm planning a murder," he said, nodding toward the front desk. "My room isn't ready yet."

"Well, that's a stroke of luck for me. I'm such an admirer of yours. May I buy you a drink while you're waiting?"


THEY SAT AT A CORNER TABLE in the downstairs bar. The waiter brought over small plates of green olives with stems and freshly made potato chips. *"Messieurs?"*

"I'll have a Negroni," Roy said.

Alec ordered a Fernet Branca.

Roy smiled. "I prefer Underberg for hangovers."

"I don't have a hangover. I need a digestive, and they don't stock Stonsdorfer."

Roy nodded approvingly. "You're certainly up on your bitters. But I suppose you'd have to be, working for Natasha. By the way, where is — "

"I don't know. Have a chip." Alec watched as Roy took the plate from him, lifted one chip, and cocked his ear as he broke it in half. Then he looked at his fingertips and rubbed them together to test for grease.

"The chips are better at the Crillon," Roy said.

"I thought you preferred the Bristol."

"You seem to be up on everything."

Alec smiled. "I try."

"Hard to believe you don't know where she — "

"Have an olive?"

They stared silently at one another as the waiter put down the drinks. Nodding, they raised their glasses and each took a sip.

Roy sat back. "I still say they make the best Negroni at the Mammounia."

"Better than Harry's Bar in Florence?"

176

"I'm glad you didn't say Venice. What a trap."

"What a trap," Alec repeated, suddenly wondering who was the spider and who was the fly.

"So you say you're an admirer."

"For years."

"Well, I've always maintained that a critic's responsibility is to keep his readers reading. No matter how many chefs are sacrificed in the line of battle, the critic must keep his readers amused. Otherwise he's out of business."

"Mr. van Golk claimed that no one could savage a chef like you did."

"You worked with van Golk?"

Damn. Now Roy would start hurling all the usual accusations. How could Alec not have known about the monstrous things Achille was doing? What clues did he have to Achille's madness? "I worked in London for a number of years. But I . . ."

Roy's face was beaming. "Well, no wonder Natasha hired you. You were privileged to work with the master. Whatever drove van Golk to do what he did, the man was an absolute genius . . ."

Alec felt a twinge in his stomach.

". . . a blaze of brilliance shining above a sea of mediocrity."

Next, a nervous thumping in his chest.

"Why didn't Natasha tell me? She knew van Golk was my idol. How adroit he was in the use of power. There wasn't anyone he couldn't break. God, I admired him for that, for never hesitating to bite the hand that fed him."

Alec's mouth became dry. The twinge in his stomach gathered force and became more intense as it pushed against his skin. He downed the Fernet Branca in a single swallow.

"I tell you," Roy continued, "to my dying day I'll regret never having had the honor of meeting the great Achille van Golk."

Uncontrollably, Alec's hand swept across the table and took hold of Roy's hand. Roy looked up in surprise. Alec couldn't let go. His fingers were locked in place. His arm refused to be pulled away. And then suddenly both men watched in astonishment as, one by one, the buttons on Alec's shirt began to pop open and *plink plink plink* their way onto the table.

10TH INTERNATIONAL CULINARY OLYMPICS
ROOM 210, GRAND PALAIS
Secretaire du presse: Eve St. Laurent
Office (555-88999); Residence (555-98211);
Lover (555-44326)


PRESS RELEASE/English


WORLD'S GREATEST GOURMET
REGAINS HIS MEMORY AND RETURNS
TO THE WORLD OF FOOD


"Something inexplicable drew me here," said Achille van Golk, renowned publisher of <u>Lucullus</u> magazine, who had been reported dead for the past three years. To the astonishment of the entire gastronomic community, van Golk turned up early this morning on the steps of the Grand Palais, banging on the door ^ %$$YOU'LL NEVER GET AWAY WITH THIS = %@

Looking drawn and undernourished, van Golk could not remember where he had been. "The last thing I recall is tasting an almond tuile that had been sent to me by the King of Spain -- you know, that is his favorite cookie -- although I do vaguely remember someone screaming, 'Fire!' I must have run from the clinic and afterward they found some poor soul and thought he was me." According to van Golk, he cannot remember his identity during this blackout period &^%YOU BAS-TARD+)(

"As Shakespeare said, 'What's past is prologue.' One must focus on the future. So many meals, so little time. It is only fitting in this year of the Olympiad that I should return to my former self."

*&^BUT WHAT ABOUT ME#@%

THE GRAND PALAIS, a fantasy of steel, stone, and glass, had been built for the 1900 World Exhibition. The space beneath its majestic glass-and-iron canopy had been transformed into an aromatic arena in which culinary gladiators and international foodies had gathered for a gargantuan banquet.

Each day six different "national" restaurants competed in the center space. Judges and visitors peered in through open kitchens to watch each team prepare the dishes on its menu. Along one wall were the cold-platter displays, along another the hot platters. Table after table was filled with candies, cakes, and pastries. Special platforms held ice carvings, butter sculptures, and exhibits of "marzipan art." Cafés, beer halls, *Kaffeehauses*, bars, and tearooms offered a place to rest before heading to lectures and demonstrations. Hundreds of booths displayed everything from cooking utensils to restaurant accounting systems.

Natasha stood at the entrance, her arm entwined in Millie's as professional excitement overwhelmed personal anxiety. The Culinary Olympics was the Oscar, the Pulitzer, and the Nobel Prize all wrapped into that most fragile of pastries — passion. It was a setting closer to academe than to commerce, a place in which *sauciers* argued with the intensity of first-year philosophy students. Teams of young cooks, institutional chefs, and world-famous instructors bonded in the search for perfection. It was the research laboratory, the university press, the art-house cinema, the senior prom of food. There was no room for the cynicism of superstar chefs whose names were inseparable from their restaurants. Everything at the Olympics, especially the awards, was taken seriously.

Just as Natasha had taken it all seriously years ago, when she was on the U.S. team. She glanced at Millie, wanting to share her feelings. But she was embarrassed by her pride at being a judge. It was as though she had returned to her alma mater to give the commencement address.

Or to be killed.

An old man with unruly white hair and a wild look in his eyes grabbed hold of Natasha. Instinctively, Millie wedged himself between them. The old man pushed him aside.

"Where have you been? I was looking everywhere for you." Professor Wladisczeucz of the Lodz Culinary Institute kissed her on each cheek. "You must take over the cold-platter competition for me."

"But Professor," Natasha asked, "what happened?"

"Ask the French what happened!" he said, nodding angrily to the man standing next to him.

The mayor of Dijon, who had married into a mustard fortune, exclaimed, "We have a right to defend our borders! *N'est-ce pas?*" He kissed Natasha on both cheeks. "The Polish team tried to smuggle in suitcases of live chickens!"

Professor Wladisczeucz looked to Natasha for help. "Airport Customs has threatened to kill all my chickens."

"*Naturellement!* What would you have us do?" the mayor asked. "Put them in jail?"

"Not without a trial first!" Wladisczeucz shouted.

Natasha glanced at Millie. "I'd like you to meet Mr. Ogden. Professor Wladisczeucz. Mayor Caron." While they all shook hands, Natasha tried to think of a solution. "Professor, let me call Maxim's. I'm sure they'll let you borrow a few — "

The Professor shook his finger in the mayor's face. "French chickens? Not in my *zupa!* Like French models, they are skin and bones. I must protect the solidarity of my team. We will march on the airport and save the chickens!" He turned and hurried away.

The mayor shrugged. "For all the good it will do. We have a *consommé de vollaile* that could win the Croix de Guerre."

Natasha whispered to Millie, "Why don't I meet you later?" But he wouldn't let go of her arm.

"Come with me," the mayor said, taking her other arm. "The committee is meeting at the Cuban café."

Millie shook his head no. Natasha pulled away sharply. "Your Honor, I'll meet you there." She glared at Millie. "I have to straighten something out first." The mayor nodded and quickly disappeared into the crowd.

"Now listen — " Natasha began.

"No, you listen. You're not going anywhere without me."

"Hold it, bub. Don't think you can boss me around like in the old days. These are the new days. Just because we're together again in Paris and we're in love again and someone is trying to kill me again, don't for a minute think — "

"Of saving your life?"

Natasha groaned. "Millie, I'm surrounded by a crowd. What could possibly happen?" She put her finger on his nose and smiled. "He's a one-on-one killer. Just like you."

Millie paused. "Do you mean what you said?"

"Every word."

"That part about being in love again?"

She kissed him on the cheek. "Let's talk about it tonight."

"You asking me for a date?"

"My treat. The sky's the limit."

"Onion soup at Au Pied du Cochon?"

Natasha smiled as she began walking backward, away from him. "You remembered."

Millie watched as she turned and headed down the aisle. Without taking his eyes from her, he raised his hand and pointed toward Natasha. A burly man in a raincoat who had been pretending to read the program followed her.

ALL THE WAITERS at the Café Castro wore beards, camouflage fatigues, and army boots. Seated under camouflage-cloth umbrellas were members of the organizing committee. A bearded waiter passed a grease-stained purple mimeographed sheet, the only copy of the menu, from person to person. There were six items listed: State Bebida No. 1, State Bebida No. 2, State Bebida No. 3, State Comida No. 1, State Comida No. 2, and State Comida No. 3.

Vera Rama Singh, credited with originating nouvelle Kashmiri cuisine, smiled and tilted her face as if to prevent the red dot on her forehead from slipping. "Can you tell me, please, what is State Bebida Number One?"

"Favorite of Hemingway," the waiter answered.

"And Number Two?"

"No more left."

"And Number Three?"

"Sold out."

Herr Professor Dr. Klaus von Rieber, former *chef de cuisine* at Spandau Prison, whose memoir, *Cooking for One*, included many of Rudolph Hess's favorite dishes, pointed to the menu. "You will tell me, please, what is State Comida Number One?"

"Hemingway favorite," the waiter replied impatiently. "No more Two and no more Three!" He grabbed back the menu and handed it to Ingmar Oooaiie, director of the Royal Scandinavian Herring Council.

Ingmar leaned over and whispered to the mayor, "I told you we should have had a smorgasbord here instead."

"I hate herring!" the mayor snapped.

"*Ja*, but he eats filthy little snails!" Ingmar shuddered.

"Chinese eat snails first," said Uncle Ho, acknowledged as a Living National Treasure in the People's Republic for his root-vegetable carving.

"Well, I'm dying of thirst," Vera said, opening her purse. "This round is on me. Five State Bebidas, if you don't mind."

The waiter snatched the menu and left.

Ingmar nodded at Vera. "Thank you. But I thought you had problems getting money from the Indian government."

"Not a bloody rupee from those *papadums*," she said. "They're so behind the times they still wear Nehru jackets. I had to hit up Air India and Ismail Merchant." As she saw Natasha approach, Vera opened her arms. "Darling, I didn't think you'd come."

Natasha embraced Vera. They had worked together in London, at the Connaught. "Wild horses couldn't keep me away. Things must be going well," she said, admiring Vera's outfit. "You're back to wearing saris."

"Please! I look like something Krishna dragged in. Did you get my book?"

"And the video! What's this I hear about your going into business? Importing caviar to Calcutta?"

"Oh, you Americans. You've got guts made of *poori*."

All of the men were standing. Natasha greeted them with kisses on each cheek. "Herr Professor Doktor."

"And my book?" he asked.

"If only the magazine reviewed books in German."

"What magazine?"

"My magazine," Natasha said proudly. *"American Cuisine."*

Von Rieber shrugged. *"Amerikanisch Küche?* A magazine for hamburgers?"

Natasha ignored him and kissed Ingmar. "Your book was wonderful. I simply had no idea herring traders were responsible for establishing the Hanseatic League."

Ingmar shook his head. "It is amazing what people don't know about herring."

"Dear Uncle Ho," Natasha said, moving on quickly.

"You like my book?"

"It's gorgeous. You're the Michelangelo of vegetables."

Vera sat Natasha next to her. "How are you doing, really? I'm absolutely distraught over those awful killings." She turned to the mayor. "I think the committee should issue a public statement of outrage that someone is killing American chefs."

The mayor sneered. "Actually, I am not certain it is even against the law."

"And," Vera continued, "we should express our gratitude that Natasha, at least for the moment, is safe."

"Certainly it is not against French law," the mayor muttered.

Vera glared at the mayor. "Apparently, the only thing against French law is good manners!"

"Or typing a menu," said von Rieber. "The *polizei* should come in the middle of the night and arrest all the owners of bistros where you cannot read the menu."

Ingmar leaned over toward him. "God knows they've locked up people for less."

"You are telling me?" von Rieber shouted irately. "Everybody forgives everybody, but no one forgave poor Rudy."

"I'd like to thank Vera," Natasha said. "Three great American chefs have been murdered, all of them Olympic gold medalists."

Grudgingly, the mayor agreed. "The least we can do is issue a statement mourning the loss of our fallen colleagues."

"If it is the least, you can be certain it will be done," Vera muttered.

"However," Ingmar said, "I think we must first clarify the term 'great chef.' "

Vera groaned. "It means they never cooked a herring!"

"A great chef," Uncle Ho said, "can turn a cucumber into the Forbidden City."

Von Rieber waved his finger. "A great chef shops for one portion as carefully as if he were feeding the entire Wehrmacht!"

"*Jamais!*" the mayor said. "A great chef charges the highest price."

All conversation stopped as a bell chimed twice over the public address system. A woman's voice announced, first in French and then in English, the opening match in the ten-event decathlon in which contestants were judged on their ability to sauté, roast, deep-fry, boil, steam, poach, bake, broil, braise, and flambé. "Ladies and gentlemen, the three-minute shellfish sauté will begin promptly at two o'clock."

Vera glanced at her watch. "Shit! I'm one of the judges. I must go." She stood up. "How do I look? Is my dot on straight?" As she kissed Natasha, she whispered, "How brave of you to come, darling. I'm just terrified you're going to be next."

Natasha was ready to scream. "Thank you." She began to think Millie was right. They should have gone back to the hotel and made X-rated love all afternoon. At least it would have taken the taste of Alec out of her mouth. Besides, her nerves were shot to hell. Natasha could have sworn she was being watched.

"We must talk," Vera said. "Why don't you meet me at four o'clock under the marzipan Jesus in Aisle Six?"


AT THE OTHER END OF THE CAFÉ, a waiter stood impatiently while a dowdy matron wearing a floppy Borsalino that nearly covered her face stared at the menu.

"My good man, would you mind telling me what State Bebida Number One is?" Beauchamp was careful to keep her features hidden from the woman she had vowed to kill.


ROY ARRIVED at the service entrance to the Grand Palais. His mouth was dry and his hands were shaking. He walked up to the burly guard, smiled anxiously, and said, "I am here to see Etienne."

The guard's eyes narrowed. *"Comment vous appelez-vous?"*

Roy cleared his throat nervously. "Louis Quatorze."

The guard opened his palm before allowing Roy to pass.

"Welcome to France." Roy reached into his pocket for some money. *"Merci,"* he said, stuffing bills into the guard's hand.

The basement of the Grand Palais had been transformed into a series of prep rooms filled with ovens, refrigerators, fish tanks, and cages with small fowl and rabbits. There was one room for dry provisions and one with misting units suspended over fruits and vegetables. Room after room was filled with flowers. An arsenal of wine and liquor was protected behind locked steel fencing. But most of all, there were hundreds of chefs all shouting at once. A gastronomic Tower of Babel. The noise was nearly deafening as they hurled greetings, insults, and instructions to one another. Roving photographers and a TV crew clogged the narrow hallway as Roy made his way to Room 301.

"Etienne?"

"Louis?"

"Yes. I mean, *oui.*"

"Your accent is not so bad," Etienne said, shaking hands. "You should hear them at Euro-Disney."

"Well," Roy said, "why don't you show me — "

Etienne shook his head and held out his palm.

"Right you are," Roy said, reaching into his jacket for the envelope filled with money. He handed it to Etienne. *"Merci."*

Etienne frowned as he opened the envelope. "I should have known there would be trouble." He looked up at Roy. "The accent is on the second syllable. *Mer-CI!*"

*"Mer-CI!"* Roy repeated.

*"Bon. Mer-CI!"* Etienne handed Roy a small detonator. "If the bomb doesn't work, you can always kill her with your accent."

"What do you mean, 'if the bomb doesn't work'?"

"A joke, *mon ami.* You press the button, and the minute she opens the top of the truffle . . ."


AS MILLIE WALKED into the American Good Foods booth, he stopped dead in his tracks. "Mrs. Nakamura?" He stood at atten-

186

tion, ready to begin the customary three bows. "Nakamura-san."
But as he leaned over, she threw her arms around his neck.

"Cut the crap. Why didn't you return my calls?"

Millie tried to disengage himself. "I was too busy returning your gifts."

"I have yet to give you the best gift of all, Ogden-san. Come with me. I have the most expensive suite at the Bristol. The kitchen is fully stocked with seaweed and eel. We never have to leave."

He still couldn't pry her arms loose. "So what brings you to Paris? A little shopping?"

"Yes. I bought the Bristol. But we can talk about that in the tub."

Millie shook himself free. "Not tonight, Nakamura-san."

"I warn you. I am not the type to sit and hum '*Un bel di.*' One way or another, I get what I want."

"Me too," he said.

"Is it still this woman on your Dupont lighter? This Natasha?"

Before he could respond, this Natasha ran screaming into his arms. "Millie! Oh, thank God you're here."

"Nat, what the hell happened?"

Natasha was trembling. "Someone's been following me." She looked over her shoulder at the man in the raincoat and whispered, "Him!"

Millie began to laugh. "I hired Alphonse to protect you. He's on our side."

She pulled back from his arms angrily. "Why didn't you tell me?"

"Babe, chill out," Millie whispered. "I've got someone I want you to meet." He turned around to introduce Mrs. Nakamura. "Where the hell did she go?"

Mrs. Nakamura had seen all she could bear. While Natasha was still in Millie's arms, she had left the booth to make a phone call. Dialing slowly, with bitter tears streaming down her cheeks, she knew that she had dishonored Fuji Food and, even worse, dishonored herself. She had no choice. In the old days she would have had to kill herself. But these were modern times.

"Find the ninja," she whispered into the phone.

A modern, Westernized woman no longer had to kill herself to save face. Instead, she would kill Natasha.

GERTA HEIL, editor of *Guten Appetit* magazine, stood on stage in the Bocuse Bowl and called the audience to attention. "Ladies and gentlemen, I'd like to welcome you to the Cold Platter Competition. Each competing chef will bring out his platter for inspection by the judges. Factors to be considered by our panel are composition, method of preparation, originality, and degree of difficulty, for a maximum of forty points. Olympic rules also state that all decorations and garnishes must harmonize in taste and color with the main dish displayed, and of course, everything on the platter must be edible."

It was standing room only. Looking around at the audience, Natasha saw Millie in the back, scanning the crowd nervously. She smiled and waved at him, wanting desperately to believe her own lie that she had nothing to worry about. But she had a lot to worry about. For starters, where the hell was Alec?

"As picked in a random drawing, our first entry is from Brazil. It was prepared by Humberto Vilfrido, master chef of the members' dining room at the Carmen Miranda Museum in Rio. His platter is entitled *Bananas Brasileiras.*" Natasha took out her pen and opened the scorepad as she glanced into the wings expecting to see the chef appear. Instead, she heard anxious voices and people running. Heil continued to read. "The platter comprises peppered shrimp and peas wrapped in banana leaves and is surrounded by — "

"Stop!" Vilfrido, a short man with a handlebar mustache, rushed on stage carrying an empty platter. "I have been eaten!"

Chefs from Denmark, Hungary, Scotland, and Italy stepped out from both sides of the wings. Stunned, they stared blankly at their empty platters. Only bits of aspic and stalks of parsley were left. The judges rose from their seats.

Heil didn't know what to say. "Ladies and gentlemen, I am certain there is an explanation."

The explanation stood outside the door, hiccuping as he peered in through a small circle of glass that framed his face. Achille stared at Natasha. It was either her or him. With Natasha out of the way, he could suppress Alec forever. He'd never be hungry again. The only question was, How to kill Natasha?

IT WAS A CLEAR NIGHT. Stars shone brightly as Natasha and Millie walked along the Seine, heading for the site of the old Les Halles just as they had done early in the morning after work at Chez Auguste. All that was long before Les Halles was torn down, the Marais restored, and the minimalist extravagance of the Beaubourg recast the landscape.

They had walked into Au Pied de Cochon expecting to be recognized. But no one did, not even Louise, who had taken their order for onion soup with a shot of cognac so many times in the past.

"She looks just like she used to," Natasha whispered, watching Louise glide through the aisles with the grace of a dancer. "Why do you think she didn't recognize us? Have we changed that much?"

Millie put down his spoon. "No. But the soup has."

"I thought it was just me. Maybe you can't go home again."

"Maybe you can't. But you can go to La Coupole." Millie left some money on the table and guided Natasha to the door.

"Oysters," she sighed.


THE CAVERNOUS LA COUPOLE was just as she remembered it. Artists to the left, dilettantes and dealers to the right. Natasha headed for a table under the posters. She looked over at Millie and took his hand. "It's still the same as it used to be."

"Exactly."

"I can't believe it. There's our waiter. Antoine. But he's so thin. Hunched over."

"*Bonjour,*" Antoine said, cleaning off the table with his dirty rag. "*La carte?*" he asked.

"Antoine?" she said hesitantly.

"*Oui.*" He looked directly at her. And through her.

"*Je voudrais mille Belons,*" she said, hoping to jog his memory.

Antoine paused, smiled, then shook his head. "*Pardon, je crois que . . . Qu'est-ce que vous avez dit? Des Belons?*"

Natasha tried again. "*Mille Belons.* Don't you remember? A thousand oysters?"

Antoine rolled his eyes. "*S'il vous plaît.*"

"Just bring us two orders of Belons," Millie said, grabbing Natasha's trembling hand. "And a bottle of Les Clos '89."

Antoine stared at him for a moment and then turned away. "Nat, it's been ten years."

"Not in my dreams."

"You don't have to settle for dreams anymore."

When Antoine came back with the oysters, Natasha leaned over the platter and inhaled deeply. Then she pushed it away. "Oh, Millie," she whimpered.

"What is it?"

"Life is not a bowl of cherries!"


FOR ONCE, the line at Berthillon was short. Natasha watched as a little girl came away from the window with an ice cream cone. "I wish I knew what happened to Alec. It's not like him."

"Hey, I thought this was to be our night. No Alec. No Olympics."

She nuzzled against his shoulder. "To tell the truth, I could use a little Olympics later on. Oh, God! They have apricot sorbet. My very favorite. I can't risk it. Millie, let's go."

"Risk what?"

She grabbed his arm and led him across the street. "Dummy. Three strikes and you're out!"

"Listen, I'm starving to death. I am standing in the middle of Paris and I am starving."

"Me too."

"So what's the answer?"

Natasha became teary. "I guess we have to try someplace new. Someplace we've never been."

"I heard about this bistro near Saint Sulpice."

"Sure." Natasha turned back to stare across the street, her eyes following the path they had taken.

"What is it?"

She shrugged. "We're like Hansel and Gretel. Someone has eaten all the crumbs, and now we'll never get home."

# HOTEL PLAZA-ATHENÉE

To Be Opened Only in the Event of My D.E.A.T.H.

I, Natasha O'Brien, being of sound mind and sound body, wish to apologize to the manufacturers of Milk Duds for all the terrible things I have said about them during my lifetime. If the truth be told, and what better time than this, I have always had a secret passion for their product and most likely would not have seen the ends of such classic films as Attack of the Killer Tomatoes, The Empire Strikes Back, and Gandhi were it not for a secret stash of candy in my purse.

I also feel compelled to confess that during my tragically short existence, I never really liked radicchio, sun-dried tomatoes, or Godiva chocolates.

Oh, Millie. What the hell happened to us? It's easy to blame career conflicts -- even murder -- for playing havoc with our emotions. But every good cook knows how to deal with a sauce that's curdled. Why didn't we? Even our bad times were better than most people's good times.

What is it, as George S. Kaufman said, that makes one man's Mede another man's Persian? And who the hell cares? Barbara Kafka loves her microwave and the Sterns love road food. Does that make them lesser humans? You know what I mean. Taste is subjective, ephemeral, easy to attack and impossible to defend. Perhaps that's why it is so deadly a weapon.

We're all guilty of elevating style and taste to a verdict rather than a preference. The jury is always coming in, breath-

191

less with judgment and ready to condemn. Such a waste of energy. Such a waste of time.

Thank God I'll be dead when you read this: Millie, you have been the Milk Dud of my life.

One more thought: what the fuck ever happened to chicken chow mein?

THE FIVE NATIONS competing in the free-style flambé were Switzerland, Brazil, Italy, France, and the Cherokee. All eyes were on Cooks With A Smile as he rolled paper-thin buffalo filets and doused them with corn liquor.

The CNN anchor team, positioned above the stage and sharing a camera feed with French National Television, had been covering all the decathlon events. "Irv, the real degree of difficulty in this dish is to flambé those filets without overcooking them."

"Yes, Chuck, that's one of the things the judges will be watching for. Hold on a minute! Bronzini from Italy has just added the grappa to his sauté pan. . . ."

"Bad luck for Bronzini. His flame is too big for those artichokes. That's going to cost him points."

"What a shame! What a heartbreaker! Especially after the way he cut the lobster medallions. I figured he was a shoo-in for the silver medal. But now . . ."

"Irv, I think Vilfrido from Brazil is just about ready."

"He's picking up the dark rum."

"Checking his bananas."

"He's raising his arm. Will you look at the angle on that bottle?"

"Not too high over the pan."

"And there he goes! Vilfrido is pouring like a real champion. First a dash over the oranges. Then a splash over the cherries. Will you just look at the way that man hits those shrimp!"

"And up comes the flame! Irv, I think we've got a winner here. Not too high. Evenly spread throughout the pan. No question about it, Vilfrido could walk away with the gold."

"What an upset that would be for the French and the Swiss."

"The word is that they're just going to cancel each other out. I've spoken to the head of the organizing committee, and they've never before had two contestants make the same dish."

"There goes Dournier from Lucerne. He's picking up the cognac."

"Chapellet just glanced over at him. You can tell this is a grudge match. Chapellet is reaching for his Armagnac . . ."

"I tell you, Chuck, I wouldn't want to be one of the judges for this event."

Neither did Natasha. She wanted to find out where Alec was. He hadn't picked up any of his messages at the hotel. Maybe he was avoiding her because he knew she had found out about Beauchamp. How could she have been so wrong about him? And how the hell long was Professor Wladisczeucz going to be at the airport with the Polish team? The last word she had was that they were holding a candlelight vigil for the chickens that were about to be executed.

The mayor of Dijon shook his head. "The world knows that *Rognons de Veau Flambés* is a French dish!" he muttered angrily. "This time the Swiss have gone too far!"

"The only thing neutral about them is that they steal from everyone," hissed Lady Redfern-Joyce, president of the British Vegetarian Alliance and host of the BBC show *Living with Broccoli*.

"No one steals from the Germans!" von Rieber challenged.

"I said they were thieves. I didn't say they were crazy."

"The Swiss steal from us. We were first to have fondue," said Uncle Ho. "Mongols bring hot pot in fourteenth century. Then Marco Polo steal noodles from us. All we have left is sweet-and-sour pork!"

As each chef finished plating his dish and presented it to the judges, the room burst into spontaneous applause. The mayor stood up. *"Mesdames et messieurs, je regrette . . ."*

Oh, no! Natasha thought. The son of a bitch was lodging a formal complaint to disqualify the Swiss. Cooks With A Smile frowned. Vilfrido banged his pan on the flambé trolley. And the Swiss chef lunged for the French chef.

Millie tapped Natasha on the shoulder. "C'mon."

"Did you find Alec?" she asked.

"No. Let's get out of here."

The crowd was turning ugly. Cheers became angry shouts as the applause took on the ominous rhythm of a quickening pulse. She held Millie's hand as he led the way toward the door, the same question having echoed in her mind for over twenty-four hours: What had happened to Alec? Suddenly aware that someone was following close behind, she nudged Millie with her elbow.

As they stepped into the corridor, he confessed. "Okay, okay. So I got someone else to watch you."

Natasha groaned. "You've hired more conscripts than George Washington!" Not that she didn't love Millie for it, but the more he tried to protect her, the more nervous she became. Assuming that was possible. Extending her hand to the stranger, she said, *"Bonjour. Et comment vous appelez-vous? Groucho, Harpo, ou Chico?"*

"Your accent is excellent." The man smiled. "I am Etienne."


ROY WORE A GRAY WIG, a mustache, and sunglasses as he stood on line to buy a ticket at the Grand Palais.

*"Combien?"* the cashier shouted.

*"Un, s'il vous plaît."*

*"S'il vous PLAÎT!"* the cashier corrected, giving Roy his change.

*"Gesundheit,"* Roy muttered, walking toward the entrance. He stopped short on seeing the metal detectors. Instinctively he put a hand into his pocket and felt for the detonator.

As soon as he stepped through the archway, the alarm sounded. The young guard handed him a small wicker basket. *"Monsieur."*

Roy had purposcly carried a lot of change. He put the detonator into the basket and covered it with coins. Very slowly, making everyone very impatient, he took out his pen, his keys, and slipped off his watch. The guard hurried him through for a second time. No alarm. *"Merci, monsieur."*

Beauchamp watched as the man put the change back into his pocket. Luckily, she had hidden her gun the day before. Not that she was prescient, or had found out that Millie had convinced the organizing committee that such precautions would be necessary. Simply, the gun frightened her too much to carry it around.

As soon as she was inside, Beauchamp hurried toward the butter sculptures. She turned left at the Little Town of Bethlehem, went two tables past Elvis, and put her hand through the opening in the drapery beneath the Loch Ness Monster. The first thing she felt was the cold steel of the silencer.

Barely breathing, she kept her eyes on the crowd to be certain no one saw her slip the gun up the full sleeve of her coat and then quickly put her hand into a pocket. With a deep sigh of relief, she leaned back against the wall to steady herself. It would soon be over. It was just a matter of time.


"I'M RUNNING OUT OF TIME!" Natasha exclaimed as she and Millie stood in front of a white chocolate Taj Mahal. "I've got to judge all these sculptures, the next event is the hors d'oeuvre competition, and there's still no Alec."

"To hell with the chocolates, to hell with the hors d'oeuvres, and most of all, to hell with Alec. The only thing you should be worried about is you. Babe, let's get out of here."

"I can't," she said between gritted teeth. "I feel as though I'm locked in a chocolate prison on my way to a chocolate electric chair."

"Don't tell anyone, but I have a chocolate key."

"If you really want to help, then please stop hiring bodyguards long enough to hire me a photographer. Alec was supposed to take care of all that."

"I ought to let you melt in the chair."

"How can I do a cover story on the U.S. team without pictures? I had it all worked out with Alec." Afraid to say anything more about Alec, she opened her scoring sheets for the chocolate sculpture. Entry No. 400. Bittersweet chocolate bust of Beethoven. Just what the world needed. No matter. It would keep her occupied. As long as she didn't mention Alec again. "I can't help feeling that he's in some sort of trouble because of me."

"How come you're not blaming yourself for the economy?"

"Millie, we've got to call the police. Alec's been missing too long. I'd never forgive myself if something happened."

"Don't look now," he said, smiling, "but it's all beginning to make sense."

"What is?"

"Turn around slowly. Two aisles over. Against the wall. Near the butter Churchill."

Natasha cleared her throat and tried to look casual as she glanced around, pretending to check the back of her shoe. She turned back to Millie and gasped, "Beauchamp!"

"Aka Mrs. Alec Gordon."

"What is she doing here?"

"I'd say it was pretty obvious. We couldn't find Mr. Gordon because he was off making whoopee with Mrs. Gordon."

"Don't be ridiculous. Alec would never . . ."

"Sleep with his own wife?"

"Take advantage of me. Let me down. Marry Beauchamp?" Was that the reason Alec had been avoiding her? Was the sleazeball screwing around with his wife? "Why didn't he tell me he was married?"

Millie stared at her. "When he did what?"

Natasha's heart began to pound. "Applied for the job," she said quickly. "I know why! Millie, he had a recommendation from Beauchamp. He couldn't very well tell me he was married to his only reference." She looked down at her sheets. Entry No. 401. Chocolate Mother Theresa.

"He could have told you after he got the job."

"What for? It didn't matter by that time. I don't care." It did matter. She did care. "It's all strictly business between us." Shut up, Natasha. Entry No. 402. Chocolate Colosseum. "The no-good bastard!" Why didn't she just hire a skywriter?

"Is there something I should know?"

"Don't you dare ever hide the fact that you're married to me!"

"I didn't. And I wouldn't. But I'm not." He stepped closer to her. "Am I?"

Natasha put a hand on his arm. "Millie, I think I ought to say something to Beauchamp."

"Like what?"

"Like congratulations and where the hell is Alec, you bitch?"

"And announce that we're on to them?"

"On to what?"

"I don't know yet. But there's something fishy here."

Entry No. 403. Chocolate octopus. "Oh, my God. Millie!"

"What is it?"

"Look. All over the octopus. Teeth marks!"

197

*    *    *

THE TROISGROS AMPHITHEATRE was filled to capacity as Natasha came onstage. She had changed into her new Valentino emerald-green suede suit, knowing that she would be photographed. *"Bonjour* and good afternoon. On behalf of the Organizing Committee for the Tenth Culinary Olympiad, I am pleased to welcome you to a most unusual event. Having been recognized for their unique showmanship as well as their brilliant culinary skills, teams from the United States of America and Japan are competing for the highest honor in international gastronomy, a special award last given to Anton Mosimann for his extraordinary bread-and-butter pudding. I refer, of course, to the Golden Truffle."

Roy, still wearing his wig and mustache, sat in the second row, just behind the judges. Instinctively, he reached into his pocket and gently fingered the detonator.

Natasha, while smiling for the cameras, scanned the audience trying to find Millie. Although she had convinced him that she was in no danger whatsoever, she still hadn't convinced herself. At least not until she had solved the Alec/Achille mystery. "I take great pleasure in presenting Captain Reed Barker and the United States Hors d'Oeuvre Team."

Reed Barker was the most successful caterer in Chicago. Michigan Avenue hostesses found his ruggedly handsome twenty-something appearance as exciting as his canapés. Once his business expanded, instead of hiring more cooks, he had recruited Chippendale dancers and turned them into a private gourmet army.

The audience broke into applause as Reed and his four-man team marched onstage. They wore pumpernickel-colored trousers, salmon shirts, cucumber-colored ascots, and pimiento-red silk field jackets embroidered with crossed celery stalks.

The team members marched around the prep counter, stamped their feet twice, and stood at attention. Reed shouted, "Mushrooms!"

As each man was called, he stepped to the counter. "Sir!"

"Potatoes!"

"Sir!"

"Cucumbers!"

"Sir!"

198

"Tomatoes!"

"Sir!"

What a to-do, Beauchamp thought as she stood near the door and reached into her pocket for the gun. Quite enough to give her a headache, if she hadn't already had one. She clenched her fingers around the silencer, eager to get it over with and sit down to a nice hot cup of tea. Of course, she'd have to be very careful to avoid hitting one of those young men. But hadn't she spent a lifetime typing perfectly margined memos for Achille, filing his correspondence according to major food groups, and keeping complete records of all his appointments, phone calls, and meals? After satisfying his every requirement, how difficult could it be to pull the trigger and fire a bullet through Natasha's heart?

"Present arms!" Reed shouted.

In rapid succession, each man unbuttoned his holster, took out a sharpening steel, and held it directly in front of his face. Then they all reached for their knives and began twirling them as the audience oohed and aahed.

"Cleaver!"

"Slicing!"

"Paring!"

"Tourné!"

Mrs. Nakamura sat back in her seat and smiled as the team began to sharpen their blades. Such children! What did Americans know about knives? No sushi master worth his wasabi would use toys of stainless steel. They were an insult to his ancestors who had forged high-quality carbon steel samurai swords. *Hai!* It was even an insult to the fish. Her ninja would use a *hon-yaki* knife sharpened only on a whetstone that had been quarried for its fine grain. A *deba-bocho?* Or a *nakiri-bocho?* Either one, a cleaver or a vegetable knife, would cut a single hair as effortlessly as it would sever Natasha's head from her body. Then Ogden-san would be hers. She had already bought him a new Dupont lighter.

"Men, name your hors d'oeuvre!"

The mushroom man took a step forward and shouted, "Hot huckleberry salsa in grilled morilles with deep-fried oregano! Sir!"

The team stamped two steps in place.

"Smoked salmon custard in roasted baby red potatoes coated with candied lemon peel! Sir!"

"Pear pâté on cucumber crescents filled with walnut steak tartare! Sir!"

"Corn meal–breaded cherry tomatoes stuffed with tequila-rhubarb guacamole! Sir!"

Roy shook his head in despair. Normally he would have got up and walked out, calling as much attention to himself as possible. But he had to finish the screenplay, no matter how much he hated Reed's cocktail-party clowns. Too much depended on the last murder. Roy's killer instincts focused on the Golden Truffle sitting on its pedestal. He saw nothing else as he allowed himself to enter the mind of a madman.

The audience burst into applause as the U.S. team presented its platters to the jury and exited running double-time around the stage. Natasha signaled to the photographers Millie had hired. She had all the shots she needed. There was nothing to worry about.

The team returned for another bow and then ran back up the aisle. Beauchamp, still standing near the door, put her finger on the trigger. Hiding the gun behind her purse, she slowly raised her hand.

"And now," Natasha began, "it is my pleasure to present the Japanese team, the Grand Sushi Masters of Tsukiji Fish Market, led by Toshio Watanabe, the 'Gourmet Ninja.' " Offstage, the Kodo drummers from Sado Island began their ritual pounding as the barefoot four-man Japanese team marched onstage in single file. They wore *judogi*, traditional white judo outfits, with bright red sashes around their waists and foreheads. The ninja wore a black sash.

Preparing to read her narration, Natasha moved to the side of the stage. Perfect, Beauchamp thought. With Natasha right there, she wouldn't have to worry about hitting any of the Japanese gentlemen.

Kabuki-like figures dressed in black marched out from the wings carrying trays of live fish. The drumbeats had reached a nearly deafening pitch as the ninja raised his cleaver and shouted a blood-curdling *"Hai! Hai! Hai!"*

Beauchamp gasped and leaned back against the door. At that precise moment, Millie swung it open.

"Beauchamp?"

Screaming as she lost her balance, Beauchamp fell back into Millie's arms and accidentally pulled the trigger. A bullet sped silently across the auditorium. Only the ninja, who could hear smoke rise and the sun set, looked up. The bullet hit his cleaver and propelled it out of his hand. The knife spun in circles, dancing in slow motion toward the audience. People began shouting as they scrambled back from the oncoming knife. They rushed up the aisles to the doors. Millie dropped Beauchamp and headed for Natasha. But he couldn't get through the oncoming crowd.

Roy pushed his way across the aisle, tripping over a Japanese woman who refused to get out of her seat. The detonator dropped to the floor. He had no time to stop and look for it.

Natasha stood frozen as she watched the knife spin out of control. The pounding of the Kodo drummers echoed the beat of her heart as a gray-haired man ran toward her.

"Natasha!" Roy shouted, ripping off his mustache and wig.

"Natasha!" Millie called out.

"Natasha," Beauchamp muttered as she ran from the auditorium.

"Na-ta-sha," Mrs. Nakamura chanted as the knife fell to the floor a few inches from her feet. She reached over to pick it up and noticed an odd-shaped small metal object.

Roy took hold of Natasha. "Come with me."

"Millie!" she screamed.

Roy glanced out at the audience and saw the Japanese woman pick up the detonator. "Oh, my God! We've got to get out of here!" He shoved Natasha into the wings and toward the side door.

Millie turned quickly as he saw Roy grab hold of Natasha. He pushed his way out the exit, planning to circle backstage and reach them.

Mrs. Nakamura was the only person still seated. The Kodo drums had stopped. The ninja, disgraced, bowed very low and walked backward into the wings. Mrs. Nakamura flicked her thumb absently against the piece of metal she had picked up. Her thoughts filled with the bitter realization that Millie's old Dupont lighter still worked.

She was alone in the Troisgros Amphitheatre as the Golden Truffle exploded, destroying most of the stage. Looking up, as though the blast were no louder than a whisper, Mrs. Nakamura began to laugh.

                        *      *      *

NATASHA TRIED TO GET AWAY as Roy pulled her down a flight
of stairs. "You need help, Roy. I know someone. I can get you into
the Menninger Clinic. I hear the food is terrific. Oh, my God, Roy,
please don't kill me!"

"Don't be ridiculous. You've got to die," he said. Suddenly the
stairs shook from the explosion. They stopped and stared at one
another. "You hear that?" he shouted. "That was my ending. Now
I have to start all over again."

"Roy, you're crazy!"

"Crazy like a fox! It was a brilliant ending!" Natasha began to
scream for help. Roy put his hand over her mouth. "Now I've got to
figure out some other way to kill you. Natasha, you have no idea
what pressure I'm under. Paramount wants to call in Billy Crystal
for a rewrite. Can you believe that? After I murdered three chefs!
Listen, you've got to pull yourself together and help me find a fun
way to kill you. Natasha, what are friends for?" He peered down the
hallway he had gone through looking for Etienne. It was empty.
Everyone had left after hearing the explosion.

Natasha gasped for air and nodded frantically.

"You'll help me?" he asked. "No screaming?"

She nodded yes, still hoping to reason with him.

"You promise not to ask for shared screenplay credit?"

She nodded again.

Roy opened the door to one of the kitchens and led her inside.
Natasha was convinced that she'd never walk out alive. She had
gone from the fire into the frying pan. Parker, Neal, and Whitey had
been killed in the kitchen. As he took his hand away from her
mouth, she knew that she was about to die.

"How are you going to do it?" she asked softly.

Roy sat down next to her. "Well, that's what we have to figure
out. I need a dynamite ending."

"You just had a dynamite ending."

He banged his fist on the table. "For God's sake, will you take this
seriously?"

"All right! But give me something to work on, Roy. At least give
me a motive."

202

"A motive? What the hell do you need a motive for? This is a movie, not Psych 101!"

"Roy, this is my life!"

"Oh, please!"

Natasha stopped breathing as she saw the pantry door behind Roy slowly begin to open. Afraid that he'd seen the look of surprise on her face, she said, "I've just had an idea."

"Tell me."

The door kept opening as she spoke. "Now listen carefully." It had to be Millie. "Suppose you were to bake me in a pie?"

Roy shook his head. "I already baked Neal in a pizza. I need something more imaginative!"

"Well, then, what about a cake?" It wasn't Millie. "Or you could chop me up in tiny pieces and put me in pastel-colored petits fours." It was Alec!

"No, no, no!" Roy said. "We've got to think big. This is the end!"

Alec put a finger to his lips as he stepped quietly toward Roy. He was holding a heavy copper skillet.

"I need something splashy," Roy said.

Natasha became giddy. "How about my doing the backstroke in a bowl of vichyssoise?" Alec stood in back of Roy. That's what he must have been doing all along, following Roy. No wonder she hadn't been able to find him. "Or you could bury me in a *tiramisu*." Alec raised the skillet. Natasha smiled nervously. "Then again, I've always wanted to be a *marron glacé*."

Before Roy could respond, Alec struck him on the head. Natasha watched Roy crumple and fall to the floor. Her eyes filled with tears as she rushed into Alec's arms. "Oh, Alec. Thank God you found me. I don't know what I would have done."

"Nor I. You know I detest *tiramisu*."

His voice was cold. Different but strangely familiar. It didn't matter. She was so relieved to see Alec that she began to laugh despite feeling somewhat uncomfortable in his arms. Not half as safe as she had expected. Understandably. So much still had to be resolved. "I ought to let Millie know I'm all right."

"Dear heart, give yourself a moment to ripen."

The voice was unmistakable. Natasha pulled back slowly. It was then that she noticed that Alec's shirt was torn. Some of the buttons had come off. His face was bloated and puffy. Jowls had begun to obscure his jawline. Something terrible had happened to him.

"I must look awful," she said, wiping the tears from her cheeks.

Alec smiled. "You just need a handkerchief." He turned around and reached into his pocket.

Natasha glanced at Roy, still unconscious on the floor. She began to tremble. Roy was not the killer.

Alec walked toward her, clutching his handkerchief. "Let me take care of it."

"Don't be silly," she said, backing away.

"I insist." He brought the handkerchief to her face.

Immediately, Natasha knew it was chloroform. She tried not to breathe as she struggled to free herself. But it was no use. Her lungs gave out. As she inhaled deeply, she looked helplessly at Alec, hoping for an explanation. Those eyes — it couldn't be. . . .

Achille caught Natasha as she collapsed. Triumphantly, he picked her up in his arms and carried her toward the dessert trolley. *"Marron glacé*, indeed!"


HE HAD TO WORK QUICKLY. The first thing he did was fill four cauldrons with water and put them on the stove. Then he put Natasha onto a display table and took off all her clothes. While the water came to a boil, Achille picked up a cleaver in each hand and began chopping blocks of bittersweet chocolate coating, the *couverture* that contained the chocolate flavor, the liquor, the cocoa butter and sugar.

He lowered the flames beneath two of the cauldrons to keep the water from boiling. Then he put the chopped chocolate into two large copper bowls and floated them over the boiling cauldrons. As the coating began to melt, he poured more chloroform onto the handkerchief over Natasha's face and wheeled her into the large walk-in freezer to lower her body temperature.

Achille hurried back to the stove with a dry wooden spoon in each hand to stir the coating. He stirred and tasted. Not his preferred Valrhona, but it would have to do. Impatient for the chunks to melt, he put down the spoons and plunged his hands into the bowls to work the shards of chocolate into a thick mass. Once the coating was melted, he tested it between his thumb and forefinger to be certain it would tighten and shrink away from his fingertips. It was ready.

First he ran his hands along the rim of the bowl to scrape off the chocolate. Then he licked his fingers and cleaned them on the front of his shirt. The clothes didn't matter; he'd soon be buying new ones in a larger size. He took the bowls from the cauldrons of boiling water and put them over the warm water. The melted chocolate had to maintain a temperature close to forty degrees centigrade.

Wondering if Natasha was dead, he wheeled her out of the freezer. No, not yet. But her breathing was very shallow. He put his hand to her stomach. She too was the right temperature.

Of all the murders, Natasha's was to be his masterpiece. He had slowed down her respiratory system with the chloroform. Once he had clogged her pores with chocolate, she would, quite painlessly, quite beautifully, and quite publicly, suffocate. The display card for Entry No. 489 in the chocolate-sculpture competition had been lettered with great care. It read

### NU AU CHOCOLAT

Achille rolled Natasha close to the stove. He plunged his hands into the melted chocolate and slathered her shoulders with the coating. Working quickly, he moved down her breasts to her stomach and then around her legs. Once he had covered the entire front of her body, he licked the chocolate off his fingers and gently turned her over.

He positioned Natasha's head on its side and bent her knees slightly, giving a more graceful curve to the buttocks. Since this was the side of her that would show, he applied the coating with a pastry brush, leaving her head for last. There was just enough chocolate to mold her hair into a sensuous swirl.

As he stood admiring his creation, chocolate still dripping from his fingers, Achille became melancholy. If only there were some way for Natasha to appreciate the poetic justice of her death. How often she'd said that when her time came, she wanted to be chocolate-covered. His moment of nostalgia was interrupted by the sound of someone opening the door in the next room. Holding his breath, he covered the drip marks on the table with a cloth and wheeled her body into the corridor.

Two uniformed porters were watching him. Achille snapped his fingers. *"Portier, portier!"* They walked over, smiling at the sight of the sculpture. One of them extended his hand toward her buttocks. *"Non! C'est un oeuvre d'art! Vite, vite, vite! Pour l'exhibition du chocolat,"* he said, pointing upstairs. *"Tout de suite!"* The porters shrugged and wheeled Natasha toward the elevator.

Achille went back to the kitchen and into the room in which he had left Roy. But Roy was no longer alone.

"Beauchamp!"

"Where is she?"

Achille smiled. Good old Beauchamp. Leave it to her to turn up just when he needed her. "Who?"

"Natasha. I saw her come in here with someone." She motioned with her head toward Roy, sprawled on the floor with a pool of blood near his head. "Him."

"My God, Beauchamp! You think she did that?"

"No." Beauchamp took a step back. "Look at you. You've got chocolate all over yourself. What have you been doing?"

"Oh yes, Beauchamp, do look at me. I'm practically plump!" He pointed to the bulges beneath his shirt and showed her that his trousers were tight. "I am getting to be more myself with every passing meal."

"Not as long as Natasha is alive."

"Precisely! That's why I had to kill her." Achille put a hand to his stomach. It was rumbling again. "Dear me, it must be nearly teatime." He headed for the refrigerator. "Come along, Beauchamp. I shall need a hand with the *zuppa di pesce*. Or should we have the *cannelloni alla napoletana?* I tell you, the Italians have been cooking brilliantly this year. I had a *polenta con funghi* for breakfast that was pure ambrosia."

"*You* killed her? *I* wanted to kill her."

"Don't be a gnocchi," he said, stepping into the refrigerator. "You haven't nearly my imagination."

She followed him inside and took the gun from her pocket. "But I do have this."

"Wherever did you get . . . oh, dear. You've been going out with that waiter again." He reached for a Genoa salami and inhaled it. "I simply must have some while we wait." He held it out toward her. "Here. Cut me a dozen thick slices. Can you believe

Natasha credited my most politically significant murders to date to a mere critic?"

Beauchamp raised the gun and pulled the trigger. She shot the salami out of his hand.

Achille was stunned. His eyes narrowed. "I wanted you to slice it, not kill it."

"They're going to take you away again," she said softly.

"Only for a short time. You know the American court system. I plead temporary insanity — although, let's face it, Beauchamp, killing the American chefs was the most rational thing I've done in years. They had to die. They had all but renounced the Holy Trinity of eggs, butter, and cream. Whatever happened to respect for classical traditions? These New World nincompoops have nearly brought decent cuisine to its knees with their trendy, flash-in-the-pan nonsense. In any event, I shall throw myself on the mercy of the ACLU and hire von Bulow's lawyer. Do you recall whether he's the one who defended that wonderful woman who killed the diet doctor?" Achille turned back to the shelves and held up a large tureen. "Let's be really wicked and have a bit of *risotto Milanese* too."

She raised her gun and aimed at the container.

"Beauchamp, this is no time for games! I am trying to get back into shape. Have you any idea what hell my life has been? First I had to endure that fool Enstein's spa cuisine. It was barely sufficient to sustain a rabbit in a coma. Then I land in America. A most disagreeable place. Its restaurants are filled with people who bite off less than they can chew."

"I can't let them take you away from me. Mr. van Golk — Achille, my darling — I can no longer live without you."

"Well, if you must, go ahead and blow your brains out, Beauchamp. But for heaven's sake, spare the poor innocent risotto!"

She pulled the trigger. And missed.

Achille put his arms around the tureen. "That does it, you old hag. You're fired!"

"I was aiming at you!"

"At me?" Achille trembled as though the air had been knocked out of him. He dropped the risotto, felt his knees give way, and sank to the floor. "Beauchamp," he gasped, staring at the blood rushing from his chest. "What have you done?"

She kneeled beside him. " 'Where is my Romeo? I will kiss thy lips. Haply some poison yet doth hang on them, to make me die. . . .' " Beauchamp kissed Achille. But instead of poison, she tasted chocolate. Picking up the gun, she whispered, " 'O happy dagger!' " She held it to her forehead. " 'This is thy sheath; there rust, and let me die.' "

Beauchamp pulled the trigger and fell on top of her Romeo.

Achille opened his eyes. He had never been so cold. Each breath was like the North Wind howling through an empty cave. His lips were dry. His throat was parched. His voice was barely audible. "Is there any risotto left?"


MILLIE WAS FRANTIC. Natasha was nowhere to be found, and he could only blame himself. The police circling the Grand Palais hadn't seen her leave. She had to be inside. But he'd spoken to everyone she knew, and no one had seen her. All he could think of was to retrace their steps.

It was on the second time around that he saw a crowd gathering at the chocolate sculptures. Millie pushed his way in. They were standing over a life-size reclining sculpture of a nude woman. "Oh, my God!" he gasped, staring at her buttocks. "I'd know that ass anywhere!"

*"Mon Dieu!"* said the man next to him. "It's breathing!"

**NEW YORK POLICE DEPARTMENT**

Division of Homicide

CASE REPORT NO. 18-5764-8976-3225-AB-218G-445

FROM: D.I. Davis, NYPD
TO: The Commissioner
    J. Oiseau, Sûreté
    D. I. Carmody, New Scotland Yard
    Det. Billy Bob Scooner, Dallas PD
    Det. Chad Stone, Los Angeles PD
RE: Achille van Golk/Alec Gordon

Enclosed, for your records, are the statement taken from Ogden upon his return to New York, the deathbed testimony of Mme. Beauchamp van Golk Gordon, and, although she was barely coherent at the time, the testimony of Ms. O'Brien as last rites were being administered.

While we have to wait for the Crown's decision to indict van Golk's solicitors as accessories to fraud before all the loose ends can be tied up, Beauchamp's testimony at least gives us a motive, not to mention her bizarre theory that inside every thin person there is a fat person trying to get out.

While it is difficult to imagine the degree of outrage that van Golk felt because of the current trend toward lighter cooking -- there is no denying the emotional price of undergoing so radical a physical change -- we have been unable to come up with any other motive for the murders.

209

A very puzzling case. There is no evidence that van Golk/ Gordon actually killed the three chefs. I am relieved that we do not have to bring this case to trial. Even the positive identification by the bakers that van Golk/Gordon was the person who bought out their cakes on the same days as the homicides merely places him in those cities on the dates in question.

The final irony in this matter is the fate of <u>American Cuisine</u>. Evidently, van Golk/Gordon was instrumental in helping to focus many of the features that caused the magazine to become an overnight success. Sadly, Natasha O'Brien has not been around to enjoy the fulfillment of her vision.

As requested, I have enclosed all of the recipes from the White House dinner -- you just can't get a copy of that first issue anymore.

PROMPTLY AT NINE A.M., Natasha sat down on her new bed and began to work. She opened the large envelope with the layout that Ester had messengered over the night before. As usual, there was a note.

Happy Anniversary. It is three months since you got out
of the hospital. It didn't take Gorbachev three months
to get over Yeltsin.

Natasha closed her eyes. Of course not. Gorbachev hadn't slept with Yeltsin.

The physical injuries she had sustained in Paris had healed quickly. The problem was the trauma of what had happened in New York. Not even scraping the floors, painting the walls, or buying a new bed had helped. She was still devastated by the knowledge that she had slept with Achille.

More than feeling that she had betrayed the chefs who had been killed, Natasha felt she had betrayed herself. She could no longer trust her instincts. Possessing the same visceral energy that had once propelled Icarus toward the sun, Natasha was accustomed to jumping off cliffs and landing on her feet. Suddenly, she realized she could not fly.

The phone rang. She sat back and waited to hear the message. It was Millie.

"Oh, come on, Nat! Pick up the damn phone. I can't go on leaving messages and sending faxes. We're communicating without communicating. Babe, please! I miss you!" He waited and then slammed down the receiver.

Millie had stayed on with her in Paris. He was at the hospital every day, fielding questions from the police and keeping the reporters at bay. He brought her back to New York and humored her determination to stay in a hotel while the apartment was renovated. Like fugitives, they slept in one another's arms without ever once mentioning the horror from which she had escaped, without ever once allowing empathy to escalate into passion. She could not have survived without Millie.

By noon she had edited the piece on "Pennsylvania Dutch Treats" and approved the layout. Reluctantly, she got dressed and went downstairs to Café des Artistes.

Jenifer Lang hugged her. "George says hello from Budapest."

"Why didn't he take me with him?"

"Over my . . . oops."

Natasha smiled. "Thanks for the chicken soup." She sighed. "I'm here to meet something named Bobby Silverstein."

"You're kidding!" Jenifer rolled her eyes. "They're over in the corner," she said, leading the way toward the table.

They? Natasha wondered. She had agreed to meet Roy's agent for a drink. He had said it was about Roy's future. How could she refuse?

Bobby, wearing a heavy knit cardigan over his shirt and tie, stood up and kissed her on the cheek. "Natasha, at last we meet."

She smiled uneasily, waiting to be introduced to the very elegant couple at the table. The woman was gorgeous. Very willowy. Milk-white skin, long blond hair, bright green eyes, and a Kay Kendall nose. The man stood up. He was tall and lean. The deep cleft in his chin led to a firm, square jaw. His handsome, tanned face was framed by a mane of silver hair.

"You know Nan and Ivan, don't you?" Bobby asked.

"Who?"

"The Lyonses. The people who wrote *Someone Is Killing . . .*"

Natasha couldn't believe it. The Lyonses were the last people she wanted to meet. Ever. "Oh, yes. How do you do?" Natasha pretended not to notice Ivan extending his hand. She sat down and turned quickly to Bobby. "You have news about Roy."

"They're letting him out of the white hotel next week. I don't know why. I did my best to convince them that he wasn't fully cooked yet. It looks as though we're going to have to be very supportive of poor Roy." Bobby winked at her and smiled. "Actually, I was hoping to get all this business settled before they put the dumb schmuck back on the menu."

"All *what* business?"

Nan leaned toward Natasha. "I want you to know how sorry we are about all you've been through."

"It's an incredible story," Ivan said.

"He doesn't mean incredible," Nan interrupted.

"What's wrong with incredible?" Ivan snapped.

"Astonishing, fantastic, remarkable — but not incredible. *Incredible* implies a lack of believability." Nan patted Ivan's hand patronizingly as the waiter came over to take their drink order.

"Miss O'Brien, the usual?"

"No. Just bring me a Perrier, please."

"Ice and lime?"

That was all he said: ice and lime. Natasha suddenly felt as though she were playing the last scene in *Brigadoon*, where every word brought back memories that were supposed to have been buried a hundred years ago. Ice and lime. Alec and Achille.

"Miss O'Brien?"

"No ice. No lime," she said for her own ears as well as the waiter's.

"Ma'am?"

"Lillet," Nan said.

Ivan began to laugh.

"What's wrong with Lillet?" she asked.

"It's such a retro drink," he said. "Pure sixties."

Nan smiled. "Natasha, don't ever work with your husband."

"I don't have a husband."

"Smart."

Ivan shook his head. "As though *I* were the difficult one." He turned to the waiter. "I'll have a Pernod. Perrier instead of water. Reverse the proportions. And I'd like it in a stemmed glass filled with ice."

The waiter nodded and looked at Bobby. "Sir?"

"Diet Pepsi. And don't forget the straw." Bobby put his hand on Natasha's. "I gotta tell you the truth. I didn't come here just to talk about Roy."

"Really?" Natasha pulled her hand out from his, pretending she

213

had to brush the hair away from her face. "And what did the Lyonses come here not to talk about?"

"We came here to talk about you."

Natasha smiled nervously. "Then perhaps I should leave."

Bobby put his hand on her arm. "Listen, I've been taking meetings with the Disney people about Roy's screenplay, and my nose is growing longer every day. Their lawyers think I have a release from you."

"And you don't."

"I don't want a release from you."

"Well, then, there's no problem, Mr. Silverstein. I'm not going to give you one."

Bobby leaned close. "I want more. I want to buy the rights to your life."

Natasha was stunned. She didn't know what to say. She stared at him until she found the right word. "Incredible."

"Let me explain," Bobby continued. "Nutsy squirrel had it all wrong. We don't start with a screenplay. We start with a book."

"Enter the Lyonses," Natasha said.

Bobby smiled. "Who said all dessert chefs were stupid?"

"I'm sure it was you, Mr. Silverstein."

He laughed. "This way we get the book, we get the paperback, we get the movie, we get the movie tie-in. I guarantee you'll be on television for years."

Natasha shook her head. "Interviewed by Barbara Walters again."

"And Donahue. And Oprah. And Sally Jessy. And Jay, Arsenio, Letterman. You name it."

"Let me get this straight, Mr. Silverstein. You say you want to buy the rights to my life?"

"It's done all the time. Otherwise you'd turn on the television and see nothing but test patterns."

"Do you want my past, my present, or my future?"

Bobby narrowed his eyes and thought. "I want it all. God knows what could happen to you tomorrow."

"And it's cheaper to buy my life than to have me sue."

Bobby leaned back and smiled at Nan and Ivan. "What did I tell you?" He tapped a finger against his forehead. "She's got a *tookis* and a half, this kid!"

214

Natasha still couldn't believe what she was hearing. "You want me to sell you my thoughts and my feelings?"

"Sweetheart, what good are they doing just sitting around in your head? Don't go melodramatic on me. It's only research."


NATASHA SAT BACK on the bed, uncertain whether to laugh or cry. She switched on the phone machine. Millie.

"You won't believe what happened. Fuji Food just bought AGF. Mrs. Nakamura also rises. Nat, I don't know what to do with my life. I put so much of myself into this damn company. I know it's crazy, but I feel as though Fuji Food just bought me. Please pick up. Help!"

The next message was also from Millie.

"Today's sermon, boys and girls, is about life after sushi. Look who I'm talking to. Nat, come out from under the covers. I need to see you. Pick up the phone, please! You can do it. That's right. Move your hand over to the receiver . . . Nat, remember me? I saved your life! Okay for you. Next time you're dipped in chocolate, call Milton Hershey!"

That was the whole problem, she thought. Even as a child, Natasha had been warned about the "next time." As though it were inevitable. Why hadn't her parents taught her about good times, new times, the best of times, instead of just the worst of times?

"Nat, let me in!"

She looked at the phone machine and suddenly realized Millie's voice was coming from downstairs. He was knocking on her door.

"Goddamn it, open up! I've got to talk to you!"

She hurried down and without a word opened the door. They stared at one another.

"I got good news and I got bad news." Millie took a deep breath. "Nat, I've been fired."

"And what's the bad news?"

"Are you gonna let me in or what?"

Natasha didn't move. "The bad news is?"

"My wife doesn't understand me."

"You don't have a wife. You don't even have a job."

"Says who?"

"You said you were fired."

"Fired and hired. It's like love and marriage. You can't have one without the other."

"Hired by whom? Don't tell me. Colonel Sanders? Burger King? Domino's Pizza?"

"Nat, I'm in a whole new area of junk food. Television! VP for daytime programming. Soaps, cooking shows, reruns."

"Don't talk to me about reruns. They're already planning *Natasha Two*."

"Oh, come on. You're not going to let them — "

"No, I'm not going to let them."

"Good. There's a whole world out there, Nat. It's time to move on."

"No more next times."

Millie took her in his arms. "Besides, I'm still in love with *Natasha One*. Let's finally put the past behind us."

Her eyes filled with tears. "That's what I'm trying to do. It's what I want most in the world."

Brushing her tears aside, he said, "You've got a pretty good track record for getting what you want. Babe, it's all out there for the taking." He whispered, "Take me. Let's get married and start all over again."

"Oh, Millie." She put her arms around his neck. "You know what I love most about you? You never listen. You haven't heard a word I've said in years. You can't imagine how comforting that's been. You never took no for an answer. I could always count on you." Natasha's tears gave way to a smile.

"You still can."

"That's my whole problem." She put a hand to his cheek and kissed him gently. "I've got to start counting on me. I'll always love you, Millie, but I've finally learned that some things have to come to an end. I made a promise to myself. No more sequels."